"Marriage?" Sandy gasped.

She was staring at him as if Drew were speaking another language.

"We work together, Drew," she said and, so far, he was with her.

"I'm a professional woman, and my professional reputation is one of my first concerns. If you think I'm coming back to Tyler after a weekend business trip with one of my co-workers to announce what went on...well, I don't even know what to say!"

Now Drew was completely lost. "Sandy, I didn't mean we have to start sending out invitations, but——"

"Besides which, do you remember who we are, Drew Stirling?"

Drew groaned. "You're not going to use that thing about Grandpa and your grandmother again, are you?"

"You are too obtuse for words," she said. "And I don't expect you ever to bring up this subject again."

"Don't you think we should talk about this?" he called to her disappearing back.

Peg Sutherland is acknowledged as the author of this work.

ISBN 0-373-82551-X

LOVE AND WAR

PEG SUTHERLAND

Love and War

Murphy women and Stirling men...
What was this strange attraction?

Harlequin Books

TORONTO • NEW YORK • LONDON
AMSTERDAM • PARIS • SYDNEY • HAMBURG
STOCKHOLM • ATHENS • TOKYO • MILAN
MADRID • WARSAW • BUDAPEST • AUCKLAND

WELCOME TO A
HOMETOWN REUNION

Twelve books set in Tyler.
Twelve unique stories. Together they form a
colorful patchwork of triumphs and trials—
the fabric of America's favorite hometown.

Around the quilting circle...

Martha Bauer and Emma Finklebaum exchanged glances, studied the faces gathered around the quilting frame, then gazed at one another again.

"Mag Murphy's still a no-show, I see," Emma said, opening the zippered pouch where she kept her quilting needle and thread.

"Third day this month she's missed," Bea Ferguson said. "She's probably busy keeping Drew Stirling away from Sandy."

Everyone nodded. The feud between the Stirlings and the Murphys was nothing new, but recent developments between Mag and Clarence's grandchildren were eclipsing even the news about the fire at the F and M these days.

Each of the women seated around the quilting frame formed an image of a wedding quilt in her mind. And then a baby quilt—baby quilts seemed more precious with each year that passed.

Emma, as the local paper's one-time social columnist, prided herself on having the inside story on everything in Tyler, and today she had a real scoop. "Well, what I find really interesting is what's going on over at Timberlake Lodge." She paused for effect. "When was the last time we had Black Hawk and his warriors in Tyler, that's what I want to know."

CHAPTER ONE

MAG MURPHY DECIDED she must be losing her marbles.

That was the only explanation for what she saw out the front window of Worthington House. At seventy and holding, she figured her eyesight was still good enough for her to recognize that devil Clarence Albert Stirling when she saw him, even if it had been more than fifty years.

The only thing giving her pause was the fact that Clarence didn't look a year older than he had the day he'd left her stranded at the altar. How else to explain it, except that Mag herself had finally started going batty?

"Nonsense. I'm as sane as I ever was," she muttered, unable to take her eyes off the tall lean fellow with the shiny dark curls who stepped onto the curb on Elm Street and stared up at Worthington House. "He must've struck a deal with the devil."

That was a much preferable explanation for this aberration than questioning her own sanity, Mag decided.

"What did you say, Gran?"

"Hmm?" Mag barely registered her granddaughter's query. She couldn't get over that scoundrel Clarence turning up after all these years. Like a bad debt, her father would have said. Must've been years since she'd even thought of him.

Or last St. Valentine's Day, at least.

Well, if he came nosing around here, she'd give him the sharp end of her quilting needle. That's exactly what she'd do.

"Gran, are you all right?"

"Yes, yes." Mag waved the hand that sported her new topaz ring. Blasted unfair, that she should have to work so hard to keep from turning into an old hag while Clarence still tap-danced around like a dandy. A young Fred Astaire, graceful enough to set her heart fluttering, she'd always thought. Disgruntled at the direction of her musings, she turned to her granddaughter. "Sakes alive, Alexandra! I'm fine. Don't get your knickers in a knot."

Sandy chuckled. Like her father, she never let Mag's sharp tongue get to her. "What are you staring at, Gran? You haven't heard a word I've said."

Mag pulled down the shade on the window, thinking it couldn't be altogether healthy for a woman her age to be experiencing such a fluttering heart. "I'm watching the snow, girl. Why don't you come back in the morning and bring your sled? We'll take a spin."

Sandy laughed and Mag enjoyed the sound despite her preoccupation with the man who had mounted the steps of Worthington House. Foolishness, thinking he was Clarence. The old fool had probably gone on to glory years ago. Or to some more appropriate afterlife, if Mag's fervent prayers had had any effect whatsoever.

"You might be up for sledding, Gran, but I'd probably throw my back out if I even tried," Sandy said, succeeding in sounding all grown-up and big-city slick.

"You're twenty-five and a long way from back trouble, young lady," Mag retorted, although it was true that her youngest granddaughter did tend to dress awfully old for her age—in severely cut wool suits and simple silk blouses, usually. To create a professional image, Mag was certain, remembering her own gabardine suits. She and Ellie Gates, who'd run the department store in the old days, had been just about the only women in town to wear tailored suits back then. In fact, they had been among the few professional women in Tyler. Ellie, however, had been a spinster, and plenty of people had thought her less fortunate than Mag, who had run the hardware store with her husband, Harry, at her side.

But Mag had known Ellie Gates quite well, and in fact had sometimes envied her friend the freedom that came from being single. Men could be a trial, unless you managed them well. And one way to manage them was to never forget you were a woman. That, as far as Mag could tell, automatically put you in the driver's seat.

"What you need's a peplum," she said to her granddaughter, and was rewarded with a bemused frown.

"A what?"

"Give you some hips," Mag said, remembering the once-stylish jackets that had flared so alluringly from a snug-fitting waist. Unlike Ellie, Mag had never figured a businesswoman had to play down her attractions to get on professionally in a man's world.

Sandy's tawny cheeks picked up a hint of color. "I've got all the hips I need, Gran."

Mag harrumphed. "You're too bony, if you ask me, all you young women today. In my time, a man liked a woman with a little flesh on her bones. Why, Marilyn Monroe was a size sixteen. Did you know that? I read it just a few months ago in one of those celebrity magazines. It's a fact."

What was also a fact was that her granddaughter, with her wide smile, dark hair and big, shining eyes, was as tall and slender and beautiful as anything Magdalena Halston Murphy had ever seen. Alexandra had her mother's dark good looks, from the strain of Winnebago Indian that had made its way down through the generations. Even Mag had always thought her daughter-in-law entirely too good-looking for Franklin, her eldest son, who was a little on the plain side like his father.

Sandy wasn't a thing like Mag, either, who had a certain flair of her own. Mag was petite, curvy instead of slim and not too shy to show off the fact. She favored bright colors, fabrics that clung and jewelry that sparkled. But her most striking feature, even to this day, was her hair. Thick and wavy, it was the color of butter, a color Tisha Olsen fussed about matching every six weeks when Mag went into the Hair Affair.

"Honey, a woman your age should go natural," Tisha always said.

"A woman my age should do whatever she darn well pleases," Mag always retorted. "Besides, Tisha, you're gaining on me. Better watch your back or I'll snatch Judson Ingalls right away from you any day now. Why, you're still getting a year older every year and I've started subtracting a year each time a birthday rolls around."

Tisha laughed. "Be careful, Mag. Before long you'll be younger than your own son."

"I can't wait."

But recently Mag had something else to enjoy. After seven long years of occasional visits, her favorite granddaughter was home to stay.

"Tell me some more about your new job, Alexandra."

Sandy shifted in the chintz-covered chair in the community room of the retirement center, like a squirmy child who could barely contain herself. She had dressed down today, in wool leggings and an oversize Ohio State Alumni Association sweatshirt. Even her hair, usually slicked back into a tidy, no-nonsense bun, was caught up in a ponytail and tied with a strand of purple yarn. To Mag, she still looked like the little girl who could barely wait for the rhubarb pie to come out of the oven.

"Oh, Gran, it's such an exciting opportunity!"

Mag remembered when her own voice had been that melodious, before it had started to creak and crack.

"Yes! Yogurt has such potential in today's market," Sandy exclaimed. "If I can position it right, I'm sure we can go international."

After almost fifty years in business herself, Mag understood the gleam in her granddaughter's eyes and the glow on her cheeks as she launched into her ideas for marketing Yes! Yogurt across the continent and beyond. Mag knew there was a big difference between keeping a small-town hardware store afloat and sailing into the deep waters of cross-border commerce. But she did know that excitement. And part of her was proud to see her granddaughter heading down that same path.

As Mag listened to her enthusiastic plans, another part of Mag prayed that Sandy wouldn't find that path as lonely as Mag herself had. The thought made her feel a little guilty. After all, Harry Murphy had been a good man. It hadn't been his fault he'd never curled her toes, never made her feel that excitement she'd so longed for.

Relying on a hardware store for fulfillment had felt a little hollow at times.

"The only thing is..." Sandy hesitated, her enthusiasm momentarily spent as she reached the end of her litany of grand ideas for new slogans and an updated logo and cable TV ad campaigns.

"What, dear?"

"Well, I know I'm young. And I know I don't have loads of experience."

"Why, you were at the top of your class," Mag protested. "You've spent the past year working in marketing for that cookie company, and I still think that ad you created is the best one on television. Everybody in this joint laughs out loud every time that dog sticks his nose in that cookie jar. And you spent so many summers working for Britt and Jake at Yes! Yogurt, who could possibly know the company better?"

Mag watched her granddaughter brighten with the reassurance.

"I know, Gran. But director of marketing is a big position. And ... what if people think I'm too young?"

"What people? Britt and Jake Marshack wouldn't have hired you if they thought you weren't qualified."

"But there might be others, like the vice president of sales. I haven't met him yet, you know. He's probably a lot more experienced, and we'll be working side by side."

Mag didn't know Yes! Yogurt's vice president of sales. Apparently he was new to Tyler, having arrived after she'd moved to Worthington House. She didn't recollect ever seeing him, and if his name had been mentioned during one of the weekly quilting-circle gossip sessions, it had probably been before she'd restyled her hair so she could begin wearing her hearing aid. But she couldn't imagine some stodgy old business poop getting the better of her granddaughter.

"Stand tall, Alexandra, speak with authority and stick to your guns. If you don't doubt yourself, girl, neither will anyone else."

LIKE EVERYTHING ELSE about Tyler, Worthington House met with Drew Stirling's approval.

The stately Victorian-era retirement home gave off a dignified but cozy air that made him relax at the idea of bringing his grandfather here to recuperate. The rooms were friendly and comfortable, with live plants and soft pastel wallpaper in the common areas of the independent-living quarters. Lively activities were going on throughout the building, from low-impact aerobics to more intense bouts of chess in the TV room. Both the extended-care unit and the assisted-living quarters seemed adequately staffed with smiling, pleasant nurses and their aides. Just the place for Grandpa to recover from his hip-replacement surgery.

"I'm sure your grandfather will find his stay at Worthington House to be a pleasurable experience," said Cecil Kellaway, the heavyset and slightly officious administrator.

Kellaway faked some kind of phony-baloney accent, but Drew didn't let that trouble him. He had a good eye for people and figured this guy would run a tight ship. Drew liked the idea of placing his sometimes truculent and always dictatorial grandfather in the hands of people who ran a tight ship.

Otherwise, Clarence Albert Stirling would be running the place himself in short order.

Drew chuckled. At Cecil Kellaway's quizzical look he cleared his throat and smiled. "You've never had a resident-led mutiny, have you?"

Slapping his clipboard against one sturdy thigh, Kellaway drew his lips into an even straighter line. "I can assure you not. Our residents are all happy and well cared for."

Drew smiled, as innocuous a smile as he could manage. He didn't want Kellaway refusing admission before his grandfather even showed up at the door. "Excellent," he said, mimicking the director's very proper tone.

How long would it be before Kellaway was calling him, frantic over some disruptive behavior from Clarence?

Drew wondered, remembering all too clearly the time his grandfather had broken down the door of the neighboring apartment in Chicago, to free a barking dog whose owner was not home. The barking had gotten on his nerves, Clarence had announced, confident in the justness of his actions.

"If you'll follow me this way, we'll make a brief survey of the kitchen. I'm sure you'll find it scrupulously clean."

It was spotless, and filled with some pretty tantalizing aromas, like baked apples, roasting chicken and homemade bread. It smelled like home cooking to Drew, who was beginning to think that everyone in Tyler must be a world-class cook. Kelsey boardinghouse, where he'd stayed the past six months, served up nothing but the best—smothered pork chops or meat loaf, real mashed potatoes and strawberry-rhubarb crisp on Tuesday nights, for example. Even Marge's Diner regularly beat anything Drew had ever eaten in a restaurant. Small towns, he was deciding, had the corner on good cooking.

He almost dreaded the day when he finished the house he was building on the outskirts of town and had to start nuking frozen dinners again.

But not nearly as much as he dreaded the day Grandpa Stirling arrived from the hospital in Chicago.

"It's only fair to tell you right now that you'll see me in blazes before I'll set foot in Tyler, Wisconsin," the old man had declared quite calmly and clearly not twenty-four hours after his surgery, when he should have been groggy from medication. Grandpa had gone straight from anesthetized to running the show, with no time in between for woozy.

"You'll like Tyler, Grandpa," Drew had said gently, exchanging glances with his sister and his mother, neither of whom had the time or the resources to care for the old man. "It's a great commun—"

"No, son, I don't believe I will. I made a solemn vow to myself fifty years ago that I would not return to that archaic little town and I most assuredly do not intend to go back on my word at this late date."

Despite being in a hospital bed, Clarence had been as immaculately groomed as ever. His mostly white hair was slicked into place, his freshly shaved cheeks smooth and pink. He had then pointed the remote control at the TV clamped to the wall and turned the volume up loud enough to drown out opposition. It was Clarence Stirling's favorite battle tactic.

Drew had exchanged confused looks with Cynthia, who had three children of her own to manage, and his mother. He'd picked up the remote from the hospital bed and clicked the TV off. "When were you in Tyler, Grandpa?"

"I told you. Fifty years ago. Now hand over that clicker."

"You never told me you visited Tyler."

"Well, there's a simple explanation for that, of course. I never told you I visited Tyler because I never did visit there."

Betty Stirling leaned closer to her father-in-law. "But you just said—"

"I am not senile, young lady. I know what I said. I never *visited* that godforsaken place, I was born and raised there. Now, could I trouble you to hand over the clicker, son?"

And that was the last the old man would say on the subject. He had adamantly refused to discuss the reason for his having left town or for the bitterness that still laced his voice after all these years.

Drew had hated taking advantage of the fact that his grandfather was still bedridden and thus unable to put up his usual spirited fight. But bringing Clarence Stirling to Tyler for the duration of his recovery and whatever therapy would be necessary to get him back on his feet was the only viable plan. One of Cynthia's three children had muscular dystrophy and needed almost constant attention as it was. And Betty Stirling lived with her sister, Evelyn Marshack, as they had all those years ago when their children were growing up. Although with their sons' help their financial circumstances were greatly improved, they still preferred living together to living alone. But Drew's mother and his paternal grandfather had never gotten along, especially after Drew's father died. Clarence thought he knew exactly how his grandchildren ought to be raised and Betty believed that was her job, so the relationship had been strained.

So Drew knew he was the most logical choice to care for his grandfather, and Clarence would simply have to get a grip, as Drew's precocious eleven-year-old niece like to remind them all from time to time.

"I hope our facility meets with your satisfaction," the slightly pompous Cecil Kellaway intoned as they completed the tour and walked back to his office.

"Absolutely," Drew said, sitting down to sign the final papers for Clarence's admission next week, when he was expected to be released from the hospital in Chicago. "I just hope my grandfather will settle in here before too long."

Kellaway smiled. "Oh, I can assure you, Mr. Stirling, he'll feel right at home at Worthington House."

Drew merely grunted as he scribbled his signature on the papers.

SANDY DROPPED a kiss on her grandmother's cheek. "Guess I'll run for now. I want to finish unpacking—I put it off all through the holidays—and there's one more journal article on the dairy industry I want to read before I go in tomorrow." She shivered. "New year, new job. It's fitting."

Mag nodded. "You get a good night's sleep. Your first day on the job is an important one. First impressions, you know. You'll want to be rested."

Sandy studied herself in the mirror on the wall behind her grandmother. The truth was she was terrified. Moving back to her hometown, to the people who still remembered when she'd been on the pep squad in high school, was far more intimidating than taking on a big job for a bunch of strangers in Atlanta. She desperately needed to succeed here in Tyler, where everyone knew her and probably still thought of her as a kid.

"I'm not sure," she said, trying for a light tone. "Maybe circles under my eyes will add a few years, give me a more mature look."

Mag chuckled. "Or make you look hung over. You'll do fine tomorrow. Now quit fretting."

"I'll call tomorrow night and let you know how it went," Sandy promised, pausing at the community-room door to wave one more time. But Mag had already raised the shade on the window, apparently once again caught up in watching the snow drifting down in the lowering dusk.

The sight of her grandmother tugged at Sandy's heart. If it weren't for Gran—and for Gin; what had happened to her former boss had played a big part, too, Sandy had to admit—she might never have returned to Tyler. She'd been happy with her job at International Baking Corporation, and she had loved working for Ginny Luckawicz. But then Gin's career had disintegrated in front of Sandy's eyes, and she hadn't felt comfortable staying on at a firm that could treat employees like that. So when Gran had decided to give up the house she'd always lived in, the tidy white frame with the wide porch and green shutters, she knew where she needed to be. Sandy and her grandmother had been inseparable, the little girl dogging the older woman's every step. From Gran, Sandy had learned to repair leaking faucets and to make tea that was never bitter and to scrutinize the sales floor at Murphy's Hardware and figure out exactly what wasn't selling and why. For Gran had remained active in the store, even after Granddad died a dozen years ago.

One thing Sandy would never forget was the way Mag communicated with her customers.

"You've got to listen to them, girl," Mag would repeat after a long talk with one of her regular patrons. "It's what they want that matters."

Classic marketing wisdom, long before anyone had ever written a marketing textbook. Mag Murphy had been Sandy's role model, her confidante and her staunchest supporter for as long as she could remember.

Hearing that Gran was retiring to Worthington House had alarmed Sandy so much that she'd jumped at the opportunity when Britt Hansen Marshack called a month ago. If Gran wasn't well, Sandy wanted to be nearby.

Seeing a lot of her grandmother over the holidays just past had reassured her some. The elderly woman's incongruous blond curls still danced softly as she spoke and she still wore jewelry that probably weighed as much as she did. Her bright blue eyes were lively and sharp. But it was her unflagging energy that really set Sandy's mind at rest. She was still glad to be here, where she could keep an eye on her grandmother. Sandy's heart swelled as she turned away.

She walked slowly down the corridor of Worthington House. Funny, you could live near a place all your life and never set foot in it. To Sandy, the old Victorian had seemed as formidable and unapproachable as the others nearby, the Ingallses' and the Phelpses' mansions. But seeing Worthington House up close had been as reassuring as seeing Gran again. Sandy was content that her grandmother was in the right place, a place where she could keep up with old friends and share activities with new ones.

Peering into smaller rooms off the main corridor, where various activities were going on, Sandy wondered if she might have overreacted, quitting an exciting job and leaving behind a comfortable life. But she was here now, and anxious or not, she was going to make the best of it, she thought as she ducked out of the aerobics room and into the softly lit activity room, lined with shelves of games and puzzles, even a table full of antique toys. A quilting frame had been pushed to one side.

The seniors at Worthington House obviously weren't into quiet activity this morning, for the room was empty. Sandy wandered in to check out the quilt, curious about the quilting circle Gran had talked about joining. While studying the red-and-blue pattern, she plucked a handful of jelly beans out of a glass decanter on a nearby table. With her other hand, she began cranking the handle on a brightly painted, old-fashioned jack-in-the-box on the table.

"I thought the candy and games were for residents only."

A silly-looking clown popped out of the box at the same moment the soft voice spoke, startling her out of her reverie. Clutching the toy, she whirled. A tall, slim man stood framed in the doorway, grinning at her.

"And you definitely don't look like a resident," he continued. "No walking stick, no bifocals, no hearing aid."

Thinking she hadn't seen a man with such a teasing gleam in his eyes for months, Sandy popped the last of her fistful of jelly beans into her mouth and simply took him in. He was dressed casually, in khakis and a crew-neck sweater in a rich shade of cranberry that played magically with his dark hair and pale, blue-gray eyes. Sandy realized as she stared that most of the men she'd seen since starting at International Baking were business types, somber in their dark suits, rushed and unsmiling in their intensity. Even the creative types in marketing had been more intent on focus groups and market share than on what fun could be had in the process.

"Stereotyping," Sandy said, shaking her head in mock disapproval. "Not a very nineties thing to do."

He helped himself to a fistful of jelly beans. "My error in judgment appalls even me. So, what are you, about sixty-nine, seventy? My grandfather arrives next week. He'll be really pleased to meet you. He's not crazy about the idea of coming here, but I think he'll change his mind."

Sandy laughed and set down the jack-in-the-box. They walked toward the door together. "Does he like jelly beans?"

The young man shook his head. "Can't handle 'em. Stick to his dentures. But I suppose you know all about that."

And he leaned over as they got to the front door and made a show of studying her teeth. "Remarkable. They look so natural."

He took a red down jacket from the hooks beside the front door and pulled a pair of gloves and a knit cap out of the pocket. He helped Sandy with her wool dress coat, the gesture of an old-fashioned gentleman. Sandy thought Gran would approve of both the courtliness and the sense of humor.

"Your grandfather will like it here," Sandy said as he opened the front door, exposing them to a burst of cold air and blowing snow.

The man shook his head. "I hope you're right. Grandpa doesn't—"

Before Sandy could find out exactly why he seemed uncertain his grandfather would like Worthington House, she heard a familiar voice and looked up to see Gran, hanging out the window of the community room and shaking her fist at them.

"Keep your paws off that girl, you two-timing so-and-so, you!"

CHAPTER TWO

EMBARRASSMENT washed over Sandy as she stared at her grandmother, leaning out the window and bellowing at this total stranger. A total stranger who, minutes before, had had Sandy entertaining thoughts of flirtation and getting acquainted and relearning the fine art of simply having fun.

With her dangling conch earrings—"Gives things a summery feel, don't you think?"—artificial-blond curls and fake eyelashes almost as long as her fake nails, Gran seemed at her flaky best, the caricature of an aging woman who still doesn't accept the fact that she'll never again look like Betty Grable. She also looked determined to launch another verbal assault on the man with the laughing eyes, but then someone from inside the community room tugged her back in by her royal-blue sleeve and slammed the window on the snowy afternoon.

The man turned laughing eyes on Sandy, raised one snow-dusted eyebrow questioningly. A corner of his mouth quirked, as if he could barely suppress his laughter. "And I thought Grandpa might find it a little dull at Worthington House. Looks as if I was wrong."

Despite her expensive college education, Sandy could figure out no way to sink into the sidewalk and disappear. She opened her mouth to deliver some clever rejoinder, but came up empty. She was grateful, at least, for the nip of damp wind on her cheeks, for it provided some excuse for her high color.

"Your fairy godmother, I presume? Guardian angel? Grandmother protector?"

"I, uh, I have to run." Hands buried deep in the pockets of her coat, Sandy began to back away. She knew she was acting silly and defensive, like an adolescent caught parading as an adult. But she couldn't seem to stop herself.

The man took a step in her direction. "Look, what she said—I don't know what she meant. I'm not—"

"It doesn't matter. I have to go." She was off the curb now and turning away. She wasn't sure why Gran's outburst had embarrassed her so, but it had. Maybe because she'd become so leery of involvement, after watching from her front-row seat while her boss and mentor lost everything she'd worked for—career, security, even her reputation.

Or maybe it was simpler than that. It could be Sandy felt flustered because the implication—that something was going on here besides a simple friendly encounter between two strangers—was closer to the truth than she wanted to admit.

After all, she had just been thinking how good it felt to be in the company of someone so devilishly cute, someone who made her smile so easily. She had been thinking that she might find time in her new life for things she had purposely shut herself off from recently. Things like men. And this man, with his sparkling eyes, lithe build and casual manner, had seemed as good a place as any to begin.

Which just showed how young and foolish she could be, letting herself get carried away by the first man to smile at her. And if Gran could see that, he could probably see it, too.

"Wait!" he called, but she was already halfway across the street, snow melting in her hair. Why on earth hadn't she worn a hat? Why on earth had she let herself get sucked into a schoolgirl fantasy in the time it took her to swallow a mouthful of jelly beans?

He called out to her once again, but the wind and snow muffled his voice. She kept walking, grateful she had gotten away before he even asked her name. Chances were he would forget her long before they ran into each other again.

DREW STARED at himself in the dresser mirror for ten full minutes the next morning, holding up for scrutiny the only tie he'd kept when he left Chicago.

"To tie or not to tie," he muttered to his reflection.

He threw a grim smile at his reflection and wrapped the tie around his neck, pretending to choke himself with the strip of paisley silk as he went into the all-too-familiar motions that resulted in a neat four-in-hand knot.

He studied the result. He was rusty.

Hadn't he left Chicago so he would no longer need a collection of silk ties in all the power colors? He almost changed his mind, then reminded himself that he had a very important statement to make in today's meeting with the new director of marketing.

After a second attempt that resulted in a passable knot, he went down to breakfast wearing a white shirt, his tweed sport coat and the lumpy necktie.

Anna Kelsey, his landlady, raised an eyebrow over the orange juice. "A necktie this morning? Did I miss something? Is the Prince of Wales passing through Tyler?"

Although still slender and attractive with her dark hair and gold-rimmed glasses, Anna Kelsey was nevertheless the motherly heart of Kelsey Boardinghouse. In fact, it was her soft-spoken warmth that had convinced Drew to take the room in the rambling Gunther Street home.

He smiled, because Anna Kelsey could draw a smile no matter what his mood. "No. Just the new marketing director for Yes! Yogurt."

Anna nodded and filled his coffee cup. "Ah. The company's really growing, then?"

"Who would have thought you could make money selling *anything* made out of goat's milk?" Glenna Kelsey McRoberts said as she took a seat across from Drew. "We all figured Britt was going a little batty, you know. A widow with four kids, growing desperate. That's what we thought." She laughed wryly, her dark hair gleaming as she shook her head. "And she probably was."

Anna gave her daughter a fond look. Divorced, with two kids of her own, Glenna had been living at the Kelsey house throughout Drew's stay. Jimmy and Megan, her young children, added a joyous, often boisterous element, and like all the other boarders, Drew was very fond of them. He was really glad Glenna had recently found such obvious happiness for herself, falling in love with Lee Nielsen, the arson investigator trying to find out what had really happened at Ingalls F and M. Lee was a lucky so-and-so, Drew thought, with a feeling of envy for his fellow emigrant from the city. But somebody else's love life was none of his business, though many people in Tyler didn't agree with him on that. That might be the only problem with small-town living.

"I know what you mean," he said with a grin. "I remember my first reaction to Jake's announcement that he was marrying the queen of goat's milk yogurt."

Anna laughed, too. Britt had created the yogurt—automatically creating an untapped market niche for her product—about four years ago when the fifth-generation

family farm was failing, the bank threatening to fore-
close, and one Jake Marshack was breathing down her
neck for payments to his dairy-feed company. Britt had not
only created a delicious and unique product, she had saved
Lakeside Farm for herself and her four kids *and* won the
heart of the heartless Jake Marshack as well.

For the first several years, Britt had managed production and Jake, distribution. But as the company grew by
leaps and bounds, they had realized they needed help and
had turned to Jake's cousin. With Drew's help, they had
built a full-scale manufacturing facility, with room to
grow, and had established an efficient network for reaching markets around the country.

Now things had grown so much they needed a full-time
marketing director. At least, that was what Jake and Britt
had decided.

Drew supposed he should feel gratified. But the truth
was he almost hated to see things change. Life in Tyler had
been so uncomplicated. It was what had drawn him here,
away from the rat race and the frustrations of city living.
Now, who knew what would happen?

In Drew's opinion, infinitely bigger wasn't necessarily
better.

"You still haven't convinced me we even need a marketing director," he had grumbled on the day Jake told
him who they'd decided to hire for the new position.

"And I never will," Jake had said. "You're still content to be a mom-and-pop operation. Britt and I think we
can do more."

Drew and his cousin rarely disagreed, at least not anymore. They had disagreed plenty as kids, growing up in the
same tiny apartment with their widowed mothers, who
were sisters, and Drew's siblings. Drew's mother had always been too stubborn to accept any of the help Grandpa

Stirling offered, so times had been tough. But now Drew knew how valuable that extended family had been. Drew had been just enough younger that Jake had wanted nothing to do with him—until Jake got old enough to realize how much Drew needed a big brother. He'd stepped in, guiding his cousin through high school, helping him line up a scholarship, then pointing him toward a career in sales. Between Jake's steady influence and Clarence's lifelong involvement, Drew had grown up a lot better adjusted than most boys without fathers.

Jake had called his cousin in as a consultant in the early days of Yes! Yogurt, when he and Britt were still struggling to get the company off the ground. So although Drew hadn't joined the business full-time until about six months ago, he had been in on it from the ground floor, giving his advice on sales and marketing techniques as it grew.

Somehow, when he'd joined them half a year ago, he'd thought they were content with the company's level of success.

"Okay," he had countered when Jake announced the decision about the marketing director, "if you're determined to do this, at least do it right. On paper, this Murphy woman looks awfully young to handle the position."

"She's twenty-five," Jake had said.

"That's barely seasoned in business and you know it."

"She's worked for us three summers, in every area of the business," Jake said. "She knows Yes! Yogurt almost as well as Britt does. Besides, she spent more than a year as an assistant at International Baking."

Drew sighed. A beginning position for a year or so at a big conglomerate meant nothing, but try telling that to Jake and Britt.

"She probably spent most of that year doing grunt work—drafting proposals for the real power in the marketing department and tracking down demographic data to support whatever conclusion somebody else wanted to prove,'' he had argued. "If we're going to have this kind of help on board, let's at least get somebody who can pull her weight in the industry.''

Jake and Britt had the final say, of course, although they sometimes made decisions based more on sentimentality than on horse sense. Drew told himself he would make the best of the situation.

But before he left the boardinghouse, he dashed back upstairs. If Anna had noticed the necktie, so would Britt and Jake. And they would also know why he'd worn it. So he left the tie on his dresser, swapping at the last minute for his usual khakis and cable-knit sweater.

He assured himself, as he stepped gingerly through the fresh snow and coaxed to life the reluctant engine of his no-longer-new sedan, that the seven years he had on Ms. Murphy would be all the advantage he needed.

The drive to Yes! Yogurt, headquartered in an old farmhouse near the edge of Britt's land, took longer than usual. The new-fallen snow had been rendered even more treacherous by a layer of sleet on top. And, as so often happened, Drew hadn't allowed extra time to get to the office, so he was pushing the clock by the time he skidded to a halt in the slick drive.

The meeting with Britt, Jake and the new marketing director was to have started five minutes ago.

Damn! Drew walked through the front door, casting off coat and gloves. He'd wanted a few minutes to collect himself, to make sure he was in the right frame of mind before he went into this meeting. He'd wanted another quick glance at the résumé of this young woman, just to make sure nothing caught him by surprise.

As usual, he was running late. As usual, he'd have to wing it.

While making a quick dash through his office to retrieve his files, Drew mentally reviewed what he knew about Alexandra Murphy. Sandy, everyone called her. Another reflection of her youth, he thought. She'd worked on some high-profile projects for International Baking, one of the giants in the food industry. And she had grown up in Tyler. That was about the extent of her credentials. Under the circumstances, establishing himself as the one in charge should be a piece of cake.

The problem was, it wasn't the kind of maneuvering Drew liked to participate in and it unsettled him. He wasn't here to play politics. He was here because he liked the challenges without the power plays that came with this level of business in the corporate world.

Nevertheless, he'd been around long enough to know that this morning's initial meeting with Ms. Alexandra Murphy would set the tone for their relationship. He intended to let her know in no uncertain terms that he was the one to whom she must prove herself. As vice president of sales, he was the one she had to please with her marketing plan. He was the one who knew how to get Yes! Yogurt into the hands of consumers. Her only role was to deliver the marketing tools he needed, when he needed them.

Despite Drew's best intentions, this felt suspiciously like the same kind of turfism and manipulation he'd left Chicago to escape.

He frowned as he searched every drawer in his desk for a pencil. Why the heck hadn't they hired a director of pencils and staples instead of a marketing person? Now that was something they needed.

The tap on his door was followed by Britt Marshack ducking her headful of strawberry-blond curls into his office. "Good. You *are* here."

"I'm here," he grumbled, finally grabbing a leaking ballpoint, the only thing he could find. "But all my pencils have taken the day off."

Britt walked over, shoved a stack of mail to one side and revealed a Chicago Bears mug filled with pens and pencils. Drew grabbed one and grinned.

"You're indispensable, Mrs. Marshack."

"I know. And you're late."

"You wouldn't notice that if you and that cousin of mine weren't so compulsive about being on time."

Feeling frazzled before things even started, Drew followed Britt to the former dining room, which they now used as a conference room. Damn, but he hadn't meant to be late today.

From his first glimpse of Alexandra Murphy, he wished he'd worn the tie.

She sat with her back to the French doors separating the conference room from the hallway, wearing a tailored red suit with a bit of white silk showing above the collar in back. Dark hair had been skinned into a neat, no-nonsense bun low on the back of her head. The suit had shoulder pads, but it wouldn't have mattered; those shoulders looked squared and no-nonsense even without the extra help.

Alexandra Murphy knew the importance of first impressions, too, and she was obviously here to impress. Drew's mood continued to sink.

He walked around the table to sit with Britt, and knew as soon as he looked Ms. Murphy in the eye that this day held more headaches than he'd dreamed.

Yes! Yogurt's new director of marketing was the impish young woman he'd flirted with at Worthington House the afternoon before—the one whose delicious smile had kept swimming before his eyes at dinnertime.

He'd already made his first impression, and he wasn't entirely sure it was the one he'd wanted to make.

CHAPTER THREE

EVERY SHRED of self-confidence Sandy had brought into the meeting vanished in the time it took her to blink twice and swallow hard.

Her red power suit didn't help. Her grandmother's choker-length pearls didn't help. Her Marian the Librarian hair didn't help. The outward composure she had mastered from mimicking Gin Luckawicz had never failed her so utterly. As the vice president of sales eased, wide-eyed, into the chair across the antique oak table from her, Sandy felt like a kid caught with her hand in the candy jar.

A jelly bean jar, to be exact.

She barely heard the introductions. But it did sink in that she was to have no reprieve, no second chance. This was Drew Stirling, the one man in town she had been most apprehensive about impressing.

Well, she had impressed him all right. Impressed him as a stammering, blushing, flirty *girl* who had a cartoon grandmother besides.

She had only one choice. She had to prove to him that yesterday had been a fluke. Sandy Murphy did not flirt, was not easily intimidated. Sandy Murphy didn't even *like* jelly beans, much less sneak them.

Thrusting her hand across the table, she told herself there was some slim chance that if she pretended they'd never met, he might even fall for it.

"I'm looking forward to working with you," she said, giving him her best corporate smile and gripping his hand firmly. It was cool and long-fingered, and served as a reminder that hers was damp and probably even shaking. "Britt tells me you've made real strides in sales over the past six months."

Sandy took in his reaction and was relieved to discover Drew Stirling had one of those faces that hid nothing. The man would be dead meat in a poker game. No wonder he'd come to Tyler, far away from corporate one-upmanship. With his boyishly open face, he would be unarmed on the boardroom battlefields. She watched, fascinated, as his mood switched from surprise to dismay to amusement.

He ended up with a look of sheer determination. Sandy wasn't sure what that meant, under the circumstances, but she made up her mind to meet him with equal determination.

With that reaction firmly in place on his mobile face, he asked, "Can I presume we'll make even greater strides in the next six months?"

What little bit of Sandy's confidence had remained now fizzled and died, but she struggled not to let it show. His challenge wasn't subtle. And she decided immediately that it rose out of his unfortunate first impression of her the evening before. Her heart began to thump fiercely. She had to do something to redeem herself and she had to do it right away, before that impression carved itself indelibly into Drew Stirling's consciousness.

"Absolutely," she said, leaning forward slightly in her chair and adopting the toughest tone at her command. "Our present marketing strategy is . . ."

She glanced at Britt, who looked a bit startled at how quickly this gambit for the upper hand had developed in Yes! Yogurt's cozy little headquarters. Sandy hadn't intended to launch into this right away. Her strategy had been to move in cautiously, allow everyone time to gain some confidence in her. Then and only then had she planned to suggest—one at a time—the changes that were so clearly needed.

Thanks to ever-outspoken Gran and a fistful of jelly beans, Sandy needed her big guns right now—as a diversionary tactic to make Yes! Yogurt's vice president of sales forget his first encounter with his new marketing director.

"Don't be shy," Drew prodded. "We're all eager to get your reaction."

Sandy doubted it. But she willed her breath to come slowly. "Frankly, you don't have much of a marketing strategy. You're shotgunning at the market."

"Shotgunning?"

Sandy had the strangest feeling, as if she and Drew were alone in the conference room. Jake had settled back in his chair, to all appearances simply intending to enjoy the unexpected show. Britt's expression said she might not enjoy the show, but it certainly had her mesmerized. The only thing Sandy knew to do was plunge ahead. If she got herself fired this morning, at least she would have the rest of the day to get on the phone and see if one of the other jobs she'd been offered was still available.

"You're sending out a lot of scattershot messages to different segments of the market," she said, growing more sure of herself as she warmed to her topic. "Even your logo isn't used consistently. I've taken a look at all your marketing materials—and there isn't much, other than your packaging and a couple of print ads in food-industry journals—and can't discern a cohesive message about what Yes! Yogurt is."

"You want to change our packaging?" Drew said, ze-roing in on one of those things she really hadn't intended to bring up right now.

Sandy refused to be sidetracked. "That's a minor point. What really concerns me—and should concern everyone at this table—is that your identity is weak in the market-place."

Drew didn't look troubled. "Dairy distributors all over the country aren't having a lot of trouble figuring out what we're all about."

"You've had some good luck," Sandy conceded, "mostly due to the fact that Britt created such a unique product to start with. But at a time when yogurt sales have mushroomed all over the country—all over the *world*—your numbers should look better. In fact, they *will* look better."

She paused to give each of the three people in the room an unwavering look. "I guarantee it."

Britt appeared surprised, Jake thoughtful. Drew seemed merely skeptical. "How?"

Some of Sandy's inner quaking returned. The voice of reason in her head screamed that now wasn't the time to do this. She didn't yet know whose toes she would be tram-pling with her suggestions and criticisms. What she was doing was corporate suicide.

She plunged ahead anyway.

"First, we'll need some market studies."

She saw him barely stop himself from rolling his eyes—a familiar look from those who didn't fully understand marketing. On him it was almost cute. This might be eas-ier, she thought, if he didn't have such compelling eyes and such a boyish smile.

"I know," she said, smiling herself as she felt the fa-miliar ground of market research beneath her feet.

"You're not alone. Most people in sales want results without the homework. They like to think the product sells based on the sheer magnetism of their personalities. But if you want to take Yes! Yogurt to the twenty-first century, you need to know what your consumers *want*, not what you want to shove down their throats."

Britt finally spoke up. "But won't that take a lot of time?" She glanced at Jake. "And money?"

Sandy turned to the friend who had given her not only this opportunity, but her first real job during college. "It doesn't have to, if you know what you're doing."

Again, Drew was there with a challenge. "And you do?"

"I certainly do."

Their gazes locked. Sandy saw respect in his bright, pale eyes, and that pleased her. But it was tempered with a touch of humor and a bit of impatience. It dawned on her that Drew Stirling didn't want her here to begin with. Young or mature, experienced or not, a marketing director wasn't exactly welcome on Drew's territory.

Something else crept into his expression, then was instantly banished. Sandy wouldn't have noticed it at all, except that she had seen the same thing in his eyes the day before. When Drew looked at her, he saw a woman. And that kind of awareness appeared to be something he wasn't willing to bring into this conference room.

Seeing that in him forced Sandy to admit that she, too, liked what she saw of the man across the table. That had never happened to her at the office, and as she'd watched her former boss's personal soap opera unfold these past six months, she'd sworn it never would. Shrewd, talented Gin had finally, with middle age staring her in the face, fallen in love. Unfortunately, she'd fallen in love with one of the vice presidents at International Baking. At first, no one had seen a problem. Then someone had suggested that Gin's department got more attention at board meetings than other departments. Next, someone questioned whether the budget for Gin's department was subject to less scrutiny than those of other department heads.

Soon the accusations became so vicious that someone had to go. That someone had been Gin.

Sandy felt the rush of anguish and anger that always came when she pondered Gin's fate.

And now, as she admitted to herself what was playing at least a small part in the friction between herself and Drew Stirling, Sandy also felt a rush of anxiety. She tried to ignore it, to tell herself that because she recognized where her thoughts were straying she could now control them. To prove it to herself, she smiled at him. It was a mistake. His determined expression turned a bit more combative.

"I'm sure you'll bring some excellent ideas to the table, Ms. Murphy," he began. "But for the moment, why don't you slow down and get your feet wet before you suggest shaking up the whole company?"

A couple of sharp responses formed in Sandy's head, none of which she considered appropriate for a business meeting. While she groped for a businesslike reaction, Drew turned to Britt and Jake, opened a folder and said, "Let's see what we can do about this outlet store Britt wants to open in town. I've got some information on a couple of buildings available to rent at a reasonable rate. Is this really the direction we want to take?"

Sandy saw her own worst-case scenario shaping up on her very first day on the job: her ideas were being dismissed, her experience called into question.

What would her mentor at International Baking tell her? For the moment, nothing came to mind. The vast reservoir of wisdom Gin had shared during the sixteen months they'd worked together had momentarily gone dry. Okay, then, what would Gran tell her?

Give 'em something to talk about, girl.

She grinned as she recalled some of Mag's advice on life and business, then looked up in time to catch Drew watching her instead of Britt, who was reviewing the reasons for opening the outlet store in Tyler. Good. Let him worry about what her own expression meant. Let those committees in his head get together and talk about what she might be up to. She deepened her smile.

He tried not to look at her during the rest of the ninety-minute meeting. But Sandy was alert enough to realize it was a struggle for him.

Let him worry about whether he really has the upper hand, she thought as the meeting came to a close. *He'll find out soon enough he's underestimated me.*

"I THINK you underestimate her," Jake said as the two men drove toward town to tour the possible sites for a Yes! Yogurt outlet store.

"No, I don't," Drew protested.

But his cousin was right. Drew had realized that the instant he saw that strange smile on her lips right after he had managed—he thought—to put her in her place.

Why he'd said what he had, so abruptly and so condescendingly, he hadn't yet figured out. Why hadn't he simply let her prattle on and hang herself?

Because it was his responsibility to keep things focused on results, he'd told himself. Britt was the dreamer and Jake held the purse strings—tightly, which was fine with Drew. Drew's role was to keep things moving forward.

Where would Alexandra Murphy fit in that mix? And why was he so adamant about not wanting to find out?

"She's a very bright young woman." Jake pulled off the highway at the empty storefront next to the Dairy King and a gas station. "Britt is convinced the two of you can be a powerful team, if you give it a chance."

"You make me sound like some kind of rigid stuffed-shirt," Drew protested, giving the car door a slam and heading toward Cordelia Rolphe, the real estate agent waiting for them at the door of the cinder block building, which had been painted a soft yellow.

Jake smiled pleasantly and clapped him on the shoulder. "If the shoe fits."

"Well, she's a bit wet behind the ears."

"Be open-minded. That's all I'm saying."

"I am open-minded."

But he wasn't, not about this. Drew stewed over the admission to himself as they toured the building. With only half his attention, he studied the refrigerated display cases and the floor, badly in need of retiling, telling himself that having little foot traffic here on the highway wouldn't be a major drawback, as customers could drive. Most of his thoughts were on the woman whose presence this morning had thrown him so. He hadn't expected that. But from the moment he'd walked around the table and recognized his new co-worker, Drew had known he had problems.

Alexandra Murphy sparked something in him that few women touched. She was beautiful in an exotic way, with that tawny complexion, dark hair and eyes, those sculpted cheekbones and that generous mouth so ready to leap into a warm smile. But her looks weren't the problem, at least not the whole problem. He'd worked with plenty of gorgeous women and never given it a moment's thought.

No, he'd seen an innocence, a girlish enthusiasm beneath her polish, and it was that that had struck a chord in him. Despite her power suit, her sedate pearls and the

Grace Kelly hairstyle that screamed she wanted to be in control, Drew couldn't get out of his mind another image of her—the leggings and the braid and the university sweatshirt worn by a young woman unable to resist the lure of candy and a jack-in-the-box. She might look sophisticated, but Drew knew something else about her.

She still had a lot of kid in her. And it was that that he was pulled toward, attracted to.

He almost groaned aloud as the thought registered. He *wasn't* attracted to her. *Couldn't* be attracted to her. Absolutely refused to even consider the possibility.

"On a scale of one to ten, what do you think?"

Jake's disconcerting question reminded Drew that his thoughts had gone far afield. Dragging himself back to the moment, he took a final sweeping look at the shop. "I think it would serve the purpose."

They walked from the chilly building into the sharp, cold breeze. Cordelia paused behind them, locking up. While they waited, Drew looked restlessly up and down the highway. In addition to the Dairy King and the gas station, a stretch of uneven sidewalk led to the Heidelberg Restaurant, Sugar Creek Park and beyond that, of course, Ingalls Farm and Machinery. Most of the walkway had already been cleared after the previous afternoon's snowfall.

In front of the F and M, however, the ice remained, making walking treacherous. Except that no one would be walking in front of the Tyler landmark. Yellow police tape still cordoned off the scene.

The site of last fall's fire remained a blight on the highway, reminding everyone as they came and went that futures were precarious in Tyler right now. With the cause of the fire still undetermined and people growing uneasy about weeks out of work turning into months, the yellow tape festered in the town's consciousness. Even Britt had begun to question whether now was the time to open their outlet shop. A slow start seemed almost guaranteed. But Jake kept reassuring her that this thing would be settled soon, that the insurance company would write the check and renovations would begin. Tyler would return to normal.

Drew wondered if that wasn't overly optimistic, but kept his worries to himself.

"Drew, look." Jake nudged him with an elbow. "Isn't that Matt?"

"Matt's in school, isn't he?"

The young man standing at the edge of the woods across the highway had pulled the collar of his jacket up and his knit cap low, so it was impossible to see his face. But Drew had to admit he looked a lot like Jake's sixteen-year-old stepson. But what would he be doing out here on the highway in the middle of the day, when he ought to be in class?

"Come on," Jake said, taking off toward the boy, who simply stared across the highway, apparently into the burned-out shell of the F and M. "I'm going to see what this is all about."

But in the time it took a truck to rumble past, the youth had disappeared, probably through the trees and back to the high school beyond.

"Damn!" Jake stood staring at the woods, a grim expression on his face. "That *was* him, wasn't it?"

"Well, it looked like him to me. But it's not like Matt to cut school, is it?"

"Well, it didn't used to be. But..."

"What?"

"Something's wrong. He's been acting weird lately."

"He's sixteen. How can you tell?"

Jake shook his head and laughed, although Drew could sense it took an effort. "You're right."

"Probably girl stuff. The head cheerleader probably won't give him the time of day. You know how it is."

"Yeah."

But Drew noticed that both he and his cousin were preoccupied as they toured the second building, this one on Main Street, between the bank and the video-rental store. And neither of them could tell Britt a thing about the second building when they got back to headquarters.

Drew knew what Jake's excuse was, but couldn't think of anything to safely blame his own inattention on.

CLARENCE ALBERT STIRLING smiled his most charming smile at the Chicago hospital nurse who wanted to stick him. "That's a frightfully big needle, Nurse Ratched."

She was a pretty young thing, round faced and dark eyed, with the most adorable pink bow of a mouth that now curved in a wry smile. "The name is Anna Grisham. And we save the biggest pains in the rear for the patients who've been the biggest pains in the rear. So, are you gonna roll over or shall I call in the SWAT crew to hoist you over and hold you down?"

Clarence chuckled and obliged. "Actually, I wouldn't complain at all, but I fear that isn't necessarily my best side any longer."

Anna Grisham laughed at the same moment Clarence grunted, and it was over.

"Need anything else while I'm here?" she asked, dropping the needle and her plastic gloves into a locked container on the wall.

"Now that you mention it," he said, "perhaps you could provide me with some information. How long would you say is the record for a hospital stay following hip-replacement surgery?''

Anna shook her head and retrieved his chart from the nearby table. ''No malingering, Mr. Stirling. You're doing very well. We'll have you out of here in less than a week, I can promise you that.''

Clarence hated frowning in front of such a pretty young thing, but he couldn't stop himself. ''What if I relapse?''

''You're not going to relapse.''

''What if I fall out of bed?''

Anna ducked her head and tried not to smile. ''Mr. Stirling, you're not gonna make me tie you down, are you?''

He smiled. ''I'm not normally into the kinky stuff, but I've been known to make exceptions.'' He wasn't typically so familiar, but had discovered during his hospital stay that the limits of acceptability had stretched some since his day.

''I'm gonna start bringing a chaperon with me.''

Clarence chuckled. ''Fine. Bring that nice Miss Lever-one, the one with the red hair.''

She paused at the door. ''Sounds to me like you're ready to be discharged right now, Mr. Stirling.''

''No, I assure you, Nurse Ratched, I'm pitiably weak.''

Then she was gone, leaving behind the sound of her laughter and the soreness in his backside.

Clarence's smile faded. He hadn't enjoyed being alone these past days, now that he knew what his grandson had in mind. He closed his eyes and tried to block memories that hadn't stirred in years—not since he'd had his heart attack in '86 and thought he was done for. The attack had turned out to be nothing but a nasty case of heartburn—as it turned out, he had the heart of a young man, according to the cardiologist—but he'd thought about her then nevertheless. Thought about forgiving her, if he happened to see her somewhere up there in the clouds.

But he hadn't died, and he hadn't allowed himself to think of Mag again.

Except maybe on Valentine's Day each year. But that was a natural thing, for a man to think of the worst day of his life from time to time.

And Drew going off to Tyler, Wisconsin, of course, had triggered more than a few memories. But Clarence had kept himself busy with his chess games and the birds in the park and sitting with the great-grandkids and taking those dance lessons once a week. Not that he didn't already know how to dance, though he'd been a little creaky ever since he took a bullet during the war. But it was company. A chance to put his arms around a member of the fairer sex. And the women did still say he looked like Fred Astaire.

Mag had been the first one to say that. Went right to his head, it had.

Magdalena. Maggie with butter-blond hair and eyes the color of Timber Lake. Mag the heartless, who had left him high and dry.

He had to change Drew's mind. He couldn't possibly go back to Tyler. At this stage of life, he didn't dare risk discovering that he still had a broken heart.

CHAPTER FOUR

SANDY LEANED OVER and took Jacob into her arms, distracting the two-year-old from his exploration of the deep recesses of the yellow Lab's mouth by swinging him over her head.

Jacob squealed in protest.

"I know exactly how you feel," she murmured in reply, sitting at the enormous, round kitchen table where the Hansen-Marshack clan gathered for meals and communication and even squabbles.

"Down!" fair-haired Jacob demanded, squirming and wiggling.

"Only if you promise not to climb down Daffy's throat again," Sandy bargained.

"Down!"

"I see the fine art of compromise is lost on you, Jacob."

Britt closed the oven door on the pot roast she was preparing for dinner and glanced at them. "You have about three seconds to make him a free man before—"

Too late. The shrieks began.

Britt grinned and stuck her head out the back door. "Christy! David! Somebody come get this screaming machine so we can converse like grown-ups in here!"

Sandy smiled. This was what she had always loved about the Marshack home, the ease with which everyone seemed to get along—despite banging screen doors, barking dogs, fussing children. And all of it, so it seemed, under the sure-handed control of Britt Hansen Marshack, with her girl-ish freckles and her disheveled strawberry-blond braid.

Of course, some things had changed since Sandy first started baby-sitting for Britt a good ten years ago. The white Victorian farmhouse with its gingerbread trim and wraparound porch had been painted and reroofed and spiffed up in countless other ways. But shopping lists and crayon artwork still adorned the fridge in the huge kitchen and family racket still provided the background music, with Britt conducting.

"Mo-om!" The exasperated voice coming from the living room belonged to fourteen-year-old Christy, already a mirror image of her petite mother. "I am on the telephone. How am I supposed to hear with both of you yelling like that?"

Britt rolled her eyes and stuck her head back out the door. "David! Matt! Somebody! *Now!*"

"I'm in the middle of an experiment, Mom!" Twelve-year-old David's voice was fainter, coming from somewhere in the vicinity of the barn.

"No arguments!"

Suddenly, a tall, broad-shouldered youth barged into the room, snatched the wailing Jacob out of Sandy's lap and said, "Come on, rug rat. Let's arm-wrestle."

Then they were gone. The crying ended almost as suddenly as the teenage boy had appeared.

"Wow. When did Matt grow up?"

Britt stared wistfully after her oldest and her youngest and sank into the chair across from Sandy. "Overnight, I think. Yesterday morning he was this awkward, skinny-chested kid with a cracking voice. Today, I looked up and Matt's almost six feet, his voice never cracks and he has to shave—*shave,* can you imagine?—almost every day."

She sighed with deep satisfaction. "The best part is, he and Jake are so close. I don't know what I would've done with a teenage boy if it weren't for Jake. He always knows exactly how to deal with a crisis. They would've had to lock me up long before now. But he handles everything like it's just another lump in the oatmeal."

Before starting to work summers during college for Yes! Yogurt, Sandy's only contact with Britt had come from her baby-sitting. She had known her in the way that small-town people know others who aren't in their age group or social circle, which is to say she knew everything there was to know about the thirty-something widow with four kids and a family farm the bank was threatening to repossess. Everything, including the romantic story of Jake Marshack coming to her rescue by bringing her goat's milk yogurt to the attention of influential people he knew in the food industry. Attention that had landed Britt on syndicated talk shows and had eventually pulled the farm out of financial difficulties.

That fairy-tale ending aside, Sandy could remember how envious she had been the summers she'd worked for Yes! Yogurt and witnessed firsthand the partnership between Britt and her new husband, Jake. Jake's obvious respect for Britt's creative bent and the thoughtful way they had listened to each other had become Sandy's ideal.

What the Marshacks had was what she demanded in a relationship. Nothing less would do.

Was it any wonder that since then she hadn't managed to date anyone for more than two months before disillusionment set in?

Was it any wonder she thought of it this afternoon, right on the heels of Drew Stirling's humiliating reaction to her at their first official meeting?

"He hates me," she said now.

"He doesn't hate you," Britt said. "He cries like that whenever he doesn't get his way."

"Not Jacob. Drew Stirling."

"Oh."

Sandy noticed that no denial was forthcoming from her friend. In fact, Britt's only response was to bring a bag of potatoes, a paring knife and a bowl to the table with her.

"I'm right, then?"

"He doesn't hate you. He just isn't sure we need a marketing director."

"Swell. That makes me feel much better."

Britt grinned. "He likes the company the way it is. Small."

"Doesn't he know small will be squeezed out in ten years or less? You have to compete to stay alive, Britt. I—"

Britt held up a hand to stem the flow of words. "Save it, Sandy. Jake and I are the ones who hired you, remember?"

Sandy stared at her friend and finally went after another knife. It took a lot of potatoes to feed this brood, she knew. "You didn't hire me out of some kind of misguided loyalty, did you?"

"We hired you because we think you have a lot of terrific experience that's going to help us go places with Yes! Yogurt. Okay?"

Sandy nodded grudgingly. "Okay."

They peeled in silence for a few minutes, then Britt asked, "How's living at home with the folks after all this time?"

Groaning, Sandy said, "Don't ask. You don't have a spare stall in the barn you're willing to rent out, do you?"

"That bad?"

"Mom and Dad are great. But they think I'm still a kid. They *worry* about me, for goodness' sake. They want me to call if I'm ten minutes late."

"You'll find a place soon. So, what kind of gossip do you need catching up on?"

While they finished preparing dinner, Britt filled Sandy in on who had married whom and which couples had already started families, the new photograph gallery in town and newcomers to Tyler. In short order, Sandy learned the latest on the young and attractive minister, Sarah Fleming, who had just married Michael Kenton, a drifter whose arrival in Tyler had set off all kinds of fireworks. Including, some people still insisted, the ones that had sparked the fire at Ingalls F and M. She found out that Pam Kelsey, the high-school football coach who also had multiple sclerosis, was still in remission and very happily pregnant, and that Ethan Trask had been appointed juvenile-court judge in Sugar Creek. Sandy's head was beginning to spin from all the news.

"And Timberlake Lodge is going great guns?" she asked as she set the table.

"Wonderful. You should go take a look around, it's really lovely out there. Sheila Lawson is the manager, you know. Wasn't she in your class?"

Sandy frowned. Not exactly a classmate: rather, her baby-sitter once upon a time. Sheila was five years older, which wasn't that much between adults. Plenty of Sandy's friends in Atlanta had been thirty and older. But how was she supposed to relate as an equal to a person who had been her baby-sitter?

How long, she wondered, did it take to feel like a grown-up in the town where you grew up?

Feeling more discouraged all the time about her prospects in Tyler, Sandy said, "What's it going to take to get Drew Stirling to come around?"

Britt paused, gazed at her, then resumed slicing the roast. "You're worrying too much about Drew Stirling. He'll come around. In the meantime, forget about him, for goodness' sake."

Sandy wasn't sure that little task would be as easy as Britt made it sound.

JAKE FOUND his stepson in his bedroom, playing with Jacob. It struck Jake that the toddler was about the only one in the family sixteen-year-old Matt had much to do with these days.

"Can we talk?"

Matt looked up only briefly, then turned his attention back to Jacob, who was intent on tasting each of a dozen empty CD boxes scattered around the bedroom floor.

"Sure. What's up?"

Jake wasn't certain how to begin. Memories began to swirl through his head, reminding him of the belligerent adolescent Matt had been when Jake first became interested in Britt romantically. For a while it had looked as if the boy would sabotage the whole relationship simply by behaving obnoxiously. Eventually, however, Matt had come around. In the almost four years since the wedding, Jake and Matt had grown close. Having the boy learn to confide in him and depend on him had been one of the most satisfying experiences of Jake's life. He felt as much like this teen's father as he did the father of the two-year-old playing so contentedly on the floor between them.

But closeness hadn't come that easily lately. Jake couldn't pinpoint exactly when things had begun to change, but he couldn't deny any longer what he was seeing. Matt didn't seem to hang out with his friends anymore, not even the new kid in town, Jon Weiss. For the first couple of months of the school year, Matt and Jon had been inseparable, especially when they both got involved in the co-op work project at the F and M. But in the past month or so, the boys didn't seem to spend any time together. Matt hadn't even been interested enough to sign up for a substitute co-op project after the fire at the F and M put an end to his first project. Gradually, that disinterest had spread to his other friends, his family, now apparently even to his schoolwork.

One thing Jake had learned quickly: you don't play games with teenagers. So he cut to the chase. "You weren't in school this morning."

Matt tensed visibly but didn't look up. "Who told you that?"

"I saw it for myself."

Matt shook shaggy brown hair out of his eyes and glanced up defiantly. "You were spying on me."

"I was out at that end of town on business. I saw you."

Matt didn't reply.

Fighting his impatience, Jake said, "Why weren't you in class, Matt?"

Screwing up his mouth on one side, Matt began pushing on the heel of one Nike with the toe of the other one. "You tell Mom?"

"So far this is between us."

The shoe came flying off and landed in the middle of the jumble of CD boxes. Startled, Jacob whimpered, studied the offending shoe and touched it gingerly.

"I cut class, that's all," Matt said at last. "Calculus. Big deal. I hate calculus. The teacher's a dork."

It sounded so reasonable, given a teenager's logic. But Matt's demeanor, now and for the past few weeks, raised a red flag for Jake. "Something bothering you, Matt? This isn't like you. In fact, you've been acting like something's eating at you for—"

"Nothing's bothering me, okay? I cut class. Wisconsin doesn't have the death penalty for cutting class, okay?"

Jake remembered his futile attempts to bulldoze his way through the wall Matt had built during the early days of Jake's relationship with Britt. Each assault had simply guaranteed that Matt would hoist up another brick, building the barricade a little higher. Jake should back off now; he knew that. But it wasn't easy. Didn't feel right.

Standing to leave, he tweaked little Jacob's nose, then said, "Dinner's on the table in ten minutes. Sandy's joining us. Think you can help make her feel welcome?"

Matt shrugged and stared at his stepfather suspiciously. "That's all? I'm not grounded or anything?"

"Not this time. But don't let it happen again." He waited for some sign of agreement from Matt, but it didn't come. "Whatever it is, I can be a good listener."

But the youth gave no indication that he was listening at all.

SANDY AND DREW butted heads again when she learned from Britt the next day that he and Jake had reached a decision about the outlet store in town. Never one to back down from a confrontation, she marched into Drew's office immediately.

"Why would you make a decision like this without consulting the marketing director?" she asked, carefully measuring forcefulness against abrasiveness. She had watched Gin, her former boss, enough to understand the fine line that separated the two, especially for women in business.

Whatever hint of amusement she had seen in Drew's eyes at their first meeting was no longer in evidence. He didn't look hostile, she decided, but he was working hard simply to remain neutral.

"We decided long before you arrived," he said. "All we've done is select a location."

Clueless, she thought. "I repeat, why would you make a decision like that without consulting the marketing director?"

He made a move to stand, then apparently changed his mind. He was unwilling to look as if he thought it necessary to flex his muscles, Sandy thought. He would prove he had the power by remaining in his chair, as if having to look up at her wasn't enough to rob him of his clout.

"What does marketing have to do with the location of a store?" he asked.

Sandy wanted to laugh, but kept it to a smile. "Marketing has to do with every decision we make that affects how we reach our customers."

"I see." He smiled back. But Sandy had seen his real smile, and this wasn't it. "I'll try to remember to keep you informed."

"I don't want to be *informed,*" she said. "I want to be *involved.* I'm going to be in your back pocket. I'm going to be inside your head when you make your decisions. We're going to be joined at the hip, Drew Stirling. That's the way marketing and sales work. And if you don't get the connection, I can recommend some basic marketing materials to read in your spare time."

He did stand now. He was taller, six feet or an inch or so over. But in her heels, Sandy barely had to look up.

"Now, look, Ms. Murphy—"

"Sandy," she said, smiling. Always smile when you have to be tough, Gin used to say. It disarms them. "We don't have to be so formal, do we?"

He clenched his jaws tightly. "Sandy. I don't need educating about marketing."

"Oh, really. Then I know you understand that location, physical layout and appearance of our facility all have an impact on its success. We've never had a retail outlet before. Shouldn't we sit down and discuss fixtures, signage, things like that?"

"Of course, of course. Whenever you want to."

"Good. How about now?"

"How about just after lunch?"

"Perfect. My office or yours?"

His, of course. You're stronger on your own turf. Sandy knew that, too. But she had demanded to be included in a major new project for the company and she had won the round. Next time, she thought, maybe he wouldn't be so quick to leave her out of the company's business.

Sandy realized as she left that she had failed to mention to him her plans for later in the afternoon, but she decided not to turn around and go back. He would find out soon enough about her appointment at the elementary school to talk with the school's dietitian about including Yes! Yogurt products in the daily menu.

Let him see how it felt to be left out, she thought, hating the idea that she sounded exactly like the pouting child she didn't want anyone viewing her as.

By the time she left the school a few hours later, with an agreement to offer free samples one day during lunch to see how the children reacted to the yogurt, Sandy had all but forgotten about Drew. She was on her way back to her car when Renee Hansen ran up, giggling and breathless, her book bag hanging off one shoulder.

"Hi!" the ten-year-old said, stumbling over her own feet in her efforts to stop. "What are you doing here?"

Sandy gave her young friend a hug. Renee was her favorite of Britt's children, probably because she had been the youngest for so long, until little Jacob came along. Quiet and easygoing, Renee had often seemed to get lost in the raucous shuffle at the Hansens', a feeling Sandy had always identified with. She remembered so clearly the little girl's somber complaints during the long, hard months after her father died, when Sandy had done plenty of babysitting for the noisy foursome.

"Nobody ever listens to me, 'cause they think I'm too little," Renee had said, sucking on the end of her pigtail. "But I talked to Daddy in heaven last night and he said he's not sad. And we shouldn't be, either."

At that moment, Sandy had pulled the little girl into her arms and made up her mind that she would listen to Renee, no matter what Renee's siblings did. Even after Sandy left for college, she had made it a point to send postcards and funny greeting cards to her young friend, filled with news of college life.

Renee had rewarded her with laboriously hand-printed notes about all the family news. Such as, "Matt says I can't come watch him at band practice because I'm too little, but I don't mind." Or, "Christy says I'm not old enough to go with her friends to the mall in Sugar Creek. But if I'm ever the big sister, I'll take my little sister everywhere with me."

Sandy had commiserated and listened and become the object of a huge case of hero worship. It was a strange feeling for someone who had herself felt left out because she was the baby of the family.

Renee might no longer be the official baby of the family, but with her plump, freckled face and the adoration in her eyes, she was still one of the cutest kids Sandy had ever met. She kept her arm around the little girl's shoulders and said, "Well, hi! I've just been convincing the school dietitian to have a Yes! Yogurt day in the lunchroom. You think the kids'll like that?"

Renee shrugged. "If you're there. Then I'll make sure they like it."

Sandy laughed and unlocked her car door. "It's a deal. Say, isn't that your bus?"

Renee looked around and saw kids piling onto the big yellow vehicle for the ride home. "Yeah, I better hurry."

"How about I give you a ride? It's on my way."

"Cool."

They had to clear the change in routine with Renee's teacher, who had once upon a time taught Sandy. Then Renee entertained Sandy most of the way home with a recitation of a comedy routine she had seen on TV the night before. Sandy suspected something had been lost in the translation, because most of the punch lines that sent Renee into a spasm of giggles didn't make much sense to her. But she still enjoyed the little girl's giddy enthusiasm.

"That's where Drew is gonna live," Renee said, pointing to a well-hidden turn off the asphalt road.

A muddy drive disappeared into the woods. "Oh, really?"

"Yep. He's building a house. It's gonna be way cool. It's got room for his wife and everything."

Sandy's heart jumped its track. "His wife?"

"Um-hmm. Can I find a new station?"

Renee began surfing for a better station on the car radio and resumed her chatter, but Sandy barely noticed. She kept thinking of what Drew Stirling had said to her outside Worthington House the day they'd met. Hadn't he said he wasn't married?

By the time she pulled up in front of the farmhouse and Renee bounded out of the car, Sandy had to know the answer. As the little girl waved goodbye, she called out, "I didn't know Drew was married."

Renee grinned. "Well, not *yet*. But I'm gonna find him somebody. 'Cause he's already said he's too old for me."

Sandy burned rubber pulling out onto the roadway. She didn't like the way relief had flooded her with Renee's clarification of Drew's marital status.

It would be better, she reflected, if he were married.

BY THE END of Sandy's first week on board, Drew had begun to remember most of his grandfather's tales about the battlefields of World War II. He discovered he wasn't comfortable living in the midst of constant skirmishes and sporadic ceasefires.

They argued about the advertising budget. They quibbled over his choice of publications for advertising. And Sandy made good her promise to live in his head. Oh, yes, she was there all right. Day and night.

Following their conversation about the new outlet store, he had taken her to the building on the highway that he and Jake had selected. She had walked around, her smile fading perceptibly as she studied the empty store. Finally, she had turned to him, shaking her head.

"I don't think this is going to do, Drew. Not at all."

They had sparred, of course. He had told her about signed contracts and she had started in on traffic flow. He had mentioned rental price and she had countered with ambience.

"Are you doing this just to prove a point?" he had muttered between clenched teeth as real estate agent Cordelia Rolphe phoned to arrange for Sandy to view the store Drew and Jake had already rejected.

Her gently arched eyebrows went up a half notch. "What point would that be?"

"That I should have brought you in on this to start with."

There it was, that damned unflappable smile of hers.

"Well, you should have. But I don't see where playing manipulative little games is necessary to prove that, do you?"

He didn't reply. She couldn't be twenty-five. No one that young could have him tied in this many knots so quickly.

Then Cordelia came back from the phone and announced that they could take a look at the other store now. And on their way out, she turned to Sandy and said, "Say, want me to be looking around for an apartment? Or maybe a house? It's a buyer's market, you know. Paying rent's a dead end."

"I know," Sandy said. "But I'm not sure I'm ready for that."

"You can't stay with your parents forever," Cordelia said.

Color came into Sandy's cheeks, and Drew realized the reference to living with her parents embarrassed her. He told himself to be a gentleman and let it go.

Then he remembered how many times she had made him look like a know-nothing these past few days, and before he could stop himself he was saying, "Still living with Mom and Dad, huh?"

"I've only been in town a few weeks," she said, her tone even.

He might never have known how deeply his comment had needled her if not for the color that continued to rise in her cheeks.

He trailed after her and Cordelia to the other store, certain that nothing she could say would convince him he and

Jake had made the wrong decision. But as soon as she started pointing out the advantages of the second building—more natural lighting for an airy feeling, a display-room configuration that would encourage browsing, the possibility of more foot traffic right in town, as well as ample parking nearby—Drew realized she had seen other things besides the financial considerations he and Jake had focused on.

She had placed herself in the customer's shoes.

Drew hated being wrong, but just this once he could admit it.

"Round one to you," he said as they got in his car and headed back to Yes! Yogurt headquarters.

"It's not about winning, Drew."

"Yes, it is. It's always about winning." *For people like you.* He didn't know what made him think that. She seemed sincere and certainly knew about being customer oriented. Her smile was warm and her eyes friendly and—

And that, he thought, was what really troubled him. Whenever he looked at her, he saw Sandy the attractive young woman instead of Sandy the capable director of marketing. That kind of thinking wasn't his style, and he didn't like himself for it right now.

But acting as if he disliked her was easier than admitting it to himself.

She placed her hands flat on the briefcase in her lap. "Am I going to need a score card?"

"I'll keep you posted," he said.

She laughed, and he found himself admiring her ability to keep her sense of humor even when she wasn't being treated very fairly. Was there anything about her he *didn't* like?

"Can you be trusted?" she asked.

"Didn't I admit when I was wrong about the building?"

"Not exactly. What you said, I believe, was, 'We'll try it your way, then.' Not exactly a ringing endorsement."

"Okay, how's this? I can see what a bonehead decision I made and I'll be forever grateful you were there to save my butt."

"That's fair, I suppose."

He laughed as well and thought maybe things were easing up between them.

But it wasn't their last skirmish of the week. She wanted to start market research and he didn't want to spend the money. She came in with a scaled-down plan that looked doable to him, although he could see it placed the burden of a lot of extra work on her. He questioned her methods and she requested a look at his sales figures.

By Friday afternoon, he couldn't wait to get out to the house he was building. Maybe he could haul lumber or something for Joe Santori. Drew was more than ready to swap mental strain for physical strain.

He was the last to leave the building. When he got out to the car, he found a stack of books in the driver's seat. Introduction-to-marketing textbooks.

Shoving the volumes into the passenger seat, he grinned. "Another point for Ms. Murphy."

CHAPTER FIVE

MAGDALENA MURPHY wasn't one for mooning over memories of days gone by. She believed in living in the present.

"These *are* the good old days," she would announce whenever one of her dotty friends in the quilting circle at Worthington House started harping on the past. "Remember wringer washers? Clotheslines in the dead of winter? Why, a pair of overalls would stand on their own when you brought 'em in. Good old days, my foot!"

Today she found her fingers slowing, stopping, her mind on anything but the Dresden Plate quilt pattern in front of her.

"Woolgathering isn't like you, Mag," Emma Finkle baum said.

Emma Finklebaum always was into everybody else's business. It came from working at the *Tyler Citizen* all those years. Mag felt no compunction to reply.

"Evelyn has asked twice now how your Sandy is doing on her new job."

Mag glanced up to discover that all eyes were on her. Sometimes it took her by surprise to find herself smack in the middle of a gaggle of old women. Emma had iron-gray hair and bifocals so thick her eyes looked twice their size. White-haired Evelyn's double chin had a double chin. And Martha Bauer must be older than dirt. Mag sighed. Most of the time, she saw them the way they'd been twenty and thirty years ago, completely overlooking the way they sagged and drooped in places where they hadn't once upon a time.

The same derangement, no doubt, that had fooled her into thinking she'd spotted Clarence Albert at the curb a week ago. She'd thought of that too much already to suit her.

"Alexandra is doing just fine," she said, turning her focus back to the quilting square in her hands. At least she didn't have hair the color of a dull nickel—her Moonspun Gold from the Hair Affair suited her just fine, thank you—and these violet-colored contacts kept her eyesight almost as sharp as it had ever been. "My granddaughter is extremely capable, you know."

"I hear they're opening an outlet store," Evelyn said. "Will there be many new jobs?"

Mag knew why Evelyn was asking about that. She glanced at Evelyn's daughter, Karen, who looked embarrassed at the mention of jobs.

"Mother," Karen chided softly, looking around at the women in the quilting circle.

"Now, where's the shame in asking?" Evelyn replied.

Evelyn's daughter visited only about once a week these days, and when she did she looked troubled and tired. Karen's husband worked at Ingalls F and M. At least, he had before the fire.

Mag gave Karen what she hoped was an encouraging smile. "I don't know whether one little store will bring many jobs or not," she admitted. "But I'm sure this can't go on much longer."

"Well, I'm certainly not hearing about much progress," Emma announced.

"Judson has stayed in town, even after the holidays," Martha Bauer said. "Things are bound to start happening now. I hear he's already sitting the family down to talk about rebuilding.''

Martha's son-in-law, Johnny Kelsey, was foreman at Ingalls F and M, so if anyone would know, she would. Everyone had expected the Ingalls family to rebuild quickly after the fire, until an arson investigator for the insurance company started poking about. In his opinion, the fire was "suspicious in nature." That meant somebody might have started it on purpose, although in Mag's opinion there wasn't a soul in Tyler who would do such a thing. But the investigator hadn't asked her opinion, and the insurance company wasn't writing any checks until the investigation was complete.

Thanks to that investigator, plenty of people had had to sit out the holidays without working, their hopes resting on the New Year. And so far, the year had brought no good news. Still, the old biddies in the Tyler Quilting Circle continued to talk the subject to death.

Mag had grown tired of the town's obsession with the topic. Tyler had always been that way, latching onto a subject and talking it dry. Folks had been that way about Judson Ingalls's murder trial. They'd been that way about Cliff Forrester, who had tried to run away from his memories of Vietnam by camping out at Timberlake Lodge before it was renovated and reopened. A lifetime ago, they'd talked themselves silly over the way Margaret Ingalls, Judson's wife, had up and vanished the night of one of her scandalous parties.

Of course, Mag had been grateful for that. That heartless troublemaker's disappearance had finally given the people of Tyler something to talk about besides Mag and Clarence.

At first, Mag had liked all the talk, all the glory that came from being engaged to Tyler's most decorated World

War II hero. Dashing with his wounded leg and the haunted look in his dark eyes, Clarence Albert Stirling had been the best catch in a town depleted of good men by Uncle Sam's call to duty. With all her nineteen-year-old heart, Mag had wanted him. Had wanted to be the belle walking by his side, absorbing the secondhand glory.

She had won him, too.

The two months of their engagement had been everything she had dreamed. They were feted and fawned over, pampered and preened. Gifts had poured in and the parties had been endless.

Until Clarence showed his true colors.

Mag jabbed her needle through the layers of fabric and felt the prick of pain, startling and sharp.

TWO PAIRS of wounded eyes stared back at Sandy, who stood in the middle of the braided rug in the Murphy family room. *Called on the carpet,* she thought, the same way she'd been at sixteen when she ran ten minutes past curfew.

"Why on earth would you want to do that?" her mother asked, an imploring note in her voice.

"No good reason I can think of, that's for certain," her father replied, his own voice gruff.

Sandy sighed. At twenty-five, having spent all but a few summers away from home since leaving for college at eighteen, she hadn't anticipated this kind of response. Or maybe she had. Maybe that was why she had waited until long after the holidays to bring up the subject of moving.

"I'm grown now," she said, trying hard to keep all hint of the little girl—*their* little girl—out of her voice. "Grown-ups don't live with their parents. I should have my own place."

Frank and Sadie Murphy exchanged troubled glances. In that moment, Sandy saw something she hadn't noticed before. Like the threadbare rug and the shiny upholstery in the house where she'd spent her childhood, her parents had grown older. Something seemed to drag down her father's lean, solemn face, giving him the appearance of a droopy-eyed basset hound. And her mother's dark good looks had faded, her hair shot through with silver and her eyes not as sparkling. Seeing them so clearly, so objectively all at once, Sandy almost backed down.

"It just seems such a waste," Sadie said, the pleading still in her voice. "Why spend money on an apartment when we have all these empty rooms?"

Being the youngest had always carried burdens that Sandy's older sister, Angela, had never appreciated. And their parents' resistance to any indication that Sandy was growing up had always been the hardest burden of all to shoulder. They'd kept her in girlish dresses, without makeup, long after other kids had started dressing like teens. Her folks hadn't wanted her to date. Hadn't seen any reason for her to work after school. Had wondered if it wouldn't be a good idea for her to stay home for a year before she went away to college.

Sandy, on the other hand, realized she had always been overeager to grow up. With a sister six years older, she had always been in a rush to catch up.

Hugging her elbows and hoping she was as right about this as she felt, Sandy said, "Mom, it's hard enough to come back and have everyone in town look at you and see the kid you used to be. I have to do some things to show people I'm not that kid anymore."

She didn't like it that the person she most wanted to impress with that point was someone who didn't even remember her from childhood. Why should she need to prove anything to Drew Stirling, beyond her professional ability? Her personal life was none of his business.

Still, it was his knowing grin that had suddenly made living at home rankle.

Frank shook his head and seemed to sink lower in his favorite lumpy armchair, where he always retired with the newspaper after closing Murphy's Hardware each day. "Whatever you want, Sandy. You know we always support your decisions."

True, Sandy thought. At least, it was true once they had hit her over the head with enough guilt to make her victories hollow. She would talk to Gran soon. Gran always helped her get things back into perspective after one of these tugs-of-war with her parents.

"What can I get you two for supper?" Sadie slid to the edge of her seat and looked at them expectantly.

"Mom, I think I'll take a walk first. You both go ahead. I'll catch something at the diner."

"But it's so cold out. And the sidewalks are still..." Sadie seemed to realize she was treating her daughter like a child, exactly what Sandy didn't want. "Well, we'll see you later then."

Sandy bundled up, laced on her boots and headed out. Having spent Christmas here before finishing up in Atlanta, she had almost grown accustomed to the idea of being back in Tyler. She waved at Nora Gates Forrester and her husband, Byron, the one Britt said had opened a photography gallery. Nora was taking the wreath down from their door, while he climbed a ladder to strip their eaves of strings of lights. And next door, Manny Niess was hauling a bedraggled-looking Christmas tree to the curb.

"Awfully cold for a stroll," the elderly man called out.

Sandy greeted him, and his friendly concern warmed her.

After nearly seven years away, first at Ohio State, then in Atlanta, she found it startling to run into familiar faces. At first, the small-town holiday decorations had amused her with their simplicity and their pervasiveness. In the city, decorations had been elaborate but sophisticated. But they had also constituted little more than backdrop to the hustle and bustle. Life went on. Christmas was quaint, but not all-consuming. In Tyler, it was different. Pausing to celebrate was part of the fabric of life here.

Now, as people up and down the street put away the last of the decorations they had been bringing down from the attic once a year for decades, Sandy began to feel the harmony and connectedness of such old-fashioned tradition.

Tyler would always be here, no matter how out of kilter the rest of the world became.

She turned down Gunther, a friendly street of well-kept working-class homes much like the one she'd grown up in, then across Main to Second, enjoying the sameness.

Another reminder of that continuity loomed a half block ahead at the corner of Elm and Second: Marge's Diner. Sandy smiled. How long since she had eaten there? Acknowledging the chill in her bones and the hunger that said it was definitely dinnertime, she entered the restaurant, pulling off her gloves and loosening her wool scarf as the door jingled shut behind her. Warm air and the smell of hot coffee greeted her.

She surveyed the room, once again noting how little things had changed. Marge Phelps supposedly didn't work here full-time anymore, since marrying Dr. Phelps. But Sandy had heard that she couldn't stay away from the place, and her touch was still evident. The radio still played, barely audible over the buzz of conversation, but still tuned to the same station Marge had always favored. The L-shaped bar and the booths with red vinyl seats had been battered a bit by the years, but no one had thought to replace them.

Even the same faces remained, although those, too, were showing the wear and tear of passing years. Judson Ingalls sat at one table with Tisha Olsen. The trial for his wife's almost-fifty-year-old murder had no doubt added to the lines and shadows that marked the years in his face. The fire had, too. Sandy spotted Joe and Susannah Santori as well, and the Youngthunders. Sandy thought she might never have left Tyler.

One table for two was free, near the front window. Shrugging out of her coat, Sandy headed for it, realizing as she approached that another table for two sat beside the one she intended to claim. It, too, had only one occupant.

Drew Stirling.

Her step faltered. He hadn't looked up yet. He was reading a book, sipping hot coffee. It wasn't too late to turn and leave.

Then she remembered where she was—in the middle of Tyler's most popular gathering place. Her presence had most certainly been noted. If she left now, having just spotted her co-worker, the story would be all over town before sundown tomorrow. Releasing a silent sigh, she made her way to the empty table. She was draping her coat over the spare chair when she noticed what he was reading—one of the introduction-to-marketing texts she had left in his car that afternoon.

So when he looked up, she was smiling. He tried to look displeased, but she caught the glint in his eyes and knew he wasn't. Not entirely, anyway.

"Are you following me, Ms. Murphy?" he asked. "Checking up on me? Making sure I'm doing my assigned reading?"

She laughed and pulled out her chair. "I'm glad to see you're willing to do *something* I suggest."

"I pick my surrenders carefully. Save the struggles for the really important stuff. That's one of the first things I learned about office politics."

If it hadn't been for his smile, Sandy wasn't sure how she would have taken his comment. But when Drew smiled, it was impossible not to be taken in by the boyishness hiding there. She sat. "I hate office politics."

"So do I." He slipped a paper napkin into the book to hold his place and closed it. "Seems silly, you know."

"What does?"

"You there. Me here."

A twinge of discomfort nudged her. "I don't want to intrude."

"You know what they'll say if you sit there eating all alone and I sit here eating all alone, don't you?" She had a pretty fair idea, but shook her head. He leaned across the narrow aisle that separated them and whispered, "That we're already feuding."

Sandy buried her smile in the menu. "Aren't we?"

"Or that we're fooling around."

Startled, she darted a fearful look at him over the top of the vinyl-covered menu.

He shrugged. "Could go either way, you know."

She shook her head again, pretending to contemplate the list of daily specials. She knew he was simply teasing, but the prospect wasn't funny to her at all. "I don't think so."

"A lovely, successful young woman. A dashing, incredibly charming bachelor."

She grunted.

"Besides, if you won't sit with me, Pat and Pam Kelsey are going to have to wait for a table."

Glancing up, Sandy caught the twinkle in his pale gray eyes before she looked over her shoulder. Sure enough, there stood the two coaches, surveying the crowded diner.

"Okay. But no business talk."

He grinned as she shifted her coat to the back of the chair opposite him and sat. "Suit yourself. Personal matters only. You have my pledge."

He seemed so close now, across this tiny table. And Sandy realized she had bargained herself into a corner with her insistence that they not discuss business. Did she really want to have a personal conversation with this man who got under her skin so easily?

His ham-and-bean soup came and she ordered beef stew. Then they were alone. Their knees brushed under the table and she inched her chair back.

"So, tell me something personal," she said, deciding the playing field looked better from an offensive standpoint.

He crushed a handful of crackers and sprinkled them into his bowl. "Gosh, with so many good things to tell, it's hard to know where to start. Do I want to intrigue you? Amaze you? Charm you?"

"I'm not easily charmed," she said. "I could go for some amazement tonight, though."

"Amazement, huh? Let's see, amazement. Okay, how's this? I walked the Appalachian Trail between my junior and senior years in college."

"You didn't." She looked at him, expecting one of his not-quite-serious expressions. She didn't see it. "You did. The whole two-thousand-mile thing?"

"Actually, it was 1,995 miles. But that doesn't count the extra miles when you need to leave the trail for, you know, showers. And stuff."

"Why'd you do it?"

"To get in touch with nature. To explore my spiritual side. To challenge myself." He broke into a grin as the waitress delivered Sandy's stew. "Actually, I did it on a dare. An outdoor company was looking for a guide for a bunch of high school kids and my roommate said I didn't have the gumption to do it. But, heck, I needed a job. So I proved my roommate wrong."

"Wow. I am amazed. And impressed." She studied him as they ate, seeing him in a different light than she had before. He still wore what she'd come to consider his uniform, khaki slacks and a crewneck sweater—this one fisherman's knit in a gray that made his eyes the color of a turbulent sky. His curly hair never quite followed directions. But he appeared more solid, somehow, more potent. For she knew now that, no matter how lightly he might regard the fact, he was someone who had challenged nature and won. "What was the hardest part?"

"Being mostly alone," he said.

Confused, Sandy frowned. "What about the high school kids?"

"They bailed out." He grinned and shrugged. "One by one, they dropped out. By the end of June, I was on my own. Sometimes you'd encounter others on the trail, trying the same stunt you were. Or you'd go into town for supplies and a shower. But mostly, you'd better like your own company."

"And did you find yourself charming?" she teased.

"Not at first. But I grew on me." He smiled. "Your turn."

Her spoon paused on the way to her mouth. "Oh, I don't have any amazing stories."

"Okay. I'll settle for intriguing."

Sandy thought about what to tell him, and nothing quite measured up to the Appalachian Trail. "Well, I was the most sought-after baby-sitter in the entire junior class."

Drew frowned, seemed to consider that, then shook his head.

"No, huh? Okay, I, uh, painted my toenails green once."

"Was it summer or winter?"

"Well, it was winter."

Another stern expression crossed his face. "Sorry. Doesn't count. If it was sandal weather, I'd consider it. But winter? I don't think so."

"Okay, I confess. The most interesting thing I ever did was Critter Crackers."

"Critter Crackers? You worked on the Critter Crackers campaign?"

She nodded, taking some satisfaction in the fact that he did, actually, look amazed after all. Critter Crackers had been the smash-hit snack food of the past year. Three-fourths of the kids in America knew the jingle by heart. The product wasn't simply tasty, it was nutritious. And it had been marketed more effectively than any product Sandy could name. In fact, the ad campaign had won the advertising industry's equivalent of the Academy Award.

"I was part of the team, yes." She saw the look that flashed across his face and decided to acknowledge it before he even had a chance to express it. "And I wasn't on the bench, either. I was a starter."

"Tell me about it."

"I thought we weren't going to talk business."

"You've introduced the subject. I now have the right to cross-examination."

"Why don't I show you the portfolio Monday?"

He shrugged. "It doesn't really matter. A small company like Yes! Yogurt can't afford to make that kind of impact on the market."

"And we don't have to," she stated. "Critter Crackers is mass market. Yes! Yogurt has a very specific target audience. We don't have to reach every household in America. So we reach the ones we want with a much smaller budget."

"Look—"

"We're probably talking about the difference between advertising on every housewife's favorite talk show four times a week versus a print ad once a month in *The Healthy Gourmet,* for example. With a new logo—"

"Oh, no!" Drew glanced around, as if aware his voice had just risen. "Look, we certainly don't need a new logo."

"Not entirely new," Sandy conceded, remembering too late that she had a very good reason for not wanting to mention the logo this soon. She knew by heart the often-told story of Britt's brainstorm for the folksy logo, a goat in a straw hat, a red rose between its teeth. "Updated, that's all."

"Have you mentioned this to Britt?"

"Not yet." The expression on his face was smug, and she guessed what he was thinking: that she'd never get it past the boss. "Look, I know this is a sacred goat I'm talking about defiling. But we can improve on it without losing its charm. Before it's over, we'll all agree that we've made a good change."

"You probably already have drawings, don't you?"

Sandy thought of the rough illustrations she'd been working on nearly every night since Britt called to offer her the job. "Listen, we were right to start with. This isn't the time to talk business."

"It's a little late to back down, Sandy." He wadded up his napkin and stuffed it under the rim of his soup bowl. "What other plans do you have? What else do you think we need to scrap?"

"I said I don't want to talk about it now." She pushed aside her half-eaten stew. "Thanks for sharing your table."

She was aware, as she made her way across the diner toward the door, that people were watching. Those who weren't at first certainly were by the time Drew followed her to the checkout, saying, "Now, this is childish, don't you think?"

"Childish?" She put a bill on the counter and turned to confront him. "I'll tell you what's childish. *Name-calling* is childish."

Then she whipped her scarf around her neck and pretended not to hear him calling after her, just as she also pretended not to hear Tisha Olsen, who, as they passed her table, said, "Guess nobody's surprised if those two are already feuding."

She heard boots crunching on the icy sidewalk behind her and crossed the street to get away. *Asinine,* she chastised herself. *A really brainless move, Murphy, throwing a logo change at him like that.*

"If I slip and fall on thin ice, let it be on your head."

She heard his voice behind her and smiled in spite of herself. "That's what happens when you try moving too fast," she called back over her shoulder.

"You should know."

Suddenly, it all seemed exactly what he'd called it: childish. She laughed and turned as he stepped onto the curb.

"I'm sorry," he said. "I shouldn't be defensive. If you didn't have new ideas, I'd be complaining that you showed no initiative."

There he went again, with that disarming humility. He didn't have to be right all the time, could admit it when he didn't have all the answers. In spite of everything, she liked that about him. She smiled. "I'll remind you of that when I bring in my logo drawings."

He chuckled. "I knew it."

They walked in silence for a block. Sandy considered the inadvisability of what she was doing, walking the silent, dark streets of Tyler with a man who unbalanced her the way Drew Stirling did. Around him, she seemed to be constantly on the verge of abandoning her common sense. Lunging forward instead of hanging back and studying the lay of the land, formulating a strategy. Reason fled, replaced by impulse.

By emotion.

Even now, when she should have remained cautious and distantly professional with him, she instead felt a push to open up. She wanted to see more of Drew the person, and wanted to show him the same.

"I know you think I have a lot to prove," she said, surprising herself with her openness.

"Maybe I'm not being fair. Just because you're young . . ." He shrugged.

There it was, as she'd expected; her age was an issue for him. She was silent as they crossed Elm Street. The elegant Ingalls mansion loomed ahead, shrouded in creeping ivy vines, looking as dark and brooding as it had always looked to her as a child.

"I always imagined the Ingalls house was haunted," she said, lowering her voice automatically to a near whisper, already forgetting that the last thing she wanted to do was remind him how recently she had been a child. How did he do that to her? Well, too late to worry about it now. "We used to sneak into the backyard in the dark, just to scare ourselves."

He studied the tall, silent house. "Maybe it is haunted. Do you know for a fact there isn't a ghost in the Ingalls mansion?"

"In a town this size, everybody would know about it."

"You don't sound entirely thrilled to be back."

She wasn't entirely thrilled with how insightful he was, either. She wasn't accustomed to that in a man, and it was one more of the things that kept her off-kilter around him.

"Strange, when I came back to Tyler to visit, all I wanted to see was how much the same everything was, how little things had changed. As if that were some kind of condemnation." They passed under a streetlight, then back into darkness. "But so many things looked different to me in recent years. I was beginning to think the old Tyler had disappeared. But now the longer I look around, the more I realize how little things have changed."

"And is it still a black mark against the town?"

"No. Not against the town. Just against me."

"What do you mean?"

Of all the people in Tyler, Drew Stirling was the one she shouldn't be saying these things to. Why give him the ammunition of knowing her fears?

"How does Tyler look to you, coming from a place like Chicago?" she asked instead. "Is it awfully small-town?"

"You might not have noticed, but that was a definite change of subject."

"Was it?"

She looked over and caught him smiling at her. Why did that smile look so intimate to her? He was a virtual stranger. Someone she wasn't entirely sure she liked, although things to like about him were turning up at an alarming rate.

"Am I walking you home, Alexandra?"

Anxiety fluttered in her heart. She hoped she sounded lighthearted. "Heaven forbid."

"It would be that bad?"

"In Tyler? That would definitely make us an item." There she went again, blurting out things she would never say if she weren't so nervous. She was losing control of this situation. And that simply couldn't happen.

"I see."

In the short silence that followed, Sandy realized her heart was pounding unnaturally fast. She tried to concentrate on all the reasons that this entire conversation was a bad idea, but she couldn't. Couldn't think.

"Then it's a good thing we're big-city folks," Drew said. "It would take a lot more than an innocuous walk for us to think of two people as an item."

"Oh, much more," she said. Her breathing had grown shallow, too.

He stopped. She stopped. Moonlight made his gray eyes more luminous than ever.

"A kiss, for example," he whispered. "A kiss would make a couple an item. Wouldn't you agree?"

"A kiss?"

He seemed to rock forward, then back. Wavering, it seemed to her. Then he grew still, and she wondered if it had been Drew who wavered or herself.

"Or would it depend on the nature of the kiss?" he asked. "Would a simple brushing of the lips constitute something serious? Or would it have to be more? Longer? Deeper?"

"I'm not sure I can answer that question," she said, aware that her voice was little more than a breath of mist on the cold night air. "Not without further research."

He smiled. "A focus group?"

She remembered then, thank heaven, who he was and why she stood on the sidewalk with him in the first place. They were co-workers. Whatever threatened to happen between them was not an option. Feeling like someone who hovered on the brink of a cliff, she took a step back and mustered a cool smile. She had to treat this offhandedly. Pretend it was nothing.

It *was* nothing.

"I'll have a recommendation on your desk Monday," she said.

"About further research?"

"On the logo. I think a focus group would work fine."

"Oh." His smile lingered.

As did the trembly, warm feelings he had elicited with his talk about long, deep kisses. Drew turned off toward the boardinghouse, leaving her alone. But all the way home, the feelings stayed with her, reminding her that perhaps she wasn't as mature as she liked to think, after all. Would a grown woman—an intelligent woman who knew the dangers—react this way?

Sometime during the long weekend, Sandy began to suspect that this must be exactly how a grown woman would react.

CHAPTER SIX

SANDY PRETENDED the reason she was spending so much time out of the office the next week was to reacquaint herself with Yes! Yogurt operations.

But as she spent a day in manufacturing, then another day on the road with their midwestern sales rep, she wasn't fooling herself for a minute. She wondered if she was fooling Drew.

That question had plagued her all weekend. Had Drew perceived what had happened between them Friday night as she had? Had he, too, felt the magnetism between them, the charged atmosphere? Or had it all been her imagination? True, he had been the one to mention kissing. He had lowered his voice, had locked gazes with her, had stood close enough to touch.

But each time Sandy relived what had happened—and she found it necessary to relive the moment countless times in the days that followed—she saw room for doubt.

He could have been teasing her. He could have meant everything he'd said in some other way, and she'd simply misinterpreted everything. He could have been testing her professionalism. In which case she'd flunked the test.

So she decided to stay out of his way until she had herself under control again.

That was easier said than done.

"Staff meeting!" Britt had chimed cheerily first thing Monday morning. "High-test coffee in the conference room, in case you aren't awake yet."

Sandy passed on the coffee. She was jittery enough without extra caffeine. Drew already sat at the conference table, looking casual and easygoing in an ice-blue cardigan, his white Oxford-cloth shirt open at the collar. He sipped juice, not coffee. Suddenly, Sandy's wool suit felt warm.

"The outer walls are up," he was saying to Jake as Sandy and Britt entered the room. "They say they're on schedule, but how am I supposed to know? At this stage, it's about as unfathomable to me as it was at the blueprint stage."

"Is this the house we're talking about?" Britt asked, filling her mug with coffee. "I drove by the other day. Looking good." She slid into the chair beside Sandy. "He's building a house, a mile or so beyond the plant. He found this terrific wooded lot with a view of the lake and Timberlake Lodge."

"A glimpse," Drew said without looking directly at Sandy. "A glimpse of the lake. And only in the fall and winter."

Sandy felt herself flush, remembering the day Renee had told her about the house. Remembering how she'd over-reacted when she thought he had a wife to put in that house. She was grateful he seemed so unwilling to look at her.

After a few more minutes of small talk, the meeting started, with sales figures and various other status reports. Drew barely acknowledged her presence, and every reminder of his calm made Sandy feel a little warmer, a little more nervous. She had no trouble mirroring his laid-back demeanor, but still found it next to impossible to concentrate on what was going on at the meeting.

Not, she told herself, that she was in any way mesmerized by Drew. No, it was simply that she wondered what he was thinking about her. If he had seen anything strange in her reaction Friday night.

When the discussion came around to Sandy and her plan of action for the week, Drew spoke before she had the chance.

"When do we get to see your ideas for the new logo?"

She could have thrown yogurt on his cardigan sweater.

"New logo?" That was Britt. Sandy heard the surprise in her voice.

"Drew is exaggerating, Britt. I mentioned to him at dinner Friday night that we might want to look at updating the logo. Nothing drastic. A refinement here and there."

Britt was either easily appeased or easily distracted. "You went to dinner Friday night?"

Jake's focus remained on the business at hand. "A logo change? Wouldn't that cost a fortune?"

"Only a small one," Drew added, ever helpful.

Sandy didn't lower herself to glare at him. "Drew is also a bit ahead of himself. We won't be making any changes until we've heard from our customers."

"That's right." Drew looked up from his notes. "We're all looking forward to some market research. When do we start?"

"This week," Sandy said, knowing she needed to wrest some kind of control over this discussion of her territory. She told them about her plans to spend time in manufacturing and with the front-line sales force. "Then the first order of business, it seems to me, is to make sure this town can support an outlet store."

"Nobody told me the two of you got together Friday night," Britt said.

"Wait a minute," Jake protested. "I thought the outlet store was a done deal."

Sandy had, indeed, decided to keep her nose out of any further plans for the outlet store unless Drew asked for her help. But as long as he saw nothing wrong with making her life a little more difficult, she saw no reason not to reciprocate. She leveled her most confident look at Jake. "Would you rather back down now or lose your shirt in eighteen months?"

"You think that's a possibility?" Britt asked.

"Of course not," Drew said.

"I don't know," Sandy said. "Nobody does. Because we haven't done our homework."

The only sound for a moment was the rapid clicking of Drew's ballpoint pen. "Okay. How long is this going to delay things?" he asked finally.

Sandy smiled. "I can have enough information for us to make a decision by this time next week."

"No longer," he warned.

"Consider it done."

To keep from pressing her luck, she decided to stay out of his way for the rest of the week. First the day in the factory, then the day on the road. And the end of the week she spent wandering Tyler, armed with a clipboard and the survey she had developed to help her come up with a recommendation on the outlet store.

The survey, it turned out, was the best distraction of all. For she might be asking questions about how many dairy products her respondents bought each week, but what she was getting in return was a quick refresher course in what was going on in her hometown.

She ran into Sheila Lawson coming out of Gates Department Store. Her former baby-sitter, still a girlish-looking blonde now working as manager of Timberlake Lodge, seemed unusually subdued, until Sandy recalled hearing about her mother's death a few months before.

"How's your father doing?" Sandy asked, remembering her own dad's comments about how hard Emil Lawson was taking the loss of his flamboyant wife.

"Hanging in there," Sheila said softly.

Sandy struggled to come up with words of comfort, but everything seemed so inadequate. "I'm so sorry about your mom," she said lamely, squeezing the other woman's arm.

Sheila's smile was wan but sincere. "Thanks. I'm keeping busy at the lodge. That helps."

"New jobs are never dull," Sandy said.

Sheila looked grateful for the change in conversation. She wrinkled her nose playfully and said, "Except in the dating department. This town has a dearth of eligible men. Britt didn't tell you that when she offered you the job, did she?"

The association was automatic. At the mention of eligible men, Drew Stirling's face came to mind, sparkling eyes, teasing grin and all. Sandy forced a casual reply. "No, she didn't."

"Of course, there is Drew Stirling," Sheila said, causing Sandy to wonder if her old acquaintance could read minds. "You'll probably work pretty closely with him. Say, maybe you could wangle an introduction sometime."

"Sure. I'll tell him you want to set up an account with Yes! Yogurt."

"Ooh, smart girl. I'm counting on it, okay?"

Sandy made a note on the survey and frowned each time she saw the note the rest of the day.

She saw Liza Forrester and her sister-in-law, Cece Baron, with their three children, preschooler Margaret Alyssa Forrester, and the twins, Annie and Belle Baron, named for their grandmother, Annabelle Scanlon. Sandy cooed and complimented the children in return for a couple of completed surveys and all the gossip she could handle, most of it delivered in Liza's typical full-speed-ahead manner.

Sandy even set up shop one afternoon at TylerTots, the day-care center her sister, Angela, ran, and interviewed parents as they came for their children. She found out who bought yogurt and who didn't, who would sheepishly admit to buying a brand other than their homegrown label, and why. She discovered that a surprising number of people in Tyler had only sampled the cheesecake or cheese Danish at Marge's Diner, and knew nothing of the other Yes! Yogurt products.

She also found out more than she wanted to know about the hard times a lot of families in Tyler were experiencing.

"Sandy, until Ingalls F and M reopens, we're doing well to keep milk in her bottle," confided an old friend from high school as she shifted her daughter from one hip to the other. "My Rick spends all day every day looking for work, but no luck. Yogurt is a luxury that'll have to wait."

Sandy heard similar comments all afternoon and mentioned it to her sister when they locked up at the end of the day. "What's going to happen to people if the F and M doesn't reopen soon?"

Angela shrugged and shook her head. "Good question. Some people are already talking about moving."

"You mean leaving town?"

"People have to have work."

"But if people start leaving town, other businesses will suffer, too, won't they?"

Angela smiled wryly. "Thanks for the reminder."

Glenna McRoberts, who hurried past in search of a pair of missing mittens, interjected, "We've already lost four families. And the impact is spreading."

All evening Sandy mulled over what she had learned. On the surface, she thought, this looked like the worst time in the town's history to expand Yes! Yogurt. On the other hand, if they could create a few jobs . . .

Alone in her room that night, she fired up the laptop computer she had used all through college and stared at the screen. Report-writing time. The success of an outlet store was too closely linked to the town's economic status for her to address one without the other. She had even made it a point to gather as much data as she could on sales trends in other small businesses around town. The fire had happened only a few months ago, so the effects were just beginning to be felt. And plenty of people didn't want to say anything, for fear of fueling a slowdown in the economy with gloom-and-doom talk.

As she began to tap out her report, Sandy saw only one way to justify such a significant expansion into the local market. They would need to add jobs to ease local unemployment. And that was going to be a tough sell.

Especially to Drew Stirling, who didn't seem inclined to buy anything Sandy had to offer.

DREW CHECKED his watch. Two hours before he needed to head out for the ninety-minute drive to Chicago to bring Grandpa Stirling back. This time he was determined to leave on time so he wouldn't be returning long after dark.

He stood, intending to track down Jake and remind him that he would be leaving early. But he passed his office window just as Sandy Murphy pulled up in front of the house, and he paused.

He'd barely seen her all week, ever since he'd been such a jerk at the staff meeting on Monday morning. She'd avoided him. Drew couldn't say he blamed her. Bringing up her intention to change the logo had been unconscionable. He'd told himself a million times he should apologize. But she hadn't been around.

He didn't know what had happened when she walked into the conference room Monday morning. He'd had no notion whatsoever of mentioning her plans for the logo. Then he saw her and rational thought had ceased.

Sandy Murphy in her prim wool suits and her slicked-back hair looked not only competent, she looked formidable. How a twenty-five-year-old woman could look formidable, Drew wasn't able to explain. But the truth of the matter was whenever he saw her he felt vulnerable. As if whatever she said he would simply agree with and to heck with the consequences. He felt like the hapless hero in some bad sci-fi flick from the fifties who fell under the spell of the alien disguised as a beautiful woman. One look in her eyes and he was mesmerized, bewitched. Sunk.

Yes, that was it. One look in Sandy Murphy's smoldering dark eyes and he was in over his head.

Why else would he have pulled such a lamebrained stunt after dinner Friday night? Talking about *kissing,* for crying out loud! He knew better than that. A sane man in today's business climate didn't go near things intimate or personal. That way lay professional suicide.

Yet in another moment, he would have been kissing her. *The kiss of death, Stirling. Remember that.*

He'd spent the entire weekend trying to convince himself how lucky he'd been that she had backed away when she did. That she hadn't started screaming for the harassment patrol right there on Second Street.

Then she'd walked into the conference room and Drew had been sucked into a momentary flight of fancy when he'd realized instantly and with no uncertainty that, given another chance, he wouldn't let Sandy Murphy slip away unkissed.

That was when he'd gone on the offensive. If he made sure she despised him, there would be no question of engaging in the kiss of death. Right?

Except that now, as she mounted the steps to the porch, Drew knew he still faced an uphill battle. The legs were long, the lips were lush, and Sandy Murphy looked tastier than anything Yes! Yogurt would ever crank off the assembly line.

He decided to give her time to reach her office—blessedly at the other end of the hall—before he went in search of Jake. He stood at the window, listened for the front door to open and close, watched snow from the evening before drip from the eaves in the January sunshine. With any luck, the roads would be clear and dry by the time he left for Chicago.

He heard a tap on his office door and turned. Sandy peered in, looking bright and fresh as she peeled off her coat.

"Just wanted you to know I've got the report ready for Monday morning," she said. "If you want a copy now, to study over the weekend, let me know."

Another surprise from the woman who could unbalance him with only a smile. Why would she give him the opportunity to study her report and arm himself against it before she had a chance to make her presentation?

"Sure," he said, already mentally adjusting his plans for the weekend, which had included plenty of time both to check on the progress of the house he was having built and to help his grandfather settle in at Worthington House. "That would be a big help."

She nodded. Drew wondered what her smooth, dark hair looked like when she freed it to spill over her shoulders.

Off-limits, Stirling.

"There might be a few...surprises," she said. "It didn't seem fair to catch you off guard first thing on a Monday morning."

The bite in her words was subtle, but he caught it. She was chiding him for doing exactly that to her this week, just as he had been chiding himself. He winced. "I'm sorry."

Her expression said she doubted it.

"I was a jerk, blindsiding you like that at the meeting," he said, taking a step in her direction before he realized it was a dangerous move. "I've wanted to apologize all week. But you've been hard to find."

"Can you blame me?"

"No. Can you forgive me?"

She walked into his office and tossed a sheaf of papers onto his desk. "I don't know. Ask me again after the staff meeting Monday."

Then she disappeared down the corridor to her office. And despite the challenge in her final words, she left him smiling.

THE SUNSHINE hung around long enough to melt most of the ice from the streets and sidewalks. So Sandy talked her grandmother into walking over to Marge's Diner with her for dinner that night. She told herself she had no ulterior motive, that there was no reason to suppose that simply because a person had dinner at Marge's Diner one Friday night, he would do so the next.

She also told herself, as she paid the tab and they walked back to Worthington House, that she was most certainly not disappointed that Drew Stirling had decided not to eat at Marge's again this week.

On the whole, the evening had been successful. Mag had talked to half the people in the diner, reveling in the attention of old friends she hadn't seen since her move to Worthington House. She flirted with Phil Wocheck, who had stopped in for coffee and pie. She taught the toddler at the next table a rhyming chant she said all the children had loved during the Depression. And she spotted Marie Innes and negotiated a rental agreement for the schoolteacher's garage apartment before Sandy could protest.

"All in all, a very pleasant dinner," Mag said, her arm linked through her granddaughter's as they reached the front steps of Worthington House.

"Thanks for your help with Mrs. Innes," Sandy said. "Mother isn't going to be happy."

"Your mother will cry," Mag said. "And Franklin will grunt and purse his lips. You're growing up. They don't want you to. They'd be doing those things no matter what, so you might as well make yourself happy."

"Gran, I'm not *growing* up," Sandy insisted as she held open the big front door. "I'm already *grown* up."

"I know, I know. But not everybody else does yet," Mag said as Sandy helped her out of her coat.

"Don't I know it." She turned to hang up her coat and heard her grandmother gasp.

"A weapon, Alexandra! A weapon! Hand me that umbrella!"

Concerned, Sandy looked around, saw murder in her grandmother's eyes. She followed the venomous glare until her own gaze landed on Drew Stirling and a lean, elegant-looking, elderly man who seemed as if he might be in the throes of a heart attack.

CHAPTER SEVEN

CLARENCE CLUTCHED the air beside him until his hand connected with his grandson's arm. There he clung for dear life.

His worst nightmare had just come true. Magdalena stood before him. And here he sat, stuck in a wheelchair like a decrepit old man. Where was justice? Why had the gods turned on him? Why the Sam Hill was she staring at him as if he were something she'd like to come after with a flyswatter?

"Son?" he said, the word coming out a dry croak, the rasp of an old man who he hadn't even realized occupied the same body he did. "My heart, I think it's giving out on me."

Drew knelt beside him. "What? Grandpa, hang in there. I'll get someone. You just hang in there."

Hang in there he did. Clarence didn't release his grip on his grandson's arm, even when Drew tried to walk away. His heart, he realized, was actually beating superbly. Extra strong, as a matter of fact. *Ah, Mag, you witchy woman.*

"I thought they had some standards in this place," he snapped, finally releasing Drew's arm and regaining his normal voice.

"Grandpa, are you...?"

"Leave it be, son. Leave it be. Now, wheel me out of this sinkhole."

She advanced on him then, and he felt her aura begin to surround him with each step she took. An aura of fury and passion, an aura of determination and confounded seductiveness. Mag had always been that way. Fifty years hadn't diminished her power one whit. Good thing, after all, that he was sitting. He felt his knees begin to shake simply from her presence.

"Clarence Albert, I thought I made myself clear," she spit out like a mean-tempered feline.

The only thing he'd ever had over her had been his charm and he figured he'd better pull it out now. He needed all the advantage he could get. "Still got the golden tresses, I see, Mag."

"You two know each other?" The young woman at Mag's side sounded incredulous.

"Grandpa, what's this all about?"

Clarence ignored Drew and noted that Mag ignored the young one at her side, too.

Mag looked older, of course. But not old. Still had that golden hair, piled up on her head the way he'd always liked it, the way he'd liked to dream about letting it down. She still had that hourglass figure, too. Her wide mouth was still painted red and those blue eyes still flashed. He thought about wrapping an arm around her waist, dragging her onto his lap and taking a spin around the lobby.

It was the kind of thing that would have set his old Mag to laughing. Lord, they had laughed. Before…before her black heart revealed itself.

"I told you never to darken my door again," she said, her voice still sharp. "I haven't changed my mind, Clarence."

"You're a beauty, you are," he said. "Too bad you're rotten to the core."

The two young people gasped, but not Mag. In fact, she began to smile. "I'll have your hide," she said. "Don't think I won't."

Then she took the young woman's arm, raised her chin and said, "Come, Alexandra. A lady must always choose carefully the company she keeps."

"But Gran...?"

Clarence watched them disappear down the long corridor. Her back was ramrod straight, but her hips still swayed like the vamp she was.

"Grandpa?"

"Can't stay here, son." He began to wheel his chair toward the door. "Come on, get me out of this place."

Drew put a hand on the chair. "What are you talking about, Grandpa? Your room is ready. The papers are all signed. There's nowhere else to go."

Mustering all the dignity he could, Clarence said, "You surely cannot expect me to remain under the same roof as that scrap of female inhumanity."

Drew shook his head. "You're getting melodramatic on me, Grandpa."

"I am setting a healthy boundary."

Drew started pushing the chair. "We're going to your room."

"I will not remain."

"Fine. Call a cab."

"This could be construed as abuse of the elderly."

Drew snorted.

They reached the room, where they had already unpacked Clarence's bags, and Drew turned on the light. "You want to tell me what this is all about?"

"None of your business," Clarence snapped, then rolled himself to the window. Streetlights glittered on what was left of the ice. What irony. Like diamonds in the night...

AN ICE STORM had come and gone the day he returned to Tyler, a conquering hero and a broken man. The gray sky matched his mood.

"The parade is tomorrow," his mother said at the supper table, her troubled eyes not lingering on her only son. "Everyone is so excited."

"I don't want a parade," he said, staring at the roast beef and potatoes and knowing he couldn't swallow.

His parents kept their eyes on their plates. His mother passed the rolls one more time. "But you're our first hometown hero, Clarence. Why—"

He stood, although not as swiftly as he would have liked. "I'm not a hero, Ma. I'm a gimp."

Then he had hobbled out the front door. But he'd realized halfway down the steps that he couldn't make it. Couldn't even run away from the things he couldn't bear to face.

He had been sitting there, backside freezing, feet gone numb, when she walked by and spotted him.

"You're Lieutenant Stirling, aren't you?"

She said it in a way that was half shy and half flirty. A jaunty red beret perched on one side of her head, perking up her brown winter coat, which stopped at her knees to reveal very shapely limbs. Her hair drifted around her shoulders like gold dust and she had the kind of smile that struck a man mute. She was a walking, talking Betty Grable poster. He didn't answer. He couldn't.

"I'm Magdalena Halston and I want you to know," she said, walking up the sidewalk toward him, "how proud all of us here in Tyler are of all our fine boys. And we're glad you're home safe and sound."

Not sound, he wanted to shout. But he didn't. For there was something in her voice that made him want to please her, that made him want to keep hearing it. So sweet and

*pure it was, it seemed to strike right at his heart. He knew
her, of course. She was his father's partner's daughter. But
when he'd left for Europe, she'd been an adolescent girl.
And that she was no longer.*

*She stood at the foot of the steps now. "Mind if I sit
with you? I just couldn't stay in on such a beautiful night.
Why, look, Lieutenant, at the way the moonlight hits the
ice. Like diamonds in the night, don't you think?"*

GRANDPA STIRLING'S cantankerous act was nothing new.
Drew propped himself against the built-in dresser and
watched his grandfather stare out the window, knowing
that the most important thing was not to let the old man
think he could get the upper hand simply by behaving un-
pleasantly.

Clarence Albert Stirling had always been something of
a mystery to Drew. Dapper and glib, like someone out of
an old Hollywood musical, Clarence could also be queru-
lous and secretive. Whereas other older people Drew knew
went on and on about the good old days, Clarence kept his
past locked up tighter, as the old man himself would say,
than Dick's hatband. Oh, he liked to tell tales about the
war, but that was it.

"Told you I didn't want to come back here," Clarence
muttered now, turning away from the window. The expression on his still-handsome face was sour.

"What'd she do? Turn you down?"

Clarence darted him a sharp glance. "Nobody likes a
wise guy."

Drew chuckled. "She must've been a real looker."

"That she was."

"Still is."

"Always did figure that gold color came out of a bottle." Something seemed to occur to Clarence and he

pointed one of his long fingers at his grandson. "You stay away from that girl of hers. I saw her. Those big eyes and a smile to make a man abandon all common sense."

Drew couldn't argue with that. In fact, it had taken him a few seconds to zero in on what was happening between his grandfather and the woman from his past. Drew had been captivated instead by Sandy's appearance, her windbitten cheeks and the bright smile she directed at the woman beside her.

How ironic, that there should be some kind of family history here neither of them knew about. "What was it, Grandpa? A Dear John letter during the war?"

"Ha! Mag Halston had more imagination than that, I'll have you know." The old man's jaw jutted out, anger evident in every line of his face. "Humiliated me in front of every soul in this town, that's what she did. Left me standing at the altar!"

"HE WHAT?" How could it be, Sandy wondered, that something this dramatic had never become a part of the often-repeated Murphy family lore?

"You heard me." Mag wrapped herself in an emerald-colored brocade bed jacket and slipped her feet into bejeweled house shoes. "You cannot imagine the abject humiliation of standing there at the altar in front of the entire world in your ivory lace gown and your Bruges lace veil— my grandmother's, for Bruges lace would have been impossible to get at the time, of course—standing there all decked out and having to explain that the groom will not make an appearance."

"Why is it I never knew about this?"

Mag fluffed up her four feather pillows, each in a satin pillowcase of a different and vivid jewel tone, and settled onto the bed like a petite queen on her oversize throne.

Mag was one of the very few residents of Worthington House to have a double bed instead of a single. She had insisted, and Cecil Kellaway had been a pushover. "Well, it isn't exactly the kind of thing a woman hopes to relive day after day."

"No, I suppose not." Sandy toyed with the concern that had been nagging her ever since the scene in the lobby and decided to confront it head-on. "Gran, what is his name?"

"I hardly think it matters. You know, if the women of Worthington House circulated a petition, stating that we feel threatened by the presence of a man like that—"

"Is he really that bad?"

Sandy watched, uncertain whether to be amused or appalled, as Mag paused, directing her penetrating gaze at the framed Dali print on the wall opposite her bed. "Well, perhaps not, by today's standards. But we needn't all sink to those standards, you understand. Clarence Stirling was a—"

Sandy's heart jumped. "Who? Clarence *who?*"

Mag looked as if she would rather eat mud than speak the name again. "Stirling. The last of the Stirlings to blight this town, I am happy to say."

Sandy sank into the only armchair in her grandmother's room, weighed down by the lead balloon that had suddenly settled in her midsection. "No, Gran. I don't think so."

"Whatever do you mean?" Mag waved a dismissive hand, her marble-size faux topaz sparkling in the dim light. "Why, that scoundrel left Tyler almost fifty years ago and hasn't been back since. The rest of them, good riddance, passed on I don't know how long ago. Probably before you were born, even. In disgrace, I might add."

Sandy shook her head. The other Stirling in Tyler, Wisconsin, had been standing beside the one who'd broken her grandmother's heart all those years ago. Tall and lean and looking remarkably like a younger version of the old man in the wheelchair, Drew Stirling had resurrected the Stirling name in town.

No wonder there had seemed to be such bad karma at work in their relationship from the very beginning.

"Gran, the man beside him—"

"I did see him." She was rummaging in her bedside drawer, piling on the bed beside her a nail buff, a hair net, a clear plastic box of various buttons, a candle, two matchbooks, a crushed package of cigarettes and a rhinestone-studded cigarette holder, a digital thermometer and a brass pencil sharpener in the shape of an alligator before surfacing with a bottle of crimson nail polish. Then she pointed a finger at Sandy, who was on the verge of chastising her about the cigarettes, and said, "And I do recall seeing you chatting with that young man some weeks ago. Not a good idea, Alexandra. They are obviously related, and my best advice to you would be to stay away from any Stirling man who crosses your path."

Uneasiness rolled around like a bowling ball in the pit of Sandy's stomach. "Gran, that's Drew."

"Drew? Drew who?"

"The vice president of sales I was telling you about at dinner."

All the color drained from Mag's face, except for the soft dusting of rose she had used to undershadow each high cheekbone. "Oh, my."

"You're just going to have to make up with Mr. Stirling."

Mag's eyes grew wide. "Never!"

"Then you'll have to stay out of his way. This is my *job*. I can't have a fifty-year-old feud interfering with my job."

After shoving all the contents back into the drawer in an unceremonious heap, the elderly woman once again studied the Dali with fierce concentration. "I suggest you look for other employment, Alexandra. You'll definitely want to stay away from this man. He looks just like Clarence and I daresay he is no more to be trusted than the old scoundrel he takes after."

MAG WAVED her red-tipped nails in the air to facilitate drying. She was having no luck keeping her mind on the foolish guests on tonight's late show. She kept thinking of Alexandra. She kept thinking of this difficult young man who was trying so to spoil her granddaughter's grand plans.

She kept thinking of Clarence.

Drat the cad, showing up again after all these years!

Seeing him had been like a physical blow to her solar plexus. She touched the place just below her breastbone, forgetting the fresh color on her nails. At least, she supposed that was her solar plexus.

"Close enough," she muttered, clicking to another channel, one featuring a foulmouthed young comic. "It's certainly not my heart."

She chuckled at an off-color punch line. If she were Alexandra's age today, that was what she'd do—go on the road with a stand-up routine. She patted her platinum curls and pondered the plan. Perhaps it wasn't out of the question, even at her age. What was it Alexandra kept harping on? Finding a niche in the market that no one else had filled?

"Not many Grinning Grannies out there," she said, burrowing into her pile of satin pillows. "And at least I wouldn't have Clarence Albert Stirling rubbing my nose in reminders every day."

Without half trying, she could imagine blue-haired Estelle Jamison making a play for Clarence the first time she heard his wheelchair squeaking down the hall. Estelle was like that. Man hungry. And men who didn't drool in their Cream of Wheat were at a premium here at Worthington House.

Of course, that would suit Clarence to a T. He always had liked keeping his options open.

The Timberlake Lodge party of 1943 had turned to disappointment for nineteen-year-old Magdalena Halston.

"Well?" her best friend asked expectantly as soon as they distanced themselves from their parents.

"Oh, hush, Cecile." Mag didn't even look at her friend, who had heard every detail of Mag's big plans and like any true friend longed to see them realized almost as fervently as Mag did.

"But did he kiss you yet?"

"I said hush," Mag hissed. "You're acting like a schoolgirl."

That had silenced Cecile.

With the return from the front of a real, live hero, Mag had been certain that this Christmas season, at last, would usher in the engagement announcement that had eluded her this past year. Men were in such short supply here in Tyler. Real men, that is. Men who weren't old enough to be your father or young enough to still be in school.

Garlands of evergreen and holly berry festooned the wall sconces and the deer-antler chandelier. Mistletoe hung from every arch and doorway in the rustic lodge. And in the corner, an enormous tree almost touched the ceiling, its limbs burdened with dozens of electric candles and strung cranberries. But the real spirit of the season flut-

tered in Mag's heart only as she watched Clarence Stirling across the Timberlake Lodge ballroom.

"There he is," Cecile whispered.

"I see him. Now quit staring."

He leaned against the mantelpiece, his carved walking stick in his hand. Thin almost to the point of gauntness, the shadows on his face making romantic statements about the horrors he had endured on his way to becoming a hero, Clarence could have been no more awe-inspiring if he had walked off the screen at the Bijou on the arm of Ginger Rogers.

And he was destined to be Mag's.

But every man-hungry woman under thirty in the whole of Tyler apparently had yet to comprehend that. Mag grimaced as that bosomy old maid Emma Finklebaum sidled up and offered him another cup of punch. Then there were Tillie and Martha, who had fluttered around Clarence all night. Both destined to be old maids as well in Mag's opinion. Even Margaret Ingalls had bestowed plenty of attention on Clarence; some said her husband, Judson, had been away at the front too long.

"Emma Finklebaum looks like a sow with those big, puffy sleeves," Cecile said, her loyalty commendable. "Besides, anybody with half a brain should be able to figure out that it's destiny for you and Lieutenant Stirling to be together."

"Of course it is." How could it be that none of these people knew that she and Clarence had been keeping steady company since his triumphant return?

"You'll be founding a dynasty," Cecile said, warming to her subject. "The Halstons and the Stirlings. Why, your dad and his are partners in half the businesses in town right now and—"

"This is not a business proposition," Mag snapped.

"I know, I know. It's just that, once you're married, you'll be more powerful, even, than the Ingallses."

Mag didn't care a fig for that. The dusty old Halston-Stirling Hardware and the S and H Creamery and all the rest were of no interest whatsoever to her. What preyed on Mag's mind was the fact that none of those foolish women flocking around Clarence knew that he had been this close to kissing her just last night, until her nosy baby sister flicked on the front-porch light.

And now, instead of having that kiss as the prelude to a proposal so that their big announcement could be the highlight of the holiday season in Tyler, here she was watching every silly goose in Tyler make a fuss over him.

"I'm going to put a stop to this," she declared.

She sashayed over to his side of the ballroom, Cecile close on her heels. Mag's cranberry-colored satin gown crackled and swished as she moved. The deep color of the dress combined with the halo of her pale curls made a dramatic statement, Cecile had assured her when they planned their wardrobes last week. The color was high in her cheeks, too. She could feel that.

The other women crowded around Clarence seemed to part and make way for Mag as she approached. She put a hand on his forearm, lightly, and bestowed her most brilliant smile. "Now, Clarence, are all these girls wearing you out? Come with me. I've found a quiet spot where we can get off our feet for a while. Wouldn't that be nice?"

She was certain that must be gratitude in his eyes. She linked her gloved hand through his arm and walked with him to the terrace, where a bench offered a view of Timber Lake.

"There. Isn't this lovely?"

"Most lovely, Miss Halston."

"Oh, please, Lieutenant. Surely you can call me Mag."

"You're much too elegant tonight for anyone to call you simply Mag."

A thrill rushed through her. His formality always struck her as so sophisticated, so worldly. She tried hard to match him in sophistication, grateful that he had been gone long enough for her to reach the maturity of nineteen. How foolish and childish she would have seemed to him even a year ago.

But now they could sit and look at the lake and she could coax out of him conversation about the coming holidays and his dreadful experiences fighting Nazis. And if he seemed to grow bored, she could touch his arm again and give him the look she had learned from Myrna Loy at the Bijou.

And before they went back in, he had indeed given her the kiss she had missed the night before. And as proper and respectful as the touch of his soft, warm lips had been, Mag knew that Clarence was hers.

Perhaps, she thought, there would still be time for a Yule-season announcement.

And a St. Valentine's Day ceremony.

CHAPTER EIGHT

SANDY WIPED the sweat from her forehead and stared at the jumble of boxes, cleaning supplies and hand-me-down furniture.

"Well, I'm moved in," she announced.

Glenna McRoberts and Angela Murphy glanced at each other. Angela opened the cooler, took out a bottle of pop and thrust it toward her sister. "You call this moved in? The heat's got to you, kid."

"It's thirty degrees outside," Sandy retorted, nevertheless gratefully accepting the soft drink.

"You aren't even close to moved in," said Angela, who was more like Mag than anyone else in the family, from her flamboyantly blond hair to her penchant for oversize jewelry. "You won't be moved in until these boxes are unpacked. Until you can sleep here. Until you know exactly where your manicure scissors are."

The three women laughed.

"Guess that speaks volumes about me," said Glenna. "Before my divorce, I lived in Beloit for five years and I never knew where my manicure scissors were."

Angela retorted, "Then you were camping out, Glenna."

"Besides," Sandy said, dropping to the floor and propping her aching back against one of the boxes they had just hauled into the apartment, "I *can* sleep here. Tonight."

Angela took off her sweatshirt and tied it around her waist. "Boy, you are eager to get away from Mom and Dad, aren't you?"

"Yes," she replied, simply and without explanation.

Arranging the details with Marie Innes and moving her few belongings, most of which had remained in boxes in the Murphy garage since she'd returned to Tyler, had taken little more than a day. She had dishes and linens, a futon and a wicker side chair for the living room, an unadorned bed and a wicker dresser for the bedroom. What served as decor included three framed posters of art prints, a fat ceramic cat—"because everyone needs a pet"—and an enormous wicker basket for books and magazines, presently empty.

As darkness settled over the Saturday afternoon, the three women sat on the floor, too tired to do much more than rest and grumble about their aching muscles.

"I told you we should've found some men to help," Glenna said. "Lee would have been glad to if he hadn't had to go to Madison this weekend."

"This is not what we need men for," Angela replied. "I have much better uses for men, if only we could find a few more."

"We didn't need men for this little bit of stuff," Sandy said.

"You can say that. You're twenty-five."

By the time they had rested and finished off the rest of the soft drinks in the cooler, hunger had set in. Angela offered to go after pizza and Glenna went with her, looking for a phone to check on her children, Megan and Jimmy, and her dad, who had taken them ice skating that afternoon. Meanwhile Sandy cleared a path to the bedroom. She was putting sheets on the bed and wondering how long a nap she could sneak in before the others returned when she heard a tapping on the front door.

Hoping it wasn't her parents—if they saw this mess they would never rest until she came back to the house for the night, or the week—Sandy headed for the door.

Her attempt at a smile fizzled as soon as she opened the door to Drew Stirling.

"I've been looking for you all day," he said abruptly.

Sandy felt prickles of irritation. "Did I misunderstand about Saturday being my day off?"

He frowned and took a step forward. Reluctantly, she edged back to allow him into the apartment, if only so she could shut out the January chill. She didn't want him here, mucking around in her personal life. Things were somehow too personal between them already.

"I needed to talk to you," he said, looking around the room as if he'd never seen moving boxes before.

"Can't this wait until Monday? I know you're probably itching to tell me what a dumb idea—"

He held up a hand to stop her. "I haven't even read your report. Actually, I forgot all about it."

Sandy wasn't sure whether she was relieved by that or not. It didn't say much about how seriously he valued her professional opinions. "Then what's the urgency?"

"I wanted to talk about my grandfather." His eyes narrowed, as if he blamed her for whatever unpleasantness had once occurred or might be about to occur. "And your grandmother. You knew about that?"

"No, I didn't." Bone-tired, she longed to sit down, but the only place to sit was on the floor or on a box and she wasn't eager to get that informal with Drew Stirling. She also wanted to ask how much he had known about his grandfather's shabby treatment of Gran, but wasn't willing to show her interest. He could get agitated about this if he wanted to, but Sandy planned to maintain her cool.

He stared at her, as if waiting for more. Hands on her hips, she decided to wait him out, giving him as unyielding a gaze as he directed at her. Finally, he said, "I don't think Grandpa is ready to accept any apologies."

Sandy's mouth almost fell open. She caught it just in time. *Calm and cool,* she coached herself. "I'm afraid I've missed something."

Drew ran a hand through his dark curls and they became more unruly than usual. In his ski jacket and jeans, he looked windblown, rumpled and boyishly appealing. "It's just, if they're going to live under the same roof, I think they need some kind of closure. Don't you?"

Sandy thought about the things Gran had said and almost smiled. A good dose of reality, that's what Drew Stirling needed. Maybe getting an idea of what it meant to deal with Mag Murphy would clue him in on what it could be like to deal with Sandy Murphy. Casually, she said, "Gran is thinking about circulating a petition."

"A what?"

"To have him removed from the premises."

Drew's face, which already looked windburned, grew redder yet. "You can tell your grandmother—"

Sandy put a finger in his chest. "Don't use that tone of voice. My grandmother has taken all she needs to from the Stirling men."

He looked startled. He backed up a foot, staggered over a box, caught himself in time. "What the hell are you talking about?"

Drawing a deep breath, Sandy reminded herself she still had to work with this man come Monday morning. "All I mean is, being left standing at the altar is—"

"What?" Drew slapped his right ear with his palm, as if to rattle some faulty wiring. "What am I hearing here?"

Sandy frowned. Was it just her, or was this conversation coming unglued? "I'm sorry. I thought you knew. The way you talked, I thought he must've told you."

"Oh, he told me all right. Told me *she* jilted *him*. Left him standing in the church in front of the whole town."

Anger blazed through Sandy. She fought to keep it under control. *Remember who this is,* she told herself. *Remember Monday morning.* This wasn't about Drew and her, it was about an old man and his failing—perhaps intentionally failing—memory. Sandy also reminded herself of what Gran had said. That the Stirling men meant trouble.

"Is your grandfather senile?"

"Se—! Listen, fifty years ago your grandmother broke my grandfather's heart. I think the least she could do, in the interest of neighborliness, is apologize. Is that too much to ask?"

"No."

"At last. Progress."

"Except that she wasn't the one who did the jilting."

Drew rolled his eyes and turned away, as if to pace. He was hemmed in by boxes and turned back. "You're telling me her version of this story is that she was the wronged party?"

Sandy used the side of her hiking boot to shove a new path through the crowded room, a path that wouldn't take her quite so close to Drew Stirling. When she reached the door, she opened it and made a sweeping gesture with her hand. She heard the crunch of tires on the icy drive. Oh, good. Her sister and Glenna were back just in time. Explaining this little scene should be a lot of fun.

"I suggest you have another conversation with your grandfather," she said. "Because he's obviously forgotten a few of the details."

He shook his head and didn't move. "You're serious, aren't you?"

"Absolutely."

Car doors slammed and the chatter of voices drew closer.

"So your grandmother has a little revisionist history going. Is that the deal?"

Angela appeared in the doorway, a large, flat box in her hands. "Pizza, anybody? Oh! Company. How nice."

"Hi, Drew," Glenna exclaimed. "Where were you when we needed you? I knocked on your door as I was heading out, but no luck."

"Mr. Stirling was just leaving," Sandy interjected coolly.

"That's too bad. We've got plenty of pizza," Angela insisted. "With extra cheese."

"Mr. Stirling has to have a conversation with his grandfather. Don't you?"

After distractedly greeting the new arrivals, Drew sidestepped through the maze of boxes and stood nose-to-nose with Sandy. "Did it ever occur to you that your grandmother might be the one who's senile?"

Angela and Glenna gasped. Angela muttered, "Now hold on, buddy!"

Sandy smiled grimly. "You're outnumbered, Drew. I'd cut my losses and withdraw from the field, if I were you."

He looked from one Murphy sister to the other, then elbowed his way between them, rolling his eyes at Glenna as he passed. Once on the sidewalk, he turned back, pointed a finger and said, "I'm getting to the bottom of this."

Sandy's insides began to quake as she watched him stalk away. As if things hadn't already been bad enough between them, this had to come up. Gran was upset and Drew had been sucked in by his grandfather's twisted version of the truth. And Sandy was stuck right in the middle.

"What on earth was that all about?" Glenna asked. "I've never seen Drew Stirling so riled up. In fact in the six months he's been living at the house, I've never seen him riled up at all."

"How dare he say Gran is senile? Who does he think he is?" Angela demanded.

Sandy sighed and once again closed the door. The pizza grew cold while she explained the surprising tale of Gran's engagement, along with the two versions of its ending.

"I'm calling Mom," Angela said. "She'll know the truth."

"The phone's not in yet." For which Sandy was grateful. She wasn't yet ready to drag the whole family into her dilemma. After all, this was *her* problem. No reason for her parents to know.

"You mean you don't believe your own grandmother?" Glenna said. "Maybe Grandma Bauer would know. Want me to call her?"

"No!" Sandy said. The fewer people who got involved in this the better, as far as she was concerned.

Angela opened the pizza box and put a slice on a paper plate. "It's not that I don't believe Gran. It's just that, well, she's old. And she is prone to embellish her stories a little."

"That wouldn't be an embellishment. That would be a lie." Glenna, too, dug into the pizza.

"Not if she's forgotten some of the details."

"Some detail. Let's see, did I walk out on the wedding or did he?"

"Let's go see Gran," Angela said. "I've got to hear more about this."

Sandy's head began to throb. "Can't we just let it rest? If this gets all stirred up, it's really going to make a mess of things at work."

"Your pal Drew already looked pretty stirred up," Angela said.

Indeed, he had. His last comment, in fact, had had all the earmarks of a threat. But Sandy felt certain that reason could prevail. After all, fifty years was a long time. The passion of the moment was long since dead. Any broken hearts were long since mended.

BY MONDAY MORNING, Drew had calmed down. He had himself in just the right frame of mind to handle whatever difficulties Sandy Murphy presented this week.

But when he and Sandy hit the conference room door at the same moment, the jitters started.

He had to do something about this.

"Clean slate?" he said, trying out a smile.

Her expression remained implacably distant. "Is that an apology?"

"Not exactly." He kept smiling, on the surface at least. This was ridiculous. Wasn't this ridiculous? You'd think *he* had left *her* at the altar. She was steaming over something that had happened half a century ago. To two other people. "More of a peace pipe."

"But not a white flag?"

Drew's smile faded. He wasn't the one at fault here. Where was it written that he was the one who had to grovel? Hell, why did anybody have to? Of course, Clarence had made it clear when they talked again on Sunday that *he* expected somebody to beg for forgiveness. Apparently, Sandy agreed. Too bad they didn't agree on who the groveler should be. "No. Not a white flag."

Sandy entered the conference room and took her usual seat, placing her papers neatly in front of her. Drew followed her in and took the seat across from her, hoping Britt and Jake wouldn't be late. He didn't want this unpleasantness to stretch out too long.

"Listen, Sandy—"

"I hope you've had a chance to read my report on the outlet store."

He had. But that wasn't the first thing on his personal agenda this morning. "I talked to my grandfather again yesterday. He's very clear on what happened in 1944. And he's never had a moment of memory problems. But regardless of who might have been at fault, I think we should encourage them to put this behind them. Don't you?"

There. That had sounded so reasonable, who could argue with it? Clarence had, of course. But Drew felt certain he could eventually work his grandfather around to a reasonable way of viewing things, too.

Sandy made a note in the margin of the report she had placed on the top of her stack, as if what he had said was of so little consequence she had let her thoughts stray to business instead. When she looked up, her face was still expressionless. He missed her smile. When she smiled, good things seemed possible. When she didn't, Drew wasn't certain what he was up against.

"My grandmother is a sweet woman who was terribly hurt and humiliated," Sandy said, sounding for all the world like a high-priced attorney arguing her case in front of a sympathetic jury. Drew would have voted her way, if he hadn't known the facts. "Some of the people who witnessed that humiliation live right there in Worthington House."

Clearly, Drew thought, he was the only one in this little foursome who understood the principle of compromise.

"Sandy, I don't think we need to get into any kind of 'he said, she said' disagreement over this. If you and I encourage our grandparents to—"

"Drew, I don't think this is the time or place to discuss our personal difficulties. Do you?"

So they didn't.

They sat in tense silence until Britt and Jake breezed in, chatting and laughing about the weekend, as cheerful as ever. Sandy managed to keep up with them, Drew noticed, which made him wonder just how phony his young co-worker could be. He himself tried, but he made a poor showing. He knew that from the puzzled look Jake gave him.

After all the pleasantries were over, they talked about Sandy's report. Drew had to admit he'd barely read it the afternoon before. And he had a hard time focusing on the discussion this morning. Frankly, he didn't give a damn about the outlet store or expanding their share of the local market, or even creating more local jobs. Right this minute, all he cared about was smoothing the rough waters between Sandy and him.

Well, no, he reminded himself, that wasn't really the issue. He wanted Clarence to be happy; that was it. After all, the move to Tyler had been Drew's idea, and he hated knowing he'd made the old fellow so miserable.

That was what had Drew troubled. The disturbance with Sandy was a side issue. Relatively unimportant in the scheme of things.

Then why did he keep glancing up, hoping she would relent and smile at him one more time?

Because he was behaving like a royal fool, that was why. What had Clarence said? Mag had been a dangerous woman. A manipulator.

Probably runs in the family, son. You watch your back.
Ridiculous.

"What's your reaction, Drew?"

Britt's voice broke through his preoccupation. Oh, yeah, he was handling things, all right. He didn't have a clue what had been said for the past five minutes. He did know, however, that he wasn't ready to let Sandy Murphy manipulate this company into deep water.

"I don't think Yes! Yogurt is financially ready to expand manufacturing, Britt."

He kept his focus on Britt, but from the corner of his eye he noted that Sandy didn't even move. Not a squirm. Not a twitch.

So they debated her proposal. And no matter what he had to say, she maintained her composure. She always had a good counterargument. Eventually, some of what she said began to make sense, even given Drew's conservative approach to spending company dollars. But he didn't give an inch.

At the end of the hour, they were at an impasse. The discussion was tabled. They were no closer to a decision than they had been when Sandy Murphy walked in two weeks ago.

Two weeks ago? In only two weeks, she had managed to create this much upheaval in his life?

He followed her into her office after the staff meeting, surprised to find himself hot under the collar at the idea that he was no longer master of the pleasant little domain he had carved out for himself.

"We have to settle this," he said.

"I don't think it's up to us. Britt and Jake have to be convinced, one way or another."

"Not that. This business with our grandparents. We have to get it settled."

"You're obsessing, Drew. Besides, it's not me you have to settle it with," she said, picking up the telephone and punching out a number. "It's your grandfather. He's the problem."

DREW WALKED through the shell of his house. Every day, it seemed, the place took on new shape. A wall went up here, a floor went down there. He stood in what would be his living room and peered through the framework that would be his picture window. The lake glittered in the distance, between the trees, a frozen, steely surface dotted by silvery patches of windblown snow. He reminded himself why he had chosen this particular spot for the house. Because the view of the lake would relax him on those rare days when eight hours at Yes! Yogurt jangled his nerves.

Today had been one of them. So had a lot of others since Sandy Murphy arrived. He didn't like the pattern that was emerging.

Restless, he turned away from the window.

He couldn't remember what it was that had seemed important enough to drive out here and check on at the end of a workday. Joe Santori and his crew had things well under control, and Joe said Drew would be in the house by Easter at the latest, even taking into account a Wisconsin winter. Drew believed him. All the walls were up now, and the insulation was going in this week, wiring the next. He felt impatience stir in him, an urgency to settle things.

He hadn't heard a car in the drive, so Jake's voice startled him. "It's coming along."

"Yeah. Thank goodness. I'm getting tired of living in a fishbowl and sharing a bathroom." He'd never thought those things before, but they seemed as good an explanation as any for what he was feeling. "Anna Kelsey runs a super boardinghouse, but . . ."

Jake stuck his head through a door that led to the kitchen. "Yeah, I know. It's not home."

They took the nickel tour. Jake made all the properly enthusiastic comments about the open, two-story living area, the eat-in kitchen, the guest bedrooms and the master bedroom suite upstairs, the decks off both the bedroom and the kitchen. It never occurred to Drew to question Jake's unexpected visit until they finished the tour and were standing beside their cars. Then Jake began to frown and fidget with his car keys.

"Drew, we've been talking, Britt and I. We feel pretty good about Sandy's proposal."

Drew tensed his jaw, his fists in his pockets. He began to wind up tightly again.

"We . . . well, we understand your reservations. But we think they're things that can be overcome. Sandy has some pretty good solutions, it seems to us."

Nodding, Drew studied his cousin. Jake had always had confidence in him. It miffed him, thinking he'd been robbed of that confidence by a girl barely out of college.

"Maybe you're right," he forced himself to say.

Jake looked relieved. "Take a closer look, will you? Let me know what you think sometime tomorrow."

"Sure."

Jake opened his car door, then turned back. "Don't take this the wrong way, Drew. But I couldn't help but wonder, is something else going on here? Something I don't know about?"

Uncertain what to make of the question, Drew first wanted to deny it. But as his cousin's words rolled around in his head, he began to understand the implications. He hadn't been fair. He walked into every confrontation with Sandy as if it must be exactly that, a confrontation. She did have some pretty good solutions, when you came right down to it.

His bias was showing. And the situation with their grandparents hadn't helped. *Damn!*

"I don't know, Jake."

Jake nodded. "She's like a kid sister to Britt. She'll be good for the company, too. Straighten it out, okay?"

Drew nodded. But as he watched his cousin pull out of the drive, he wasn't sure he knew how to straighten things out. Things were out of hand on a half dozen fronts, it seemed to him.

Where did he start?

SANDY WAS HALFWAY through her nightly ritual of fifty leg lifts and forty sit-ups when she heard the pounding on her front door. Not a knock, a definite pounding.

Frowning, she lay on the floor staring up at the ceiling, contemplating the unwelcome interruption. She did another sit-up. The pounding intensified.

Grunting out a barely audible "Keep your shirt on," she pulled herself off the floor and headed for the door. Empty boxes were piled along one wall and the room now looked practically livable, to her eyes anyway, after only two days. At least she could now offer whoever threatened to demolish her front door a seat on the futon.

Drew Stirling had his fist raised and aimed at the door when she opened it.

Acutely conscious of the damp turquoise sweatband around her forehead and the faded workout clothes she had thrown on after shedding her charcoal suit, she was about to snap out a greeting that was anything but welcoming. Then he held up his copy of her report and said, "You're right. Let's talk."

Disarmed, unable now to use unpleasantness on him, Sandy still wasn't willing to invite him into her apartment at nine-thirty in the evening, wearing her sweats and at a clear disadvantage. "Couldn't this wait until tomorrow?"

He suddenly looked and sounded tired. "I suppose. I just...I don't think I can sleep. I wanted you to know and I couldn't get a phone number for you and..."

Sighing, Sandy swept the door open. "They hook me up tomorrow. Come on in. I've got a pot of decaf."

So she poured coffee into pottery mugs and they sat over the tiny dining table and discussed her plan for expanding both manufacturing and sales in Tyler. He had some good ideas, saw holes in her plan that she hadn't anticipated and suggested solid solutions to them. The hands of the clock had edged toward midnight by the time they finished, and her respect for his business acumen had edged up, as well. This was almost as good, she thought, as a brainstorming session with Gin had been.

"Thanks, Drew," she said, standing as she retrieved their empty cups and headed for the sink. "We had a workable plan before. Now I think it's a great one."

He smiled, still looking tired. "Thanks. Maybe we'll make a good team, after all."

She leaned against the counter and he stood beside his chair. Sandy had known the apartment was small, but his closeness pointed up just how small. A good team? She wondered. It had been easy, these past two-and-a-half hours, to think of Drew only as a colleague. But now that their reports were closed and their pencils put away, the atmosphere in the room felt different.

Increasingly uneasy, she moved toward the door. But as she brushed past him, he put a hand on her arm. She froze.

"Sorry I've been so hard to live with."

She glanced up, knowing she should move away but finding her limbs unwilling to budge. If he had looked anything but unsure himself, she thought, it would have been easy. But there he was, his eyes full of questions and his lips forming such an uncertain half smile.

"Things will get better," she said, although she had no real reason to believe it was so.

They hovered there, his fingers resting lightly on her arm, his breath close to her cheek. *Move. See him to the door. It's late and that's why things feel so weird.*

But she didn't move. She waited, heart thumping, watching his face waver in her direction. She saw his lips, which no longer smiled. Her gaze flickered to his eyes, which looked unfocused. An ache spread through her and she recognized it with a shock.

He wanted to kiss, and so did she.

She whispered, "Our grandparents wouldn't approve of this."

He grinned, then lowered his lips to hers. They touched so briefly she later wondered whether they had touched at all. Then, abruptly, he backed away.

He was no longer grinning and his eyes were suddenly so focused they looked almost startled. "I'd better go."

She stood alone, propped against her locked front door, a few minutes later. She told herself she should be grateful one of them had shown good sense. She only wished it had been her.

She also wished it could have happened a minute or two earlier, so she wouldn't now be wondering quite so achingly about the taste and texture of his lips.

But she would still be wondering if it had happened this way for Gin.

DREW'S HEAD SPUN angrily all the way home. Dammit, why hadn't he thought of this before?

Our grandparents wouldn't approve of this, she had said. That was when something had occurred to him. And no matter how strong the pull of her soft, full lips, he had known instantly that he had to get as far away from her as possible.

If their grandparents had been engaged, why couldn't they have been lovers, as well? And what would make a woman of any generation more bitter than being left behind in disgrace? Pregnant?

Who's to say that Sandy and I aren't related?

CHAPTER NINE

"GRANDPA, IT'S JUST dinner." Drew tried to make his own voice soothing in response to the recalcitrant voice on the phone. "I promise, it's not going to turn into the Inquisition."

At least, not in the way Clarence expected, Drew thought.

"Yet another indication that you do not know this town," Clarence replied. "As soon as they spot me, the game of twenty questions will proceed. They will demand answers."

Drew wanted answers, too, but he wasn't about to admit that to his grandfather. He would have to be shrewd to get anything out of Clarence that Clarence wasn't ready to share. And he'd made it abundantly clear that he had nothing more to say on the subject of Magdalena Halston Murphy. Besides, there were other issues Drew needed to address with his grandfather. Sighing, he shoved his paperwork to the corner of his desk and leaned back in his chair. "Look, I talked to Mr. Kellaway today and he said you haven't left your room since you arrived."

"As I suspected, the busybodies have begun their work already. Privacy is an alien concept in this burg."

"You won't even go for your physical therapy. Don't you want to get better?"

There was a long silence, then Clarence answered, "I warned you not to bring me here."

"I'll be there at six."

"Six? You've been in Tyler too long, son. Your mother raised you better than to dine at such an uncivilized hour."

Drew didn't point out that his family had eaten late when he was a child only because his mother couldn't finish her shift at the department store and get home on the bus any earlier than seven.

"Dress warm, Grandpa."

Clarence continued his protests, but Drew hung up. He'd already heard the entire routine.

He looked up to discover Sandy standing in his office doorway, looking efficient and all-business in a royal-blue suit. God, she was more than just intelligent and entertaining and challenging. She was gorgeous! Even in those baggy sweats the night before, face scrubbed clean and hair damp with perspiration, she had been gorgeous.

Yeah, but is Clarence her grandfather, too?

"Britt and Jake have a few minutes," she said, "if you want to go over the plan with them."

"Oh. Well, why don't you do it?" He was too rattled to sit in the conference room and act as if they were nothing more than colleagues. Not when he had come so close to kissing her senseless not twelve hours earlier. Not with things so up in the air. Not with those milky-pink pearls resting lightly against her perfect neck. He cleared his throat and pulled his paperwork back to the center of his desk. "It's your plan, really."

She frowned. "I think we should present it together. So they know we're in agreement."

She was right, of course. Wasn't she always? Why was he falling apart like this? Had Sandy's grandmother affected his grandfather this way, too? Was there a twelve-step recovery group for men who suddenly found themselves powerless around clever, dark-haired women with soft-as-silk skin?

She stepped into his office and closed the door. Drew's pulse began to race. Being alone with her was not a good plan.

"What happened last night, Drew?"

He remembered the old admonition to never let 'em see you sweat. Not good for the business image. But this thing with Sandy had gone way beyond business. And way beyond his control. He felt nervous and he doubted he could hide it.

"Nothing. I . . . nothing."

She never changed expressions and she didn't move a muscle, but somehow Drew understood that she had no intention of leaving until she heard what she wanted to hear. "What was that kiss about?" she asked.

His mouth went dry. If she intended to push, he had no choice but to push back. "Did I kiss you?"

Her placid, lovely face gave no clue to what was going on behind it. But the silence stretched out so long it was clear something went on. At last she smiled without revealing a thing, merely deepening the mystery. "I guess we'll never know, will we?"

This was it; she had him by the scruff of the neck. She knew it; he knew it. Game, set and match; hand her the trophy. He resisted the urge to tug at his turtleneck, which seemed to be slowly choking him.

"Come on," he said, standing abruptly. "We'll talk to Britt and Jake."

So she'd seen him sweat. Big deal. That was the least of his problems.

MATT HANSEN poked a spoon into his goulash, but he was certain he couldn't swallow another bite.

He had to tell his mom he was flunking two courses. He would rather vacuum the floors every day for the rest of his life. As a matter of fact, it wouldn't surprise him if that was the sentence.

As if having the threat of terminal housework and parental disapproval hanging over his head weren't bad enough, tonight's dinner topic was how Yes! Yogurt could help with the unemployment problem in Tyler.

Maybe he could volunteer now for the toilet-scrubbing chain gang.

"Anyway," Britt said as she walked around the table refilling bowls, "if Sandy and Drew are right, we're talking about ten new jobs. That's something."

"Surely the investigation will reach some kind of conclusion soon," Jake said. "In the meantime, even a little bit of good news might raise spirits in town."

Matt's own spirits sank lower. He could feel the shackles on his ankles.

"Matt, you've hardly eaten a bite." His mom stopped behind his chair. "Are you all right?"

"Fine. I'm fine, okay?"

Britt's arm came around and she pressed her wrist to his forehead. Matt cringed.

"You don't feel warm."

"I told you! Jeez. Can I be excused?"

"But you haven't eaten."

Then, in case the jury hadn't heard enough, his fourteen-year-old sister added her testimony. "He acts weird at school, too," Christy said.

He glared at her. She made a face at him. Little Jacob pointed and laughed at her. For once, Matt didn't think his baby brother was funny. Matt shoved a bite of goulash into his mouth and prayed everybody would stop staring at him.

For a change, his prayers were answered. Jacob knocked over his glass of milk and the phone rang, creating instant pandemonium. Relieved to have the attention diverted, Matt took advantage of the chaos to ease from his chair and slip out the back door.

He heard David calling his name as he opened the door. "Where'd Matt go? Matt! Telephone! It's Jon Weiss!"

Matt's pulse skittered. Jon Weiss. The last person he wanted to talk to. He pulled the door silently shut and stood shivering in the dark, listening to the happy commotion behind him and knowing there was no way he deserved to be a part of it.

DREW WAS TIRED of the small talk. He twisted his coffee mug back and forth, dreading moving on to the topic he really wanted to discuss. He'd had about all the confrontation he wanted in recent weeks and he wasn't looking forward to locking horns—again—with his grandfather.

The waitress stopped to refill their cups, providing the reprieve of another handy, meaningless topic.

"This establishment has not changed one iota in fifty years," Clarence said, stirring a liberal portion of creamer into his fresh coffee. "The name, of course. It was the Knife and Fork Diner in those days. What did you say they call it now?"

"Marge's."

Clarence shook his head. "Lacks a certain originality, don't you think? Marge's Diner. The Knife and Fork, now that had character."

Despite complaining all the way about coming out in public in a wheelchair, Clarence had dressed to kill for the occasion. He wore his best tweed jacket with the plaid vest and worsted trousers that remained from an old suit. He wore a hat with the brim dipped low in front, the kind last seen when Humphrey Bogart was a leading man. His silk necktie was knotted crisply and his shirt was so heavily starched it must be rubbing his neck raw.

"I thought we were dining out," he had said when Drew arrived at Worthington House. He had eyed disapprovingly his grandson's crewneck sweater and the khakis that no doubt didn't crease well enough to suit him.

"Few people dress for dinner at Marge's, Grandpa."

That didn't mean Clarence had to approve their slovenly manners, however.

He had already asked the name and circumstance of every person over fifty he saw at Marge's. A few he obviously recognized, most he didn't.

He had already demanded every detail of the fire at Ingalls F and M and expressed appropriate, if not altogether sincere, sympathy for those who remained out of work.

"The scoundrel should be caught," he had stated. "And justice served promptly."

"No one knows for sure it was arson, Grandpa. They're still trying to make that determination."

"I heard it was a drifter. We never used to have that element in Tyler."

Drew saw nothing to gain from pointing out that the drifter in question was married to one of the town's most popular ministers. Although some still stared and wondered and even talked when Michael Kenton came down the street, others had quietly accepted the fact that anyone upstanding enough to capture the heart of the Reverend Sarah wasn't likely to be an arsonist.

Clarence pointed his steak knife across the table. "Personally, I would look closer to home for the culprit."

"I hope you aren't pointing that knife at me," Drew said, trying to lighten the conversation.

"Nonsense. One of the Ingallses. That's where you'll find the motive."

"Their business is shut down. Where's the motive in that?"

"Insurance, son. Insurance."

Drew didn't care for that particular theory, either. He liked every single member of the Ingalls family, even gruff old Judson Ingalls. They might once have been the town's moneyed elite, but today they were simply its doctors and lawyers, family people whose lives were comfortably intertwined with those of many other folks in the community.

"I could have been there myself, you know," Clarence said, capturing Drew's attention with his strange claim.

"Been where? What are you talking about?"

"Bigger than Judson Ingalls."

Clarence was prone to grandiose ideas, but this was news to Drew. And a very improbable suggestion. "What are you talking about?" he repeated.

Sitting across the table from his grandfather, he saw a familiar, faraway look come into Clarence's soft gray eyes—the same look he got on those rare occasions when he talked about the war. Drew knew a story was about to commence.

"Ah, son, if it hadn't been for the war, I don't think the thing would have had nearly the same consequences." Clarence absently stirred his coffee. "The war, that's what made all the difference."

"Why was that, Grandpa?" Drew asked softly, knowing his prompting wouldn't even be necessary in another moment or two, once the tale truly captured the old man's attention.

"Why, because there were pitifully few weddings during the war, of course. And what few there were were slapdash affairs. You know, grab the justice of the peace on the way to the train depot, that kind of thing."

Drew listened raptly as the story unfolded, of a wounded war hero returning to a small town hungry for good news, where a whole passel of young women were starved for the sight of a man—any man—who was older than fifteen and younger than forty. The fairest of the starved young women was the daughter of the business partner of the war hero's father, so the match seemed a natural to everyone. The two families ran quite an empire in the small town, everything from the hardware store to the creamery to the first auto dealership in the county. The wedding was to be the event of the season.

But once he had painted the scenario, Clarence grew silent. Drew waited, but the old man seemed content to brood.

"So what happened, Grandpa?"

"What happened? Why, the fickle young girl called the whole thing off, that's what happened."

Impatient for the rest, Drew waved off the waitress who approached. "Are you sure?"

Clarence's eyes widened. "Am I *sure?* Was I not the wronged party? Was mine not the broken heart?"

"Well..."

"The woman in question was a chronic prevaricator. It appears time and age have not altered her basic nature."

"You still insist she's lying?"

"As a gentleman, I can only say her memory is not all that it should be in this particular instance."

Drew pressed for details, but Clarence could not be budged. They ordered dessert, Marge's famous apple pie for Drew and coconut cream for Clarence. Halfway through the pie, Drew decided on a different tack.

"But what about the business partnerships, Grandpa?"

Clarence savored a bite of coconut cream, then dabbed at the corners of his mouth with the paper napkin he had complained about when they had sat down at the table. Drew recognized the pause for dramatic effect and waited patiently.

"Everyone tried to carry on as usual, of course," Clarence said at last. "Much was at stake. But there was too much bitterness. The Stirlings blamed the Halstons and the Halstons blamed the Stirlings. It was a fine mess."

The upshot was that, with the families bickering so much, one by one the businesses began to fail. Finally, all that was left was the hardware store. The Halstons, according to Clarence, stole it away from the Stirlings and gave it to their daughter when she married Harry Murphy.

"Another returning war hero, I might add," Clarence said. "Of course, I don't recall much of the feuding. I left town myself."

"And never came back?"

"Only for funerals, son. Only for funerals."

"So there are no Stirlings left in Tyler?"

Clarence frowned. "Not until recently. I warn you, that family deals under the table. I would not do business with a Halston."

"They're Murphys now, Grandpa."

"Blood will tell. That's all you need to know."

Drew pushed aside his half-eaten pie and tried to absorb this chunk of family history he'd never been told. It was a classic tale of love and betrayal, complete with fortunes lost. The problem was he had only his grandfather's word about who were the villains and who the victims. Drew knew his grandfather well enough to be sure that there wasn't a dishonest bone in his body. But he'd also heard the old man tell enough battle stories over the years to realize that some embellishments grew with each telling.

The truth about the ill-fated wedding and all that came after might never be known.

But there was one truth Drew needed to know.

"Grandpa, just one more thing. Is it possible..." This was delicate. Not the usual grandfather-grandson topic of conversation. "You don't suppose that... Is there any chance at all that I'm related to Sandy Murphy?"

Clarence finished his coffee, folded his napkin neatly beside his dessert plate and stared at his grandson. "Young man, there are certain questions a gentleman does not entertain."

"But—"

"Unless you have a pressing need to know. Is there some romantic intrigue between you and that young woman?"

"No, sir. That is—"

"My advice is simple. Extricate yourself, son."

Drew felt his uneasiness turn to queasiness. "Then it is possible? That Sandy and I—"

But another elderly man was looming over their table— Phil Wocheck, a former groundskeeper at Timberlake and father of the present owner of the lodge. "Excuse me if I intrude," Phil said in his faintly accented voice, "but if I am not mistaken, you are the Stirling boy."

He spoke, of course, to Clarence. Drew smiled. The Stirling boy, now well over seventy, white-haired and not exactly smooth of skin, did not appear delighted at the reunion.

"That's right."

Phil put out his weathered hand and introduced himself. A brief conversation followed, but Drew barely listened. He was too consumed with his own anxiety about his possible blood relationship to Sandy Murphy. But how to get the information he needed out of a stubborn old man?

"Imagine this," Phil said as he waved and headed back to the table he shared with one of his old cronies. "We never thought to see you back home again. Won't people be surprised?"

When he was out of earshot, Clarence said, "You know what that means, don't you? It means won't people be talking about this, once word gets out. It means the whole town is going to rehash the story all over again."

"It was fifty years ago, Grandpa." Drew stood and began maneuvering his grandfather's wheelchair through the crowded diner. "Nobody's going to care anymore."

"They'll care! Even you care. Even you want to know what happened."

"I have reasons."

They left the bright warmth of the diner for the biting cold of a January evening.

Clarence said, "You have reasons. This woman has you under her spell, that's your reason. Because you're not related to her to my knowledge. You can't deny you're under her spell, can you?"

Drew wished he had another answer for his grandfather, but he didn't.

THE ELEMENTARY and high schools were among Sandy's first targets. If the children of Tyler learned to love the healthy treats Yes! Yogurt produced, how could parents turn their backs on them?

Standing in the lunchroom handing out free samples, she was grateful for the distraction a hundred noisy youngsters provided. Her cool demeanor might fool Drew Stirling, although she wouldn't have bet good money on that. But what she managed to project bore no relation whatsoever to what whirled beneath the surface.

What had she been thinking yesterday morning, even bringing up to Drew what had happened, what hadn't happened, what might have been only in her very vivid imagination that night at her apartment? They had worked together—really worked together—for the first time since her arrival. And for the second time she had managed to convince herself that he wanted to kiss her.

But he *had* kissed her, hadn't he? Hadn't his lips brushed hers? Could she possibly have conjured up those feelings, those sensations, if it hadn't happened?

By the following morning Sandy had felt so confused and agitated that anything seemed better than remaining in turmoil over something she couldn't explain. So she had blurted out her question, hoping he would explain to her why one moment he had seemed intent on seducing her and the next had vanished without a backward glance.

At least she had satisfied herself that he, too, had felt the disturbing power of what had happened—or not happened—between them. With his expressive face, he hadn't fooled her for a second.

But she was still no closer to understanding what was going on between them. And maybe it was just as well. All she needed to remember was that her professional standing was at stake. Besides, there was too much history. Murphy women and Stirling men needed to steer clear of one another. Maybe it was that simple.

So Sandy concentrated on the task at hand, marketing. Attracting young consumers with free samples of a wholesome, nutritious snack. The product tasted so good, they would never know it was also healthy. And if the samples were well received, which Sandy never doubted for a moment, Yes! Yogurt would make a substantial product donation to the Tyler public schools. That tax-deductible donation would create an immediate need to pump up production, which would create an immediate need for additional workers. Increased product recognition would also contribute to sales at the brand-new outlet store, leading to even more production. Clearly, it was a win-win situation. Even Drew agreed, at last.

Sandy scooped yogurt into small cups, topped it with crunchy granola and smiled at the youngsters who trooped by her tiny stand. They were variously excited, intrigued, skeptical and downright resistant. But the yogurt went fast. Plenty of students came back for seconds. Sandy's dipping arm grew weary, but the children's response kept her smile enthusiastic.

Especially one particular child. Renee Hansen, Britt's ten-year-old, made sure that all her schoolmates sampled the yogurt. And to each she announced, "This is my best friend, Sandy. She helps my mom make yogurt."

"From goats?" asked one little girl, making a disgusted face and pointing to the picture on the sign.

Renee gave her young friend a withering look. "Well, what did you think, it came out of a rock?"

As the lunch hour drew to a close, Renee came back to the cart, where Sandy was getting ready herself for the next group. "They all liked it."

"Good." She gave Renee a quick hug.

The bell rang to signal the end of lunch break, but Renee continued to dawdle, straightening cups and wiping up spills on the surface of the cart.

"You'd better run," Sandy said. "You don't want to be late for class."

Renee shrugged. "It's only geography. I don't like geography, because Mrs. Malpern says we have to spell every country and every city perfectly or it counts off."

"Gee, that is tough. But I'll bet you can do it."

"Maybe."

"I'll help you practice this weekend, if you like."

"Yeah? Cool. Um, Sandy? Can I ask a question?"

"Sure."

"Are you going to get married soon and have babies?"

The query startled Sandy. She had always taken it for granted that sometime, in some far distant moment in time—way past the age of thirty, for example—she might marry, become a mother. But that all seemed so far away. Her first instinct was to brush off Renee's curiosity. But the full impact of the question began to settle on her like a weight. Married? As in sharing a bathroom and looking at each other over the morning paper every single day? Babies? As in diapers and mashed bananas? Strange reactions swamped her. "Well, gee. I don't know. Why?"

"'Cause when you do, I want to be the baby-sitter for you."

Sandy laughed, but she was aware of the nervous flutter in her middle. Why was it that all of a sudden, the very idea of marriage and babies sounded so completely plausible? Desirable, even? "I see. Well, I promise if I need a baby-sitter, you're it. How's that?"

Renee didn't look satisfied. "Then you'll have to hurry. Because I'll have to go away to college in eight years. See what I mean?"

"Yes, I do. But I'd have to be in love first." Now why had she said that? Why did she even think that?

"Like Mom and Jake?"

"Like your mom and Jake." And no matter how valiantly she tried to keep the thought from entering her mind, she couldn't; he was there. His smile. The hot brush of his lips over hers. Drew. Damn him!

"I could help."

Sandy shook off the sensations. "Help what?"

"Help you find somebody."

Recalling her young friend's expressed interest in her uncle Drew's marital status the day she'd given Renee a ride home, Sandy grew agitated. "Oh. Well, I appreciate that, but...but I think you'd better get going to class, don't you?"

Reluctantly, Renee nodded. "Okay."

The little girl dashed across the cafeteria, grabbed her backpack and darted to the door. From there, she paused and called out, "I'll think of somebody. You can count on me."

Sandy gave her a thumbs-up and realized her hand was trembling.

In the hollow silence of the momentarily empty cafeteria, she gave herself a mental pep talk. She was not in the market for settling down, for becoming a parent, for having a man in her life. Especially not for a certain man.

But the images wouldn't leave her the rest of the day. Images of two cups of coffee and the morning paper.

CHAPTER TEN

SANDY HEARD her first version of the Wedding That Never Was from Annabelle Scanlon, Tyler's postmistress and gossip extraordinaire.

Sandy had gone to the post office to get the most recent information on bulk-mail regulations, which she needed in order to prepare a proposal for a promotional mailing. First she had to listen to the latest on Raine Peterson, an old high-school acquaintance whose Broadway play had opened—and closed—the previous week.

"I heard she was devastated," Annabelle said. "The reviews were extremely harsh."

"That's rough," Sandy replied, feeling a pang of sympathy for her classmate. All through high school, Raine had talked of little else but dancing. While Sandy had thrown herself into the pep squad and Future Business Leaders of America, Raine had lived and breathed dance, which was one reason Sandy hadn't known her very well, even in their small class. How must she feel if she thought that dream might now be dying? "But if I know Raine, she'll come through it," she declared.

Annabelle shook her head. "I'm not so sure. The darn thing closed after the first night. I don't know what Raine'll do now. And Marge, her mom, isn't talking."

It occurred to Sandy that anyone with good sense wouldn't talk to Annabelle Scanlon about personal problems. The woman meant no harm, but she certainly managed to keep the rumor mills in Tyler well supplied.

"Did you have a chance to pull out the bulk-mail regulations so I could get a copy?" Sandy asked, trying to get the conversation back on track without wasting any more time on chitchat. She had a million things to do this week, including finding a designer to work on the logo update and working up another survey to continue the market research Yes! Yogurt so desperately needed.

"Oh, yeah. It's right—" Annabelle shuffled through the piles of paper on her jumbled desk "—here."

Sandy had begun to scan the regulations when Annabelle said, "I'll bet nobody was more surprised than your grandmother when Clarence Stirling showed up over at Worthington House."

"Um, yes." Sandy frowned at the document in her hands, refusing to look up. "Can you give me some idea what size mailing would fit these weight requirements?"

"Oh, sure. I've got some samples here somewhere."

Annabelle began to rummage around the back room, stopping once to help a customer who dropped in with a package to mail. Sandy half listened, amused, as the postmistress managed to coax plenty of details about the package out of her unsuspecting customer. The next person through the post office door would probably hear all about the birthday present Renata Youngthunder had just sent to a friend in Lubbock, Texas.

When Annabelle returned with the samples Sandy had asked to see, it was as if there had been no interruption in her conversation about Mag and Clarence. "You know, I was just a child at the time—twelve or thirteen, I think—but I never will forget what a ruckus that wedding stirred up."

Sandy didn't reply, although she had to admit a part of her was beginning to wonder what Annabelle might remember about the incident that had launched this fifty-year-old feud.

"My mother was a seamstress, you know," Annabelle continued, clearly needed no prompting. "She probably made half the wedding dresses in Tyler from 1935 until she retired in 1963. I remember when Mag and her mother came in for the fitting. Already something was wrong. You could see it in Mag's face."

Sandy couldn't help herself. "Oh?"

Annabelle nodded. "She'd been crying. I felt so sorry for her, she was such a sweet, pretty young thing. I stood there holding the box of pins for my mother, the way I always did, and I heard Mag's mother say, 'Young lady, now is not the time for tantrums. There is more than a wedding at stake here and I'll thank you to remember it. We'll *all* thank you to remember it.' Those were her exact words."

Stunned, Sandy let the postal-service documents fall into her lap. "What in the world would she have meant by that?"

A satisfied smile settled onto the postmistress's face. "Of course, I didn't understand it at the time myself. But I heard Mother and Daddy talking later. The Halstons and the Stirlings were founding a dynasty, you see. And they didn't care one little bit about sacrificing their children."

"A dynasty?" This was news to Sandy. Astonishing news.

"Why, sure. Those two families owned everything in this town that the Ingallses and the Barons didn't. Shoot, the whole thing was nothing but a business arrangement. Mag was smart to get herself out of it, if you ask me."

"Get herself out of it? You mean *she* called it off?"

Annabelle's laughter echoed off the post office's high ceiling. "Well, it might have been better if she had. Honey, that child simply didn't show up. She locked herself in her bedroom and didn't come out for three days. Oh, it was delicious, that's for sure. Today the only thing scandals have is sex. Back in the old days, scandals had *mystery.*"

UPSET AT THE IDEA that she was going to have to apologize to Drew Stirling for the things she'd said about his grandfather, Sandy marched straight from the post office to Worthington House. A glance at her watch told her it was time for the twice-weekly meeting of the Tyler Quilting Circle. But she had a few things to discuss with her grandmother before she threw herself on Drew Stirling's mercy.

The quilting circle was holding court in the activity room—Martha Bauer, Emma Finklebaum, wheel chairbound Bea Ferguson, plus Mag and a few others Sandy didn't know very well. Once again Sandy was struck by how much younger and more energetic her grandmother looked than most of the other women present. Mag Murphy sparkled, from her bright blond hair and her ivory complexion to the glitzy jewelry and clothes she wore.

This morning she had on a fuchsia satin caftan, plus a teal-and-fuchsia turban dotted with rhinestones.

Sandy slipped into a seat behind her grandmother. "Gran, we need to talk."

"Fine. Talk."

"Privately."

The murmur of voices grew distinctly softer. Mag held her needle up to the light and squinted as she attempted to rethread it. "I have no secrets."

Sandy lowered her voice. "It's about Mr. Stirling."

Emma Finklebaum leaned across the expanse of quilt and said, "We didn't catch that."

Emma had written the social column for the local paper for as long as Sandy could remember. The woman still thought the public had the right to know anything and everything.

"It's about Clarence," said Bea Ferguson, who was a good deal younger than the rest of them and possessed much better hearing.

Emma nodded her iron-gray head. "I told you so. I knew as soon as word got around that he's back that Clarence Stirling was all we'd hear about for weeks."

"I don't want to talk about that cad," Mag said, still struggling with her thread.

Taking the needle, Sandy slipped the thread through the eye and handed it back to her. "Well, I do. It's causing me problems at work."

"I warned you about that Stirling man."

"After the way Clarence treated your grandmother, I should think you'd have the good sense to listen to what she's telling you," Emma said.

Sandy felt her irritation rising. "Okay, Emma. Why don't *you* tell me how he treated Gran?"

Emma arched a brow at Mag and waited for her quilting partner's curt nod. Then she jabbed her needle into the fabric to hold her place and sat back comfortably in her chair.

"I remember it very well because I was new on the social beat at the time, of course," she said. "And this was one of the biggest stories of the day. I had to fight to keep that lowlife Medgar Wojhoski from stealing it for his business pages. In those days, men were inclined to treat women shabbily in both personal and professional situations. Am I right, girls?"

Everyone nodded gravely, except for Martha Bauer.

"When I heard about Margaret Ingalls, I was crushed, because I knew I could never print that, not in those days. And I knew the chances were very good that I'd never get the chance to do the wedding story, either."

"Margaret Ingalls?" Sandy said. "What about Margaret Ingalls?"

"Well, you've heard the stories about her, I'm sure. Judson Ingalls's wife was quite the femme fatale. If she saw a man, she wanted him. Or at least she wanted to make sure he wanted her. Clarence didn't stand a chance."

"Don't excuse him," Mag protested. "He was as culpable as that floozy."

"Well, of course he was. All I meant was the flesh is weak, especially if it's male flesh."

Sandy sighed. That explained the teary, reluctant bride at the seamstress shop. "So he was fooling around and you backed out."

Emma straightened abruptly. "Oh, my stars, no! Mag didn't suspect a thing. Nobody would have dreamed of breathing a word to her face, not in those days. Why, she didn't know anything about it until she was standing there in the church in that ivory lace gown and discovered there was no groom to be found."

Emma sighed and retrieved her needle. "I must say, that was my personal favorite of all the stories I wrote—no offense intended, Mag. But the town was in an uproar over it, and I got the scoop."

THE CONFRONTATION CAME at lunchtime, in the dining room at Worthington House. How they had managed to avoid each other until then was a mystery to Mag. All she knew was that her luck had run out. There she stood with her teacup and saucer in hand, on her way to join a friend at another table, and there he sat.

And half the occupants of the Worthington House dining hall seemed to freeze in place as she and Clarence came face-to-face.

Mag remembered distinctly the last time she had been the object of such undivided attention. She had behaved with dignity then and she intended to do so now. With a nod, she smiled at Clarence and prepared to sweep past him. But as her crinkled rayon skirt brushed his chair, he said, "You're prettier than ever, Magdalena."

Delight bubbled up in Mag's heart, instantly followed by outrage at how easily she had allowed him to manipulate her emotions. The scoundrel, thinking he could get her to come around by flattering her! The anger almost spewed out before she caught herself.

Dignity, she reminded herself. *The one thing he cannot rob me of without my permission is my dignity.*

She stopped and looked directly at him, which was more disconcerting than she had imagined. His gray eyes were still so clear and bright, sparkling with the same vitality he'd had fifty years ago. Oh, she saw the lines on his face and the gray that dominated his hair. But somehow she saw most clearly not with her eyes, but with her heart. And her treacherous old heart still saw him the way she'd seen him then. When she had loved him.

How could that be? Unless she loved him still?

Ignoring the churning in her breast, she said, "How gentlemanly of you to say so, Clarence."

She turned away then, hoping that would be the end of it. She didn't feel confident she could keep up this civility for long. But before she could take a step, he spoke again.

"Could I ask one favor, Mag?"

His nerve astounded her. It shouldn't have, she supposed. "And what would that be?"

"Call off your granddaughter."

Suddenly Mag wanted to grab him by the scarf knotted casually at his throat and drag him up to eye level. How dare he mention Alexandra! Her teacup began to rattle in its saucer as her hands trembled. "What are you insinuating?"

"That you've set her after my grandson. The same way you launched yourself at me once upon a time."

That was it—the final straw! Mag slammed her teacup on a nearby table, effectively drowning out the ripple of reaction that traveled through the lunchroom. "That may qualify as the most despicable thing you've ever said, Clarence Albert Stirling."

He had the nerve to chuckle. "But I'm right and you can't deny it."

She started to do exactly that, but reminded herself of the importance of dignity. "Such an absurdity needs no denial."

"I don't know if your perfidy runs in your granddaughter's veins, but I don't want Drew finding out the hard way. Is that clear enough?"

Mag had never before punched anyone in the nose, but she looked down at her oversize emerald ring and allowed herself a momentary fantasy. If it had been a real gemstone, she might have risked it. But with her luck, the green glass would crack all over the place and simply embarrass her.

"My Alexandra's only interest in your grandson is in trying to save him from his own professional incompetence," she retorted. "And you may share that information with him at your earliest convenience."

Then she decided to hell with her dignity. She dumped the contents of her teacup into his lap and left the dining room. The roar of reaction as she exited was most satisfying.

DREW HEADED down the darkened hallway, drawn by Sandy's murmuring voice.

He had seen the light on at Yes! Yogurt's headquarters as he drove back from another evening visit checking on the progress on his house. He had told himself he simply needed to make sure there was nothing amiss at the office, but the truth was he had known what he would find.

Having worked like a fiend to get her next survey ready, Sandy had begun the calls that would help them develop a strategy for reaching their best audiences. For the rest of this week she would be on the phone late into the evening, talking to people all over the country who fit the profile of health food consumers.

He reached the door to her office and looked inside. She sat at her desk, telephone pressed to one ear, looking as crisp and professional as she had at eight o'clock that morning. The only concessions she had made to the long day and the late hour were removing her earrings and draping her suit jacket over the back of her swivel chair. Even her voice didn't sound weary, as might be expected after a workday this long. No, Sandy Murphy still managed to sound upbeat and enthusiastic as she queried the person on the other end of the line.

Were there no chinks in her armor? No human failings to bring her down to the level of mere mortals?

She didn't even hang up when she finished the survey, but depressed the disconnect button, released it and began to dial the next number on her list. Only a long sigh signaled her weariness.

"Sounds like break time," he said. "What do you think?"

The expression on her face was wary when she looked up. "What are you doing here?"

"I drove by and saw the light."

She kept her finger on the next name on her list. "Well, I'm not a burglar. But thanks for checking."

"Haven't you been at this long enough for one night?" Why couldn't he let it go? Drew wondered. Why couldn't he wish her luck, tell her he'd see her sometime tomorrow and leave? How she chose to do her job was none of his business.

The truth was, now that his grandfather had assured him there was no chance he and Sandy were related, he felt the last reason to distance himself from her had been removed. He was attracted to her and she to him. They were consenting adults. Where was the problem? "I won't tell the boss if you call it quits."

Ignoring his weak attempt at humor, she shook her head. "I need to complete four more surveys before I call it quits tonight."

He knew enough about market research to know that completing four more surveys could easily mean dialing another thirty or forty numbers. And that the reason she was doing this herself instead of hiring a few college kids was because he'd made such a big deal about the budget.

"I've got an idea," he said. "Why don't we talk to Jake tomorrow? As long as we're making a commitment to Tyler's economy, we might as well hire a crew to do some of this research for you."

She replaced the phone in its cradle. "Training them will take time."

"Even so, you can wrap up the project quicker with some assistance."

She nodded. He could almost see weariness envelop her as the awareness sank in that she might not have to do all the work herself. Knowing that caring too much would be a mistake, Drew walked over to her desk, picked up her jacket and took her by the hand.

"Come on. You're beat. Let's get you home."

"I really should—"

"No, you shouldn't." And she acquiesced as he helped her into her jacket.

The gesture was a mistake. Her nearness was disconcerting. Wanting her was still out of bounds for so many reasons. Way out of bounds. But some part of Drew wasn't processing that information. Some part of him insisted on wanting her anyway. He thought of how she would feel, leaning against his chest, her hair against his cheek.

He stepped back.

He didn't help her into her overcoat when they reached the front door. He didn't open her car door.

"Drew?"

The uncertainty in her voice tugged at him. He took one more step in her direction. Moonlight cast a silvery glow on her skin, her eyes. Oh, Lord, why her? Why now? Why not a dozen other women in Tyler instead?

"Drew, I think I owe you an apology. Maybe."

"For what?"

"For the things I said about your grandfather."

Drew's spirits sank. Actually, he had just about decided that he was the one who owed her an apology. But he'd hesitated to bring it up, reasoning that it would be better all around to leave this personal issue outside the walls of Yes! Yogurt.

"Maybe not," he said.

She shook her head. "I talked to some people today.... Well, the truth is, they talked to me."

"They do seem eager to talk about it, don't they?"

She looked surprised, then amused. "You, too?"

"Afraid so."

She sagged against her car. "And what did you hear?"

How could he explain that what he'd heard had raised more questions than it answered? "Judson Ingalls...he was the best man."

"Was supposed to be the best man."

Drew grinned. "Right. That was the plan, anyway. Judson said Grandpa was touchy about his injury. He'd been wounded in the war, was having a hard time thinking of himself as anything but a permanent cripple. That's why Grandpa backed down, according to Judson. He didn't want to saddle your grandmother with half a man."

The revelation didn't seem to please Sandy. In fact, her usually cheerful expression grew glum, when he'd thought she would be delighted to have her grandmother's version of things confirmed.

"So I guess you're right," he added. "Which is beginning to be the story of my life. I do need to talk to Grandpa about all this, see if he can't be persuaded to smooth things over with your grandmother."

Hugging her coat more tightly around her, Sandy shook her head. "Something really screwy is going on around here."

"What?"

"Well, Annabelle Scanlon told me Gran locked herself in her room the day of the wedding and refused to come out."

"Mrs. Scanlon must've been a child then. She probably doesn't remember."

"No, she seemed pretty sure of herself."

"Well, maybe that is what happened. After Grandpa—"

"There's more."

"Oh?"

"Emma Finklebaum remembers the day, too."

"Who?"

"From the Tyler Quilting Circle. She was social columnist for the *Tyler Citizen* at the time." Sandy put her palm to her forehead, as if combating the pressure of a headache.

"And?"

"She said your grandfather... Well, apparently there was some talk about him and Margaret Ingalls."

"Judson's wife?"

She nodded. "And that's why he never showed up the day of the wedding."

Drew automatically wanted to deny the implication. But deep inside, he knew his grandfather had always viewed himself as a charmer, an enthusiastic—if harmless —ladies' man. "Seeing as it was fifty years ago, I guess anything's possible."

"The point is nobody's telling the same story. So where does that leave us?"

Drew studied her, a pastime that was rapidly becoming one of his favorites. With her brow furrowed in worry, she looked younger and more defenseless than ever. But at the moment that didn't trouble him. He wanted to brush his thumb over the crease in her forehead, erasing the sign of anxiety. He wanted to kiss the corners of her lips until they turned up in her usual smile.

Maybe Grandpa was right. Maybe the Stirling women did exert some kind of powerful hold that wasn't entirely normal. And maybe Drew himself was crazy.

Nevertheless, if he didn't see her smile before she got into her car and drove away, he wouldn't be able to sleep tonight. A desperation play, that was what he needed. "Maybe we should encourage them to elope."

She looked suddenly alert, her eyes wide. But she didn't smile. "What?"

"You know—elope. Do you think your grandmother could make it out the window and down a ladder before old Cecil Kellaway caught them?"

That did it. She laughed, a rich, infectious sound. Drew felt the tension in his chest melt away.

"Oh, yes, I think she could make it. But I think a much more likely scenario is her throwing your grandfather out the window."

"I don't know. If they're still this angry fifty years later, I'd say they never got over each other. Yep, I suspect they could be convinced to bury the hatchet."

"In your grandfather's back, maybe."

He laughed at her wry statement and decided he didn't care what kind of black magic was at work here, he was falling for Sandy Murphy. Heck, he might as well enjoy the process. He leaned an elbow on the roof of her car and inhaled her scent. She wasn't a perfume kind of woman. All he breathed in was her skin, her hair, her essence.

"That much anger hides a lot of emotion," he said.

"She hates him."

He shook his head. "She only thinks she hates him. Don't you ever watch the romantic movies, where they think they hate each other but everybody else knows it's only because they're so attracted and fighting it tooth and nail?"

"No."

"No? Oh, Sandy, you've obviously experienced a misspent youth."

"I like courtroom dramas."

"It's all the same. What do you think drives people to murder and mayhem?"

"Greed."

Again he shook his head. "Grand passion."

She looked away. "I wouldn't know."

He took a chance. After all, how many chances did a guy get in one lifetime? He touched her cheek with his knuckles, her soft, cool cheek. Need became an insistent ache. "Find out."

"I'm not a motivated buyer," she said, her voice suddenly lower and deeper. She didn't back away from his touch.

"I think you are." Her eyes met his again, and he saw reflected there the tug of war going on within her. He leaned closer, felt her breath mingle with his. "Maybe this is just an impulse purchase."

"You're crazy," she said.

"Yeah."

And she moved the inch closer he'd been waiting for. He touched his lips to hers, waited for the next signal that she was willing. Her lips moved, the beginning of a soft, slow mating. He took her head in his hand and pulled her close, deepening the kiss, finding her tongue, drinking in her heat. Her body pressed closer to his, although her curves were hard to find beneath her overcoat.

But he wasn't in any hurry. He figured this was madness, and madness wouldn't last long. He needed to savor each minute.

By the time she pulled away, her breath was coming in short, uneven gasps. "We're both crazy," she said, backing away.

"I can't argue with that."

He followed her home, a silly urge to make sure she made it safely. He figured she wouldn't like it, but at the moment, he was operating solely on gut instinct. Reason was not part of his mental software just now, not where Sandy Murphy was concerned.

Apparently his grandfather was right. The Murphy women were dangerous. And Drew jumped into the fire willingly.

CHAPTER ELEVEN

IN A TOWN THAT NEEDED a break from the depressing lack of progress on the mystery of the Ingalls F and M fire, the gossip about Mag Murphy and Clarence Stirling became a welcome diversion.

Annabelle Scanlon's childhood memories became more vivid and more poignant with each retelling. "I never will forget how that poor child trembled, hesitated about even *trying on* that wedding dress. As if she knew what was to come."

Marge Phelps hung out at the diner more than she had in months, dishing up her version of the story with each helping of her famous hamburgers or apple pie.

"Magdalena Halston was a spoiled, pampered girl," she recalled with perfect clarity for anyone willing to listen— and that included almost everyone in Tyler. "She chased him till he caught her, and when she had him she didn't want him anymore. Game over. That simple."

According to Marge, Mag had called the whole thing off on a whim, because she'd suddenly realized married women didn't enjoy the whirl of parties unmarried girls were invited to. No one asked how Marge knew any of this, since she would've barely been out of training pants at the time.

Phil Wocheck, who had definitely been around at the time, recalled it another way. "For the parents, this was a business arrangement. These two young people, they were so in love. Yet everywhere they turned, the talk was of business and money. Soon, who believes in love any longer?''

Phil said he knew for a certainty that the couple had made a pact to stay away from the showy wedding their parents had planned, an event supposedly to cement the contract between their families. Mag and Clarence had plotted to run away and marry quietly, he declared, but their furious parents put a stop to the elopement.

More than one well-informed senior citizen in Tyler confirmed the story that young, naive Clarence had been lured into the web of the flirtatious Margaret Ingalls, notorious for her parties and her young male playthings. But even there no one could agree on exactly how that story concluded. Some claimed Margaret Ingalls herself had marched into the church and disrupted the ceremony when the minister asked if anyone knew of a reason why Clarence and Mag should not be joined in holy matrimony. Some said Mag had heard the truth and threatened to blow both guilty parties to Kingdom Come with a shotgun from what was then Halston-Stirling Hardware. Yet another version said Clarence spent the morning of the wedding waiting in a rowboat on Timber Lake for Margaret Ingalls, who had promised to run away with him. She never showed, of course. But she had accomplished her purpose.

Sandy even checked the morgue at the *Tyler Citizen*, hoping the official version would shed some light on all the rumors. But the yellowed clippings disappointed her. Emma Finklebaum's reporting turned out to be a very circumspect recitation of the dry details. The wedding had been postponed. No one was blamed. No mention was made of infidelities or coercive parents or tears in the church.

Of course, there were also a dozen versions of what had happened to the Halston-Stirling business partnerships. Everyone was a villain in one version or another.

All Sandy knew was that she hoped something else would happen soon to divert all the busybodies' attention. She also hoped that no one would begin to wonder if history might be repeating itself. No one except for herself, that is.

Sandy's inner turmoil, plus the gossip raging through Tyler, wasn't helping her relationship with Drew one bit.

Tension had continued to build between them the morning after the kiss. Sandy had driven to work in an emotional uproar, unsure how to behave when she next laid eyes on Drew. She hadn't had to wonder for long. He was waiting in her office, lounging in a chair, long legs stretched out in front of him. She had to step over them to get to her desk. She hadn't been certain her knees were steady enough to manage the maneuver, since she was quivering all over, inside and out.

He didn't say a word and neither did she. Leaving her office door ajar, she made it safely to her own chair, which left her well protected, at least theoretically, by the barrier of her desk. He was smiling, one of those warm and winning smiles that made her want to trust him with her grandmother's pearls—and other things equally valuable.

Why hadn't someone warned her it could be so easy to fall for a Boy Scout?

She stopped herself. She hadn't *fallen* for him, exactly. Wanting someone, even madly and desperately, did not constitute *falling* for him. Falling for someone was serious. And that was *not* what was happening here.

"Good morning." The way he said it turned the words into an intimate caress.

"Stop it," she said, lowering her voice to make sure it didn't carry into the corridor.

His smile transformed into a grin, as if he were a Boy Scout with a prank to play.

"Ah, good," he said. "You are feeling guilty this morning. I was afraid you'd handle this with your usual cool aplomb. I was afraid I'd be the only one feeling like a high school freshman with a crush on the English teacher."

"This is not appropriate," Sandy replied, hearing the prissy indignation in her voice and hating it.

"Lighten up, Sandy. I only wanted to let you know that I have no intention of bringing this into the office."

She opened her mouth but discovered she had no idea how to respond. That was her real problem. She hadn't been able to resolve the conflict between what she wanted to happen and what she knew should happen. Did she begin a surreptitious relationship with a co-worker, knowing the folly of it, knowing how easily that could jeopardize her position here at Yes! Yogurt? Did she launch into this knowing full well nothing could come of it, given the bitterness of the family feud separating them? She'd hoped for a day's reprieve, even a few hours more to figure out what should happen next.

Naturally, here was Drew Stirling, in her face first thing, with everything all figured out.

"What exactly does that mean?" she asked, stalling.

He didn't move a muscle. He remained sprawled in the chair, relaxed and comfortable. Maybe office flings were nothing new for him. Like grandfather, like grandson.

"It means whatever happens between us out there has nothing to do with our work. The two don't have to cross over."

She stared at him, baffled. He was either naive or in serious denial. "How old are you?"

"Thirty."

"Thirty." Okay, she was beginning to regain some control here. This was just another negotiation, and she was catching a glimmer of her goal. She had to put a stop to this, and now. Yes, that was the best plan. The only plan. "You're thirty years old and you honestly believe we can have a personal relationship outside this building and still conduct ourselves impersonally inside? Don't you think it's time to give up the fairy tales, Drew?"

Her words didn't faze him. He grinned back at her. "Well, I'm a pro. How about you?"

Sandy told herself anger wouldn't solve a thing. "Are you thinking with your brain, or with some more...volatile part of your anatomy?"

He sat up then and his grin vanished. Good. She'd hit her target. "If I thought sex was all this is about I wouldn't have a bit of trouble turning my back on it. If you were nothing but the prospect of a hot tumble, this wouldn't be worth the bother. But there's something more than that going on here and you know it. So don't pretend this is something you're above, Sandy. It won't fly."

The safe footing upon which her moral indignation rested melted out from under Sandy. This was not a man who would let her get away with games or manipulation or even self-deception. Which made this whole thing just that much more complicated.

Sighing, she said as much. "Don't you see? That just makes it harder?"

His face relaxed. "I know that. But we don't have to have all the answers to all the problems today. All we have to do today is agree that whatever this is, it won't follow us through the doors of Yes! Yogurt."

"It's not that simple."

"It's not as complicated as you want to make it," he countered.

"What about our grandparents?"

"That's them. This is us. It doesn't have to be the same thing."

She stared at him, wanting to believe in the simple sincerity she saw in his pale gray eyes. How tempting the notion that she could show up here every day, be the consummate professional, then walk out the door and into his arms. The fantasy of a grand passion, intensified by the need for secrecy from both family and co-workers, beckoned, delicious as only a taboo could be.

Resisting the temptation, she shook her head. "I don't need this, Drew. Britt and Jake don't deserve it, either. I *am* a pro. How about you?"

Then, before she had the chance to weaken, she turned and walked away from him.

Her bold assertion didn't last long, however. She could maintain the facade when he was there in front of her, tempting but forbidden. But when she was alone with her thoughts, her turmoil continued. Eventually, her silence fed the problem, which became so big she found herself dialing Ginny Luckawicz's apartment in Atlanta.

Maybe, she thought, Gin could tell her what to do. Hadn't Gin always come through before?

Sandy wondered if she only imagined the strain in her former mentor's voice when the woman answered. But she was relieved when Gin's old enthusiasm returned at the sound of Sandy's voice.

"Gosh, it feels like a year instead of a month!" Gin said. "How's it going? Have you taken over the company yet?"

Sandy laughed, wondered if the other woman could tell that laughing was as hard for her as it sounded for Gin.

"It's slow going," she admitted. "But it's great being around Britt and Jake again."

"And the other fellow? The sales VP? How's he turning out?"

Grateful Gin couldn't see the expression on her face, Sandy said, "Fine. No problem. How are you?"

The silence continued a beat too long. "I guess you didn't call for the cleaned-up version, did you?"

Sandy's heart plummeted. "Not as long as we're friends, Gin."

"You're sure you can stand the heat? I wouldn't say my name is poison in this business, but I understand they're looking for my mug shot to include in the newest Webster's, under arsenic."

Sandy knew precisely the expression Gin's face would twist itself into with that wry statement. She listened as Gin described all that had happened since she'd been asked to hand in her resignation at International Baking. After twenty years in the industry, she knew plenty of colleagues and friends to turn to when she needed a job. But virtually all of them had listened to her, smiled politely and promised to get back to her as soon as something came up. These days, Gin said, most of them were out when she phoned. Few got around to returning her calls.

"I'm thinking of leaving Atlanta," she confessed. "I was thinking Austin might be a good place to start over. What do you think?"

Sandy didn't want to ask the question, but she couldn't stop herself. "But what about Ted? Can't he help? You couldn't leave Ted, could you? After all this?"

Gin's laughter sounded bitter. "Ted? He was the first one to stop returning my calls. Take it from me, Sandy, if you're looking for a way to wreck your life, an office affair is the shortest route."

Sandy hung up without mentioning Drew. She didn't have to. She had all the advice she needed without saying a word. This craziness could go no further. The only thing she didn't know was how to stop feeling the way she'd felt since she and Drew had kissed. Being near him yet keeping her emotional distance was becoming a virtual impossibility. They were thrown together constantly. They worked together to hire and train a team to complete her market research. They met with a designer who was implementing some of Sandy's ideas for an updated logo and signage, which would be needed ASAP for the new outlet facility. They sat down frequently with the contractor who was making the necessary structural changes in the store.

Sandy was spending more time with Drew Stirling than with anyone else. And each moment seemed to stretch into eternity, an agony of feeling either humiliated by her own weakness or exhilarated by his closeness. She wavered between wanting to forget what had happened between them and wanting it to happen all over again.

Except that wasn't entirely accurate. She didn't want it to happen again. What she wanted was to pick up where that night had left off. Instead of halting with that one heart-stopping kiss, she wanted more.

She wanted Drew for her lover.

But that wasn't an option, especially not after his crazy assertion that this thing between them wasn't about sex. The implication being that there might be some kind of emotional thing going on here.

Well, the sex business Sandy might have been able to handle. But anything more, forget it. Look what falling in love had done to Gin Luckawicz.

DREW SUPPOSED that Sandy had made her bold declaration about being a pro easily enough. He wondered if backing it up had been harder.

For himself, he knew being near her, having to make decisions and think on his feet with her only an arm's length away, was beginning to take its toll on his sanity.

When he was supposed to be looking at artist's renderings, he was considering instead the curve of her lips and, yes, damn his sorry, sex-obsessed male hide, the swell of her breasts beneath one of those sedate yet sensuous silk blouses she wore every damn day.

At least, thank heavens, she wore her skirts to her knees, ever demure, ever the professional. No thigh-skimming, skintight skirts for Ms. Alexandra Murphy. So he had no alluring display of slender thigh to tempt him.

In fact, if she had been that type he might've had no problem to begin with. He'd worked with plenty like that without turning a hair. A woman who flaunted it didn't push any of his buttons.

Buttons. Tiny, silk-covered buttons. He contemplated them as he and Sandy pored over the preliminary results of the market research she had initiated. Pondered how easily they would slip free of their buttonholes, revealing the tailored satin camisole he imagined lay beneath. Satin the color of chilled champagne, against her tawny flesh.

Sandy was not a peekaboo-lace kind of person, Drew had determined.

He kicked himself for that. For degenerating into adolescent activities like fantasizing about her in her lingerie. She would have his scalp if she knew. He was a man out of control. A man whose thoughts were no longer his own. A man driven by passion.

He liked the sound of that.

The worst part was having to bottle it up. He had no one he could talk to about this.

"Something troubling you?" Jake asked one afternoon as they made a walk-through of manufacturing. "You seem preoccupied by something."

Drew had to squelch his instinct to confess. His cousin had long been his best friend. And being secretive wasn't part of Drew's nature. But even though he felt he could confide in Jake, he knew that wouldn't be fair to Sandy. She deserved her privacy.

"No."

Jake grunted. "You wouldn't make much of a poker player."

"I know."

Drew tried pointing out a problem with the milking machines that might slow them down in their new plans to step up production. Jake made a note and they discussed a couple of possible solutions. Then they headed back to the car.

"So?" Jake said. "What is it?"

"I don't know." Drew sighed, searching for something plausible, something with a nugget of truth in it. "Maybe it's all the changes. Things are happening awfully fast."

Jake studied his face, and Drew hoped his expression passed muster.

"You sure that's it?"

"Sure I'm sure."

"Know what Britt said?"

Drew didn't bother to reply. He knew he'd hear it anyway.

"She thinks it's got something to do with Sandy."

Drew tried to imagine how he would want to look if he had just drawn a straight flush and didn't want anyone else to know. That was the expression he tried for. The poker face everyone said he didn't have.

"Well, maybe so," he said. "After all, she's the one behind all the change." •

"I don't think that's what Britt meant."

Drew tried to stare his cousin down, then decided he really didn't want Jake to say it aloud anyway. "Britt's a daydreamer."

"Britt knows people."

"Britt's a romantic."

Jake stared at him and a slow grin spread across his face. "Britt knows people," he repeated, then didn't say another word all the way back to headquarters.

Drew had much the same conversation with his grandfather a few days later.

"You might as well speak up, son," Clarence said. "Something is disturbing you. It's written all over your face."

"I know, I know," Drew said, by now peeved with his inability to develop an inscrutable visage, the lack of which was clearly his most serious shortcoming.

"It's that Murphy woman, isn't it?"

"Yes. No! Of course not."

Clarence chuckled. "Playing you good, is she?"

"It's not like that, Grandpa." Drew was growing tired of this refrain and suspected it sounded as weak to his grandfather as it did to him.

"She will operate this way, you know. Precisely as her grandmother did. I could predict this perfectly."

"You're way off base."

"First she runs hot, then she runs cold. A little kiss, perhaps, followed by a complete retreat. You're probably in the retreat stage. That's always problematic. Never mind, son. She'll move into the next stage soon." Clarence smoothed the scarf he had knotted at his throat and tucked it into his jacket. "That come-hither look is so effective. Steel yourself, my boy. Steel yourself!"

As Drew drove out to Jake and Britt's later, he told himself his grandfather might, after all, be skirting the edges of senility. He honestly seemed to believe that what had happened between him and Magdalena Murphy was destined to happen all over again between Drew and Sandy.

The two situations were entirely different, of course. Why was it Drew seemed to be the only one who could see that?

When he pulled up at the farmhouse, the only other car in sight was Sandy Murphy's sedan. Frowning, he went in through the kitchen door, as he always did. Ten-year-old Renee sat at the table, working a jigsaw puzzle with Sandy, who bounced Jacob on her knee.

"What are you doing here?"

They spoke as one. Probably the only time they'd ever reached consensus, Drew thought.

"Jake asked if I could stay with the kids," he said.

Sandy gave him a suspicious glance. "Britt asked me to stay."

Drew wondered if there was more to this mix-up than met the eye. In all the time he'd known Jake and Britt, they'd never asked him to baby-sit. He had never changed a diaper in his life, for one thing. Tonight, Jake had explained, both Christy and Matt had plans. Renee and twelve-year-old David were still too young to stay alone all evening, though they could help out taking care of the baby.

"Maybe I ought to go, then," Drew said, at which point Jacob scrambled down from Sandy's lap and hurled himself at Drew's knees.

"Dwew don't go! Dwew stay!"

Renee grinned at him. Sandy didn't.

"Maybe *I* should go," she said.

"No!" Renee protested. "You can't go! And leave me all alone in a house full of *guys?* Yuck!"

Drew watched Sandy squirm. Without her usual corporate attire, she almost looked in need of a baby-sitter herself tonight. She wore a pair of red wool leggings and a fleecy red-and-purple striped tunic. Her hair was still up, but had lost some of its severity in the process of her changing clothes or working out before coming over. Strands feathered around her face and the bun itself was slightly askew. Her cheeks were scrubbed and her boots had been kicked off under the table, revealing a pair of thick purple socks. Her gaze never left his face. He smiled as he leaned over to pick up Jacob.

"Sure, kiddo," Sandy said at last. "You and I will finish our puzzle and Drew can go do guy stuff with David."

Renee shook her head and tried to find the right spot for a corner piece of the puzzle. "He's doing his biology report. He said he'd put a dissected frog in my bed if I bothered him. I'd leave him alone if I were you."

Drew debated the pros and cons of dissected frogs versus the forbidding look in Sandy's brown eyes and said, "Come on, Jacob. Let's make sure David doesn't need a hand with his biology."

Renee, as it turned out, had given excellent advice. David had barricaded himself in his room. His only reply to Drew's knock was to turn up his music and to shove under the door a sheet of notebook paper carrying the felt-tipped message Top Secret, Keep Out! In fine print was the further disclaimer: This Applies to All Grown-ups and Especially Kid Sisters.

Uncertain how a sitter should handle such a situation, Drew identified himself in a voice loud enough to carry over the music. The sound level came down and the twelve-year-old's face appeared in the doorway.

"I'm studying, man. Be cool, okay?"

Drew cocked his head to one side to peer inside the room. "Yeah, but I'm the sitter. Gotta make sure there's nothing illegal going on. Know what I mean?"

David grinned. "Yeah. Like I might be having on-line sex with cartoon characters all over the world. Right?"

Drew couldn't help himself. He grinned in return. "Yeah, something like that. I'd never work as a baby-sitter in this town again."

"You've got my pledge, man. No on-line sex. Just poking around in frog guts, okay?"

"No sex. Fwog guts," Jacob repeated, as usual picking up on the most provocative part of the conversation to memorize and repeat at day care.

Drew wandered back downstairs. What now? His thoughts strayed to the kitchen. To Sandy. He had promised not to drag any personal stuff through the doors of Yes! Yogurt. He hadn't promised not to remind her of it elsewhere.

It was, however, the gentlemanly thing to do. She'd said she wasn't interested. He should leave it at that.

Even when I know she doesn't mean it?

And he did know. She had given herself away in the heat of her response when they'd kissed. He'd felt the hunger in her lips. He'd seen the longing in her eyes. And he'd noted the way she shied away ever since, as if afraid to trust herself around him.

Drew supposed he could be fooling himself on this, but he thought not. If the in-control Ms. Murphy wasn't interested, she would have no trouble whatsoever giving him the brush-off. But if he affected her enough to rob her of her cool...

He and Jacob played with the plastic train in the living room for a while. They watched a Winnie the Pooh video for fourteen minutes, until Jacob grew tired of sitting still. They discussed the merits of leaving the clean laundry where they'd found it, neatly folded in a basket at the foot of the steps; that was not Jacob's preference.

The only alternative Jacob would accept to strewing laundry around was helping Renee and Sandy with the jigsaw puzzle.

"Good thinking, my man," Drew said, picking up the toddler and swinging him overhead.

"We've done all the guy stuff we can think of," he said, dropping into the kitchen chair next to Sandy.

"Did David show you his frogs?" Renee asked.

"Fwog guts," Jacob replied.

Renee crinkled her face. "I knew it. That is so gross. I'm going to be a conscientious objector when I get to seventh-grade biology."

"Biology's not so bad," Drew said, studying Sandy's long, lithe fingers as she searched out a home for her puzzle piece. She wore her nails short and rounded, and they gleamed pale against her dark skin. He wanted to feel the touch of those fingers, wondered if she lost her famous control easily under certain circumstances. "You might like it by the time you get to the seventh grade."

Renee didn't seem to notice the tension Drew felt in the room. She chatted almost without stopping about her best friend's CD-ROM, which she coveted, and her growing prowess with a basketball and a dozen other things. Drew and Sandy alternated inserting a comment when the little girl paused to take a breath. Mostly, however, Drew's attention was on Sandy. And hers, he thought, was on studiously avoiding notice of him.

He'd read in novels about women with lilting voices, and he decided Sandy's qualified. Listening to her and being anything but happy would be no easy task. Combine that with her infectious smile and it would be easier to stop the earth in its orbit than it would be to feel grumpy around her.

He liked the way she handled herself with Renee, too. She didn't talk down to her, which was something he'd noticed and admired about Britt when he first got to know her. Sandy asked questions and listened to the answers and never once lapsed into anything that sounded like a lecture. And when it came time to put Jacob to bed for the night, she asked for Renee's help and let the little girl take the lead.

Drew sat at the kitchen table and waited for them to return. He liked the way this felt, being here in this rambling, lived-in farmhouse littered with kids' toys and pets and other remnants of family life. Wet galoshes by the back door and a broken cereal bowl on the counter and a stack of clothes hangers on the edge of the table. He liked the creak and thump of feet overhead, the flash of a little girl's giggle.

And he liked knowing that Sandy would walk back down the stairs and warm the room again.

"You're getting in deep, Stirling," he muttered, jumping up and checking the coffeepot. It was cold. That was okay. He should go now. No reason to stay, with Jacob tucked in bed.

He wondered what real parents did when the kids went to sleep. Did they curl up on the couch and watch an old black-and-white movie? Did they smooch? Did they go to bed early themselves sometimes?

He went back to the table, picked up a puzzle piece and absently toyed with it. He heard footsteps on the stairs. He forced himself not to look up, to pretend he wasn't standing there holding his breath until she returned.

She stood on the opposite side of the table and spoke softly. "Renee decided to read for a while."

He looked up. "I didn't know kids still did that."

Her smile looked uncertain, as did her eyes.

He should give her a reprieve. "I might as well go." He hoped she would discourage him.

"That's probably a good idea."

Damn! "You could at least *pretend* you hate to see me go." He dropped the puzzle piece.

She quit attempting to smile. "Don't start."

She looked down and picked up another puzzle piece, turning it over and over. Drew headed for the door, but changed his mind. He walked back to where she stood, put his hand on hers and guided the puzzle piece into place. He felt the tremble of her fingers but didn't let go. He stood there until she turned toward him.

"It's too late *not* to start," he whispered.

Her eyes pleaded with him for the one thing he was not willing to do.

"Don't ask me to play games," he said. "I've been trying. It's not working."

"This won't work, either," she said, quiet desperation in her voice.

"Ha! Just watch."

He lowered his lips to hers. She didn't back away, didn't flinch. Her lips softened against his, warm and pliant and damp. He slid his arms around her and pressed her to him, as he had wanted to before, savoring the way her gentle curves melted into him. Her arms crept up; those long fingers buried themselves in his hair. The movement lifted her breasts, and he knew he was dangerously close to taking this one step further. Here and now, however, was not the right time.

"This must be it," he murmured against her lips.

Her response was a gentle moan. "What?"

"The black magic my grandfather warned me about."

Her chuckle was breathless as she pulled away. "So you got the warning, too?" Her hands trailed down his chest as she backed up, then broke the connection.

"I think we should show them they're wrong."

"Didn't you hear what happened to Romeo and Juliet?"

"Ah, but their problem was they tried to sneak around," he said, feeling regret as she moved to place the table between them again. "If they'd been up-front about things, old Will Shakespeare would've had an entirely different story to tell."

But Drew saw from the look in her eyes that he was wasting his breath.

"Maybe I'd better go," he said.

She nodded.

The January wind had never felt so cold.

RENEE HUDDLED halfway down the stairs, ear strained toward the kitchen. The things they said didn't make much sense, but she knew exactly what to make of the long silence. She hugged her knees and grinned.

Sandy and Drew were kissing. Falling in love. Right here in her very own kitchen.

It was working. First, she'd suggested that her mom ask Sandy to baby-sit tonight. Then she'd suggested that her stepdad ask Drew. By the time everybody realized the mix-up, which was smack in the middle of the chaos of people leaving the house tonight, well, everybody had been grateful when Renee offered to call Drew and Sandy and straighten everything out. Since Matt was the one assigned to stay home until the baby-sitter arrived and he had been oblivious to the earlier confusion, pulling it off had turned out to be easier than Renee had ever imagined.

Content that she was the first to know about this fairy-tale ending brewing right here under everyone's nose, Renee started to creep back up the stairs. Then she heard them talking again, heard the change in their voices. They weren't fighting, exactly. But they weren't going to kiss anymore.

She heard the back door closing and dashed up the stairs.

From her window, she watched Drew walk toward his car, head down. He looked back toward the house before he got in the car, and Renee held her breath. Maybe Sandy would change her mind, would run after him and fling herself into his arms.

Drew gave up on that hope before Renee did.

CHAPTER TWELVE

ANOTHER MONDAY-MORNING staff meeting, another confrontation. That was the way Sandy was beginning to view the start of each week.

This morning she could still taste Drew's lips on hers, still feel the heat of his lean body pressed against hers, when he tossed the fact sheet on Food World, an international food show in Chicago, onto the conference table.

"Will you be ready?" he asked without preamble.

She picked up the flyer, avoiding his eyes. He was doing his best to look impersonal and unemotional. His best wasn't good enough. What he looked was miserable. Sandy felt a corresponding tug on her own heart. What sense did it make for both of them to feel this way, when the apparent solution seemed so simple?

Pushing aside her reactions to him, Sandy studied the information about the food show, the largest and most prestigious trade show in the industry. This convention could make or break new products, and regularly did both. It was the place where restaurants and grocery stores decided what foods to serve or sell to the American public during the next year.

It was just weeks away.

Sandy needed Food World. If her efforts to revamp Yes! Yogurt's marketing strategies were to show quick results, she needed to launch them at this show. Otherwise, any major impact her work might have was easily a year away.

But three weeks to prepare was an impossible deadline, especially with the grand opening of the outlet store just two weeks away.

She swallowed hard and looked around the table at Britt's expectant smile, Jake's encouraging nod. Drew's challenging frown.

"I'll be ready."

Britt settled back in her chair, relaxed. Jake looked surprised but pleased. Drew leaned forward and forced Sandy to look him squarely in the eye.

"You'll be ready? With the new logo? New packaging? Signage? An entire campaign? Everything?"

Heart racing uncomfortably, Sandy felt herself drawn into his intense gaze. His kisses were like that, an irresistible force, sweeping her into a maelstrom of emotion. Her own gaze flickered to his lips. She stopped the direction of her thoughts. The show. That's where her focus had to be, day and night, for the next few weeks.

"I said I'd be ready. You can count on it."

She could panic later.

MAG SWIRLED to give Emma Finklebaum the full effect of her cherry red circle skirt.

"My ankles are still trim for an old dame, don't you think?" she asked, catching a glimpse of herself in the mirror.

"You certainly are going all out today," Emma commented.

Mag noticed that her old friend hadn't bothered to give her the compliment she'd been fishing for, but she decided to let it pass. Today was too important for trifles. Besides, she *knew* her legs were dynamite. It would be natural for Emma to resent that. Emma had always been plain, even when she was young. Why, from her first day as the social columnist, she had worn those wire-rimmed glasses on that horsey face of hers, not to mention that flat, mousy-colored page-boy and those suits with the football-pad shoulders, the ones she thought gave her a Joan Crawford look. In her dreams.

"Well, it's not every day my youngest granddaughter has a grand opening," Mag said, feeling charitable today toward this woman who'd probably never heard a wolf whistle in her life. "She's worked like a fiend these past few weeks, getting this outlet store ready."

"Working with Drew Stirling, I hear."

Leaning toward the mirror, Mag checked her makeup. At her age, she had to make sure her mascara didn't smudge against her upper eyelids. She should've had that surgery when Annabelle Scanlon suggested it. If she had, she could pass for fifty-five. Wouldn't that scoundrel Clarence Stirling chew nails over that?

Blast it! There I go again, thinking about that man! But not today, she told herself.

"Don't be silly," she said to Emma. "This is entirely Sandy's baby. And she's getting ready for a big world-wide show in Chicago in—" she paused to calculate "—about a week, I believe. The dear girl has worn herself to a frazzle."

"Well, you'll wow 'em, Mag. No doubt about it."

Mag smiled at her friend. "Thanks, Emma. Now, come on, let's shake a leg. I told Sandy I'd be waiting at the door."

Mag's heels clicked as they started down the hall. It had been weeks since she'd worn high heels. Her friends told her it was foolish at her age—broken hips and all that. Mag told them all she'd rather break her neck in a pair of come-kiss-me pumps than live to be a hundred wearing rubber-soled lace-ups and support hose.

Her stockings today were red, too. Her earrings were bright red plastic ribbons and her blouse was black with red ice-cream cones. Emma had called her crazy for buying the silly thing out of a catalog three months ago, but Mag had known as soon as she saw it that sometime or another it would be the perfect thing to wear. And she had been right, of course. She even had a red chiffon sash wrapped around her head, with curls spilling out the top. She looked like a movie star today and she knew it. A glamorous movie star, from the old days, back when stars really knew how to make an entrance.

Sandy made a fuss, of course, telling her as they drove over to the new store how good she looked.

"I dressed in those darn business suits all my life," Mag said, eyeing the charcoal-gray item her granddaughter was wearing. "Got tired of being stodgy. A girl owes herself a little fun. You know, I could whip off this scarf and we could slip it into that waist pocket on your jacket and just let it trail. Now, that would make a statement, don't you think, Emma?"

Sandy grinned, but to Mag she still looked distracted. Pressure, of course. "Thanks, Gran. But I think I'll stick with the stodgy image today."

"Fine. But if you change your mind, look for me in the crowd. I'll be easy to spot."

They all three got a chuckle out of that.

Location was everything, Mag knew, and the location for the new Yes! Yogurt outlet was perfect. Next door to the video store, the old red brick building had been dressed up with a yellow-and-white awning and a cheery yellow-and-white sign featuring an abstract-looking goat munching on a rose.

Mag grabbed her granddaughter's hand and squeezed. "That's it, isn't it? The new logo? It's stunning! So nineties! You'll knock 'em dead in Chicago, Alexandra."

"Thanks, Gran. I hope you're right."

"Forty-five years in retail—of course I'm right."

The little shop was already full of people milling around, eating free samples of frozen yogurt and cheesecake and sipping coffee. Half of Tyler had gathered, it seemed to Mag. She floated about the room on a cloud of excitement, cooing over new babies—"Gracious, but breeding does seem to be in vogue again, doesn't it?" she said to Alyssa Wocheck, who had a passel of grandbabies with her—and catching up on the latest with Annabelle Scanlon.

"You know they say Pam Kelsey is pregnant, don't you?" Annabelle asked from the corner of her mouth. "What do you think of that?"

Mag pretended to be hurt. "You mean they've already stopped talking about Clarence and me?"

"Well, the talk has died down." Annabelle inclined her head toward the front window, where a row of metal ice-cream-parlor chairs was obscured by the crush of people. "You could spark things up again, if you've a mind to."

Mag's gaze followed the direction of Annabelle's gesture. At first all she could see was parkas and overcoats and a knit cap here and there. Then, as Marie Innes walked off and the Reverend Sarah bent over, she saw what Annabelle had seen: Clarence Stirling.

He sat at one of those little tables like an aristocratic lord. He wore a camel-hair topcoat and a wide-brimmed brown fedora, with one gloved hand resting on the carved head of a walking stick. He was smiling at Emma Finklebaum's sister, Tessie, with all the charm of a prince.

The sight of him evaporated Mag's happy cloud. She landed on the ground with a thud.

"Still a handsome devil, isn't he?" Annabelle whispered. "Look at the way Tessie is preening over him. What are you going to do, Mag?"

"Why, nothing."

Apparently disappointed, Annabelle wandered off a few minutes later. Suddenly, Mag could find no one to talk to. Whichever direction she turned, it seemed, she ended up facing the window, catching a glimpse of jovial Clarence Stirling. Everyone else she saw, she thought of good reasons to avoid. Whatever would she say to them, when all she seemed to have on her mind was Clarence Stirling? What was he saying to all these people he had turned his back on fifty years ago? What could they possibly be laughing about? What was an old man like that thinking, flirting so blatantly with women who hadn't even been born when he ran off? Mag began to consider leaving.

She had spotted Sandy and was headed in her direction to make excuses when she overheard Cece Baron talking to her husband, Jeff.

"I don't know, but he certainly doesn't *look* worried about running into Mrs. Murphy, does he?"

That did it. If Mag left now, everyone would think she was running away. That she couldn't handle being in the same room with Clarence Stirling.

And they'd be right, wouldn't they?

Fluffing her hair, Mag squared her shoulders, raised her chin and did what she should have done at the start. She swirled through the crowd, marched right to the front of the store and placed herself in front of Clarence. Then, with her flirtiest smile, she said, "Hi, there, sailor. I thought maybe you'd buy me a frozen yogurt."

"IT'S A HIT," Drew said, squeezing behind the counter again to pick up another tray of cheesecake samples.

Sandy cursed her luck in choosing this moment to step out of the crowd herself. Why was it that no matter how careful she tried to be, she always ended up in Drew's path? Granted, they worked together. But it was more than that. It was almost as if some force greater than her own best common sense kept placing them together.

Thank goodness she'd had no less than a million things to do these past few weeks. Working eighteen-hour days, she'd had no time to think. No time to feel, even.

But the truth remained that no matter where they ended up—in the kitchen at Britt's with a houseful of kids or in a bustling store with half the town as witnesses—Sandy felt an instant and electric intimacy.

"It's a hit *today*," she said as briskly as she could manage. "We're giving it away today. Let's see what happens a week from now."

"A week from now we'll be in Chicago," he said. "Still think you can be ready?"

"Of course I'll... What do you mean, *we'll* be in Chicago?"

"We. As in I the vice president of sales and you the director of marketing."

She stared at him, stunned. "I thought Britt was going with me."

"She was. Then Renee reminded her of some big pageant at the school and did the sad-faced-kid routine. You know Britt. No way is she going to miss one of her kids being in the spotlight. So you're stuck with me."

He didn't look the least bit disturbed about it, either. He looked rested and happy and as if it would take a lot more than her mere presence to distract him. She, on the other hand, felt worn-out and ragged and ready to lose what little control she had if he so much as breathed in her direction. She could not handle—would not put up with—a trip to Chicago with him at her side.

She groped for an alternative plan, but kept coming up empty.

She could quit her job.

There had to be a better way.

She could ask Britt to ask Jake to go in Drew's place.

And have to explain her request?

She could give in. She could do what every fiber of her being kept suggesting in those rare moments when she wasn't thinking about market research and logo slicks. Those moments at night when she closed her eyes and could see only Drew's smile. Those moments when she did her sit-ups and could feel only Drew's touch. Yes, she could give in to the temptation. And that was exactly what she feared.

A pesky part of her mind—sometimes she worried that it wasn't her mind at all, but her heart—kept asking her what would be so tragic about doing that very thing. Sometimes that little voice argued so persuasively that Sandy became convinced her professionalism wouldn't suffer permanent damage if she sank to the depths of admitting she was not just a marketing director, but a woman as well.

But every time Sandy almost bought her traitorous mind's arguments, she received a reminder that there was more to the problem than just her professional conflicts. Like right now, when she looked across the room and saw her grandmother sitting at a table with Drew's grandfather.

Oh, Lord. Was Yes! Yogurt's grand opening about to disintegrate into an angry free-for-all right in front of her eyes?

CLARENCE KNEW how to behave like a gentleman. He also knew that sometimes it was easier than others. That was the mark of a true gentleman, he had always believed—the ability to act like one even under difficult circumstances.

Mag Halston Murphy definitely constituted a difficult circumstance.

So he did what his breeding dictated. He snapped his fingers at one of the young people walking around with trays of frozen yogurt and procured one for his erstwhile fiancée.

"You're looking well this morning," he said.

She sat across from him and took a small bite of the yogurt. "Last time you said I was as beautiful as ever. I've moved all the way down to 'looking well'?"

She *would* go out of her way to make this being-a-gentleman business even harder. As a matter of fact, she did look beautiful. She still looked soft and round, as did those curls of hers, the kind of fluffy curls a man longed to crush in his fist. Even a seventy-something man with a touch of arthritis in that fist, as it turned out.

"Ah, Mag, you're a stunning woman. But I don't want to be responsible for contributing to your vanity."

"I promise not to hold you responsible."

He caught the teasing gleam in her eye and chuckled. "Still have that sharp tongue, I see."

"Never change a winning game. That's what my father always taught me."

The mention of the man whom he blamed for ruining his own father stirred unpleasant emotions, so Clarence decided to change the subject. "Looks as if our grandchildren make a good team."

"Alexandra has my business acumen."

"I don't doubt it."

In response, Mag smiled that featherheaded smile of hers that had gotten him into so much trouble all those years ago. Because Mag was no featherhead at all. Far from it. He thought, for the first time in many years, about the other side of Mag, the side he had allowed himself to forget so he could concentrate on her childishness, her betrayal. Mag had also been the kind of young woman who set her sights on a goal and knew exactly how to hit her target. She had a sharp mind and she hadn't been shy about using it, even in the days when women weren't encouraged to think for themselves.

As a dreamer accustomed to getting by principally on his charm, Clarence had thought in those days that the two of them made the perfect match. What he lacked, she had. What she lacked, he had. Between them, they could knock the world to its knees.

Well, one of them had been knocked to his knees, that was a certainty.

"What did you do with yourself all these years, Mag?"

She looked surprised at the question. "Oh, about what you'd expect. Raised a family, ran the store—the things people did in our day."

"The old hardware's still going strong."

She nodded. "My boy Franklin has a good head."

He kept asking questions and soon had a picture of the life they might have shared. The children and the grandchildren and the peaceful life in Tyler. He found, as he listened, that he didn't feel the bitterness he had expected to. Her life had been good, but so had his. He had struggled more, perhaps. But he had needed to, to get his head out of the clouds.

"Are you changed much, Mag?"

"Changed?" She cocked her head to one side and appeared to mull over his question. "Well, I guess we all change some. I like to think I'm not as self-centered now."

He smiled, thinking how right it felt to sit here and talk to her as easily as they once had. "Nineteen's a time for being self-centered, isn't it?"

"What about you, Clarence? Tell me about you."

He didn't really want to tell her, because it wasn't all pretty, especially the years right after he'd left Tyler. But he looked into her bright eyes and saw the same rapt interest that had lured him to her all those years ago, and he was lost. He wanted her to know about his life, just as he had once wanted her to know about the darkness he'd felt coming back from the war a broken man. That was why he had fallen for her—she made it easy for him to talk. And what he said she seemed to understand. And she loved him, anyway.

Or so he'd thought. Ah, but disillusionment wounded so deeply at that age.

But the disillusionment was not nearly so real at this moment as the look in her eyes, so he began to talk. He told her about the struggles to get on his feet in Chicago, made easier because he was a veteran at a time when patriotism ran high and made harder because of his own bitterness and reluctance to fail. He told her about the good, if uninspiring, woman he had shared his life with. She had been nothing like Mag and, at the time, that had seemed like the best qualification for a wife. He told her about the children and the grandchildren, glossing over the tragedies, such as losing his only son, Drew's father, in a car accident.

And he didn't mention that sometimes he'd longed for something more in the good woman he'd wed. A fire, a flare that he'd missed.

When he finished, he realized her eyes had never left him.

"So we both survived," she said.

"And better for it, I'm sure." But he didn't believe that. Not now, looking into her eyes and remembering . . .

"I suppose," she said. A trifle wistfully? "Although it took a while before I could see that."

He didn't want to ask. He'd hoped she would tell him of her own free will. But it appeared she wouldn't, and the wondering had plagued him for so many years that finally his resolve broke down.

"Why'd you do it, Mag?"

"Do what?"

"Stand me up like that? If you didn't want to go through with it, you could've come to me and told me."

"What are you talking about?"

"You can't imagine the agony of it, standing there waiting with half the town looking on."

She pointed her plastic spoon at him. Her eyes were no longer soft with memories, they were shooting sparks. He remembered that, too.

"You've lost your mind, do you know that, Clarence Albert Stirling? The one left standing was me. And I think it's high time you made your apologies."

"Apologies? Me?"

She crossed her arms. "I'm waiting. You'd best jump in here while I'm in a forgiving mood."

Clarence asked himself what a gentleman would do in this situation. The answer was clear. But he couldn't bring himself to do it. Instead, he braced himself on his walking stick and the wrought-iron table and pushed himself to his feet. "You'll excuse me, Mrs. Murphy. But *my* forgiving mood just vanished."

CHAPTER THIRTEEN

DREW PLOWED through the opening-night crowds at Food World, impatient to find the Yes! Yogurt exhibit. He would have hated admitting it, but it wasn't so much his company's booth he was impatient to see. It was the woman at the booth.

Two aisles over, above the heads, he saw a bright yellow helium balloon in the approximate shape of a goat. His heart leaped. He smiled for the first time in days as he quickened his pace.

He stopped a few yards away just to take her in. She wore a body-skimming dress instead of her usual suit. The sophisticated winter white made a stunning contrast to her dark skin and hair. She had also softened her hairstyle tonight, although she still wore it up, captured on one side with a curve of silver. Often at shows such as this, a good many of the women staffing booths were stunning young models hired to attract attention, an obligation they fulfilled at least in part by wearing clinging, skimpy outfits. Beside them, Sandy looked like a class act in high heels.

What she wore best, he thought, was her smile. Gracious and real and absolutely captivating, her smile was given out freely with every sample of frozen yogurt, cheesecake and cheese Danish that left the booth.

Drew thought he would personally buy anything she offered, if he were on the receiving end of that smile.

"Some exhibit, isn't it?"

Drew turned toward an unfamiliar voice, which belonged to an equally unfamiliar middle-aged man in expensive charcoal pinstripes and a solid gold collar pin.

"You were looking at the yogurt booth, weren't you?"

Drew nodded, still trying to figure out if he was supposed to know him. "Yes."

"So was I. Impressive for a small company." The businessman shook his head. "I tried to get Alexandra when she was still with International Baking, but she'd already signed on with these guys somewhere out in Wisconsin. I hated losing her, but she wouldn't discuss it."

As unobtrusively as possible, Drew checked out the man's name tag. R. D. Wernikoff. Recognition dawned instantly. This man was CEO of one of the largest food manufacturing conglomerates in the country. And he knew Sandy? Not only knew her, but wanted to hire her?

"Why?" Drew asked, without stopping to think how impertinent the question was. "Why her?"

Wernikoff chuckled. "You have to ask? Look at that exhibit. That logo, that slogan, will appeal to every twenty-something consumer in this country. Plus it has the sophistication to speak to the thirty-five-to-fifty market. Alexandra knows how to take the pulse of her generation—after all, she *is* the target consumer. But she can do it without losing track of what the Boomers like because she has an innate maturity, as well. We're all going to have to do that, if we expect to capture the younger crowd without sacrificing the established market. The key is people like Alexandra."

Drew looked back at Sandy with new eyes. And he saw the exhibit she had created—*really* saw it—for the first time. He remembered the hours she had spent with the graphic artist and the designer from the exhibit company, articulating exactly what she wanted to accomplish with every detail. The colors, the type style, every nuance had a purpose. He'd heard more than one of their vendors leave Yes! Yogurt grousing about her being such a stickler for details. But as Drew studied the exhibit now, and compared it with the others around it, he could see that Sandy had accomplished exactly what she wanted. The Yes! Yogurt exhibit stood out from the rest. It said the company was both fresh and stable. It said the products not only tasted good, they were good for you, too. If Drew had been a first-time customer, he would have both trusted this company and been enthusiastic about what it offered.

And all of that was Sandy's doing.

He ambled toward her, more enthralled than ever by this young woman with her radiant smile and brilliant mind. She spotted him. Her smile wavered for only a second, then she refocused on the people milling about the booth. He was close enough now to hear how enthusiastically she introduced everyone to Yes! Yogurt. He stepped into the open, U-shaped exhibit with her, found another tray and began helping. When he could snatch a moment between chatting with visitors, he leaned toward her and whispered, "You're a genius."

She looked startled at first. Then her smile deepened and she said, "I wondered how long it was going to take you to figure that out."

He laughed. They worked side by side for the rest of the evening. Drew thought he'd never before enjoyed being part of a team as much as he did this night.

"TIRED?" SANDY ASKED, although personally it was all she could do to keep from skipping down the broad downtown sidewalk. They'd taken the shuttle from Chicago's convention center to the small hotel where they were staying, but she knew as soon as it dropped them off that she wasn't yet ready for the silence of her room.

"No," Drew said, sounding surprised. "I thought I would be, but actually..."

"You're wired."

He looked at her and grinned. "Yeah. That's it."

"Then let's walk."

"Walk? Aren't your feet killing you?"

She laughed and gestured toward the walking shoes she'd slipped out of her tote bag and onto her feet as soon as the show ended. Drew grinned.

So they walked.

"I always feel this way after opening night of a show," Sandy said. "It takes me hours to come down. I love meeting all those people, trying to get them excited about my product."

"And you're good at it."

"A genius, actually. I have that on very good authority."

She paused as they crossed a bridge over the Chicago River and stared at the lights reflected in the water, at the mirror-image of towering buildings shimmering in the dark depths. The sounds of traffic behind her—a random horn, the chug of a decrepit cab engine, the screech of brakes— gave her a sense of having come home.

She sighed contentedly despite the frigid bite of Chicago's famous wind, and smiled. "Don't you miss the city?"

"No."

"But you grew up here. How could you not miss it?"

He shrugged. "Maybe because I know what else is out there, besides all the sparkle."

"Well, I miss the bright lights," she declared. "Everything's so alive in a city, especially Chicago."

Especially tonight. And it was more than the success of their exhibit; she couldn't deny that, if she was honest with herself. It was because of Drew. His presence at her side tonight had magnified everything.

"Then what are you doing back in Tyler?"

"It's a good job."

She had better reasons, but hesitated to spoil the mood. Tonight felt too perfect, too magical. She wanted to keep it that way, despite the faint warning bell in her head that told her this was crazy, walking at his side like this, talking to him in a way that left her open for examination. *You're nuts, Alexandra.*

"Better than the job R. D. Wernikoff offered you?"

See? Definitely nuts, to think she could both open up to him and keep him from getting too close. "How did you know about that?"

"Okay, let me get this straight," he said, ignoring her question. "You're ambitious and talented. You'd rather be in the city than back in Tyler. You had a major-league job offer, which no doubt came with major-league money attached, versus a small-potatoes job with money to match. You took the small job in the small town you're glad to be out of. I'm sure there's logic somewhere in there, but I'll be darned if I can find it."

Nothing could rattle her tonight, she decided. Not even Drew Stirling's probing. "What are *you* doing in Tyler?"

"Are you being evasive?"

She grinned. "Do you plan on giving up the inquisition anytime soon?"

"Are you ever going to run out of questions to answer my questions?"

"No." She laughed at the bemused expression on his face and he joined her. Why was she fighting it? If there was karma at work here, as she sometimes found herself thinking, maybe it wasn't *bad* karma. Maybe it was just unfinished business. Maybe this was the way it was supposed to work out, after all these years.

And maybe you've used up every single one of your brain cells these past few weeks. That seemed a more plausible explanation for the ease with which she was caving in to Drew's pressure. Finally, she said, "I'm there because of my grandmother."

"Okay. This sounds promising."

"We've always been close. Very close." He was studying her so intently that she couldn't look into his eyes and keep her train of thought. His intensity was too disconcerting, as if he could see through her and into her. "When Gran moved into Worthington House a few months ago, I guess I got worried that maybe she wouldn't be around long."

"Some people might have thought she had plenty of family in town to take care of her."

The way he said it made Sandy think it wasn't what he himself thought. After all, there were probably others who could have taken on responsibility for his grandfather, too. But reading so much into what Drew said was probably nothing more than fanciful thinking on her part.

"I know," she admitted. "But I didn't want to wake up one morning and find out I'd lost precious time with Gran all for the sake of some big-bucks career move. That made no sense to me."

"Wow," he said, so softly she almost missed it in the rumble of a truck on the bridge behind them. "That's good. I like that."

His approval shouldn't have created such a warm spot in her heart. But it did.

"We'd better get back," she said, moving toward the hotel again.

"Why?"

"Because it's late. And we have an early morning and a long day ahead of us."

He fell into step again beside her. His arm brushed hers as they walked. Sandy felt the instantaneous charge she had come to expect every time they touched. She had hoped that reaction would disappear during these past weeks, as she'd overworked herself to the point of exhaustion. A crazy emotion she could only identify as elation burst forth in her chest when she realized it hadn't. She tried to squelch the feeling, and once again questioned her decision to fight this thing that happened between them so effortlessly, so naturally.

"So, I guess you'll fall asleep as soon as your head hits the pillow?" he said.

He knew the answer to that as well as she did, so she gave him a look instead of a response.

"Then what's the hurry? We should go dancing." He did an impromptu cha-cha, minus a partner, as they crossed the street. "Or we could sit up and read to each other from the serial-murder thriller I have in my suitcase. Purchased on your advice, I might add. Or how about this? We could eat overpriced cashews from the minibar in your room and lick the salt from each other's fingers."

Sandy laughed. "I think the smart thing would be to soak my feet and call it a night."

"Do you always do the smart thing?"

The answer, of course, was yes, usually. But she couldn't bring herself to tell him that.

He walked her all the way to her room, which she knew was a mistake; but he was adamant about his misplaced gentlemanly impulses. He stood in the doorway looking forlorn, the twinkle in his eyes telling her he hoped she would take pity. She closed the door, whispering, "Good night, Drew. You'll thank me for this in the morning. Six a.m. comes awfully early."

She leaned against the door, eyes closed, listening to her heart pounding and wishing her exuberant spirits hadn't just ebbed away, leaving her feeling empty and alone.

She hung her dress neatly in the closet beside the others she had brought, pulled on her flannel pajamas and the ratty robe that didn't match. She washed her face and brushed out her hair and began trying to convince herself that a few dozen sit-ups would get her ready for sleep.

She'd done ten when she heard the soft knock on her door. She dropped back to the carpet and let her arms flop at her sides. She knew who it was, of course.

The next knock was a little louder than the first.

This was insane. She couldn't even consider opening her door to him. This was a hotel room, for heaven's sake. She was in her pajamas. Her *flannel* pajamas. Nope, opening the door wasn't even a remote possibility.

The third knock was loud enough that Sandy figured people up and down the hall must be checking their doors now. How long before someone called Security? She dragged herself up off the floor, went to the door and peeked through the peephole. Yep, there he stood.

"Go away!" she said, pressing her forehead to the door.

"Can't do that," he said.

"You certainly can!"

"No. No, I can't. I have something of a crisis here, Sandy. You're the only one around I can turn to."

She knew better. She heard it in his voice: this was one of his sneaky little ploys. But she opened the door and peered out over the chain, which was still in place. "What kind of crisis?"

He turned his head, glancing up and down the hall. The dim overhead light gleamed off his unruly curls. When he looked back, his sheepish smile was as irresistible as a little boy's. "Not out here, okay?"

The only crisis going on, Sandy thought, was the one inside her own head.

Even as she lifted the chain and opened the door, she knew she wasn't letting him in because she believed for one minute that he had some kind of problem. She was letting him in because she wanted to. Because his grin reached inside her and tweaked at those little-girl places she didn't visit often.

And because his eyes suggested that she acknowledge those womanly places she also tended to stay away from.

Yes, a crisis was brewing, but it had nothing to do with whatever excuse Drew had concocted.

He closed the door and sagged against it. "Thank goodness."

"What is it, Drew?"

"If I hadn't known you were here, I'm not sure what I would've done."

"I'm waiting."

"My minibar. It was out of cashews. But I knew you'd have some. You do, don't you?"

She wanted to laugh at the melodrama with which he delivered his lines. But she discovered she didn't have enough breath in her to laugh. Her chest felt constricted, tight. Maybe because her heart was still pounding too fast. Way too fast for the few sit-ups she had done.

She tried to look and sound severe. "If I give you cashews, will you leave?"

Obviously, she had not pulled it off. He gazed into her eyes and shook his head.

"Drew . . ."

He took a step in her direction, and she found herself paralyzed, unable to retreat.

"You're ravishing in flannel. You know that, don't you?"

"Nobody likes a wise guy, Drew."

He grinned. "I wouldn't say that again if I were you. I think your nose just grew a quarter of an inch. What's the truth, do you think? That you find it endearing when I'm a wise guy?"

"I really want you to leave."

He crinkled his face and groaned. "Oh, no! There it goes again. Now, personally, I don't mind a prominent nose on a woman. But you probably don't want this getting out of hand."

Shaking her head, she walked over to the minibar, retrieved a small can and thrust it at him. "Here are the cashews. There's the door."

He took the can without touching her fingers, studied it, then studied her again. "If you really mean it, I'm gone."

For the second time that evening, Sandy felt something begin to ebb out of her, something she felt only when Drew Stirling was nearby. She had felt it as soon as he stepped behind the booth with her at the convention center, an elation that was absent when he was not around. Oh, she knew she was capable and complete all on her own. She'd learned the value of self-reliance from Gran a long time ago. But somehow, when Drew was near, the whole world suddenly became more vivid. Music had more melody and sunshine more warmth and her own heart more lilt. It was almost the way she'd felt when she went away to college and fell in love for the first time with some shallow but pretty college boy, as if the world were suddenly new and fresh.

Almost that way, but not quite. No, this was different. This felt quieter, more serene, more real.

This felt like a grown-up, make-a-commitment kind of thing. Why did that frighten her so? She was an adult. If she didn't want this to get out of hand, she was perfectly capable of keeping it under control. Wasn't she?

"So what'll it be?" Drew asked quietly. "Am I out of here?"

She smiled and said, "And let all this flannel go to waste?"

CHAPTER FOURTEEN

SANDY HEARD all the voices of reason that clamored for her attention as Drew took her into his arms. Gin's voice. Gran's voice. Sandy didn't want to listen to them.

"What about all those stories about office love affairs?" she murmured as she hurriedly plucked at the buttons on his shirt. "What about—"

"That was them," Drew said, his arms becoming entangled with hers as he tried to pull off her pajama top at the same time she worked to rid him of his dress shirt. "This is us."

He had to be right, she thought, drowning in the warmth of his lips, shivering at the touch of his hand on her breast.

They fell onto the bed, casting off pajama bottoms and trousers, satin panties and boxer shorts. He still wore socks, and one leg of her pajamas still coiled around her foot. But those minor difficulties were no more important at this instant than her grandmother's warnings.

"Oh!" Sandy said, feeling his touch between her legs and knowing that reason was about to run out entirely. Even as she arched to meet him, she knew she needed reassurance....

"What Gran said..." She sighed. "You Stirling men..." She moaned.

"Ancient history," he murmured.

Sandy felt the quivers rising in her, taking her. His heat seeped into her. She touched him and found his body spare and hard and rough with springy curls, and she couldn't caress him in enough places at once.

Love, she thought. *So this is love.*

Thank goodness she was beyond speech. Those weren't words she wanted to let slip.

Then he lifted her legs and she wrapped them instinctively around his waist, pulling him to her, into her. And they moved together, a frenzied thrusting that pushed her over the edge. She cried out, clutching him, grasping at him, wanting him closer and deeper and harder, until she at last relaxed completely and lay still.

He lay still, too, his pulse pounding in her ear, which was squashed against his chest, and waited for her to open her eyes. Then he said, "I had no idea flannel was such an aphrodisiac."

All she could manage was a breathless laugh before he began to move again, slowly this time. Deep and slow, so that the madness built only gradually. But it built, grew, quickened, until, together, they tumbled over the next edge.

SANDY LEANED BACK against the four fat pillows in the hotel's king-size bed and managed to hold the telephone to her ear in spite of Drew Stirling.

He sat at the foot of the bed, her feet in his lap, massaging them with the hotel's fragranced body lotion. With firm, circular motions, he touched her and soothed her and made it darn near impossible to think of anything but the feel of his skin on hers.

Since opening night she had spent the entire food show under the spell of his touch, his voice, the magnetic pull of his presence. Why should now be any different?

Because she had told herself it would. Because she had promised herself that leaving Chicago would be the end of it, and their Chicago stay was almost over. Once this trip was behind them, so was this interlude. Back home and back to normal.

No one, she told herself, needed to know that anything had even happened between her and Drew. Sure, she'd had that moment—more than one, actually—these past few days when she'd entertained the crazy notion that she and Drew were different. That these feelings between them were strong and pure. And permanent.

But all she had to do was remind herself that Gin had surely thought the same, in the beginning. For that matter, so had Gran.

No, Sandy wouldn't repeat their mistakes. This thing with Drew was a one-time aberration. An exciting memory, nothing more.

She'd told herself that a lot these past couple of days.

From the other end of the phone line Britt Marshack's voice called to Sandy, but so did Drew's touch, from the foot of the bed. Deciding which call to answer was the toughest thing she'd ever done.

"Oh, yes," she said to Britt, hoping her voice sounded normal. "Wildly, um, successful. I think even Drew will have to admit we made more of this show than either of us ever expected."

She wiggled her toes at him.

Drew didn't let go. Instead, he placed her bare foot on his bare chest.

"Well, tell me all about it." Britt's voice seemed to come from a great distance, a sensation Sandy knew had very little to do with long-distance phone lines or hotel switchboards. "Who did you meet? Did you actually sign new customers? How many new prospects?"

"Britt, I'm not sure I can think straight enough right now to even tell you about it." Too true. Not with Drew massaging her feet. Actually, he now seemed to be inching up, working out the tension in her tight calf muscles. He seemed to know exactly where she ached, exactly where she needed his touch. One of his many talents.

"Come on, Sandy," Britt said. "I know it's been an exhausting few days, but don't leave me hanging like this."

Waving Drew's hands off so she could think more coherently, Sandy began reviewing their successes at the show, which had ended a few short hours ago. Drew wouldn't cooperate, of course. He kept up the gentle but insistent massage, which made it increasingly difficult for Sandy to keep her thoughts on business. He grinned lazily at her the whole time, because he knew precisely how hard it was for her to think about the restaurant chain they had signed and the upscale grocery-store conglomerate that wanted so much to carry Yes! Yogurt products that it had agreed to a very advantageous co-op ad campaign. Not to mention the two foreign markets that looked like a sure thing.

As she recounted the litany of their successes—hers and Drew's, together—Sandy came to realize she could now see the end of this exciting interlude with him. She could now sense the way her emotions would besiege her Monday morning, sitting across the conference table from him and knowing they had had their fling and it was over.

The emptiness was devastating.

But it was the only alternative. She knew that. She assumed he did, too. And she told herself to put the whole problem away for the moment. There would be plenty of time for emptiness and loneliness when they returned to Tyler.

"What a time you've had!" Britt said when she had finished relating their success story. "My head is spinning!"

If only Britt knew the rest of it, Sandy thought. She had left out the best parts. "Mmm," she murmured, wondering when Drew's hands had managed to inch above her knees without her noticing it. She noticed it now. "Mine, too."

"How about Drew?"

"Hmm?" She shot up in the bed, abruptly pulling away from Drew's touch, guilty at the mention of his name. "What about Drew?"

He raised his eyebrows and crawled up beside her to listen, tucking his arms around her as he did so.

"Did the two of you work okay together? I know it's been tough for both of you, with all this stuff about your grandparents. I hated bailing out on you like that."

Relieved, Sandy said, "Oh, well, no problem. Yes, I'd say we made a pretty good team." He kissed her neck, and Sandy felt the need to clarify her position. "At the food show."

He trailed the tip of his tongue along the pulse at the base of her throat. Sandy felt her grip slacken. He caught the phone for her, pressed it back into her hand. She looked into his face, which was always a mistake. Those silvery, expressive eyes made it so hard for her to think clearly, to behave the way she knew she should.

"I'm sorry," she said to Britt, "what was that?"

"What is going on there?"

"Nothing. Nothing's going on here."

Drew gave her a wicked smile and began to loosen the buttons on her silk shirt.

"Are you sure?" Britt asked. "You sound distracted."

"I'm, ah, getting undressed."

Which apparently was true. Her shirt was now open and Drew was brushing soft kisses above her camisole.

"Okay, I get the picture," Britt said. "It's late and you're ready for bed. I'll have to wait till you get back tomorrow for the whole story."

Tomorrow. Back to the real world. Sandy told herself not to even consider the plan that had begun to form in her head when she woke up early this morning, Drew's sleeping form curled warmly against hers, his breath at the back of her neck. It wasn't a possibility, she told herself firmly.

"About tomorrow," she said, recognizing that she was caving in even as she coached herself not to. She was turning out to be a spineless hedonist, at the mercy of her passions. "I was thinking. Since I've been working nonstop, and for half the weekend, maybe I'll take a day in the city tomorrow. To relax, since it's Sunday, after all. Would that be a problem?"

"Of course not. That's a good idea. What about Drew?"

He was tugging the strap of her camisole off her shoulder, that's what.

"Drew? Well, uh, Drew. I think he needs to stay over, too. I think he wants to...I think there are people...." She struggled for a way to obscure the truth without telling an out-and-out lie to her friend. Drew, who had pulled back to enjoy her difficulty, grinned and provided no help whatsoever. "Drew probably wants to stay in bed all day."

He rolled back on the bed in silent laughter.

"Oh. Well, we'll see you two when you get back."

Sandy hung up with a sigh of relief.

"Let me say it again. You are a genius," Drew exclaimed, easing close again. The camisole fell away with his touch. "How did you know I wanted to stay in bed all day?"

"That was just for Britt's benefit," she said, hearing the sounds in his throat as he uncovered her nipple and took it in his mouth. "Sight-seeing," she breathed. "That's what I had in mind."

"We'll take a vote," he said.

The decision was unanimous.

RENEE SPRAWLED on the living room rug and pretended to keep her attention on the video. But she lost track of the story. She was more interested in listening to her mother's phone conversation with Sandy. Renee had hatched a plot of her own and couldn't wait to find out if it had worked.

"Well, that was a strange conversation," Britt said, hanging up.

"How's that?" Jake asked.

"Sandy sounded *very* distracted."

"She's just tired. You know how those shows can be."

"I swear, it was more than that."

Renee imagined that Drew was bringing Sandy piles of long-stemmed roses at the very minute her mother had called. She'd seen that in a movie once and it had been *so* romantic.

"And she said they're going to stay over an extra day," Britt continued.

"Good. They've been on fast-forward for weeks. It'll do them good."

Renee smiled. They would walk around the city and hold hands, take the elevator to the top of the Hancock Building to view the whole length of beautiful Michigan Avenue. Jake had taken the family there once. By the time Uncle Drew and Sandy came home, maybe he would have kissed her again and they would be in love. They would have a big wedding and lots of babies.

If Drew and Sandy had babies, she wondered, would that make her an aunt? Aunt Renee? Maybe not.

"But the two of them, Jake?" Britt sounded confused. "They barely get along. You know I never would have asked them to go together if it hadn't been for that mix-up about Renee's school program."

Renee compressed her lips, trying not to smile. Who would have thought it would work, pretending that her school program was a week earlier than it actually was, just to keep her mom and stepdad at home? Renee remembered how she had crossed her fingers, hoping that would mean Drew would have to go instead. And it had. Everything had worked perfectly. Her mom hadn't even been mad when the "mistake" came out.

"Be grateful they're getting along," Jake said.

"Dream on," Britt retorted.

"Who knows," Jake said, "maybe they'll fall madly in love."

Her mother and stepfather both laughed at that. Renee only smiled.

THEY DIDN'T STAY in bed the *entire* day.

They did get up late in the morning, bundle up and wander out into the city in search of breakfast or lunch. They ended up with chili cheese dogs and a walk through the Shedd Aquarium. They found a spot in Grant Park where they could get close enough to the lake to feel the spray from the waves pounding against the ice-shrouded break water, then they wandered through Drew's old neighborhood, listened to the deafening rumble of elevated trains along the Loop.

"See how wonderful cities are?" Sandy said as they walked, hand in hand, back down the bustling sidewalk toward their hotel.

"To visit," Drew conceded. "But if we lived here, we'd have to contend with the traffic and the noise and the pollution."

Sandy shrugged. It hardly mattered. They still had half a day together, stretching out before them like an eternity. She refused to have it spoiled by their differences.

"And that's why you're in Tyler? Because it's quiet and clean and small?"

"Sort of. Actually, I'm there because I got fed up with the rat race."

"At work, you mean?"

He nodded. "Do you know how many over-fifty men I saw my company ease out just because they could pay a younger person less? Do you know how many of the people I worked with swallowed ulcer medication by the truckload? I hated it. That's not the way I wanted to live my life."

"That's business. There's no way around it."

"Sure there is. Look at Yes! Yogurt."

"But not many people are willing to sacrifice success to work for a small company like ours."

"I guess it depends on how you define success."

Sandy liked the earnestness in his eyes when he said that. "And how do you define success?"

"Not by the number of deals I cut in a day or a week or a year."

"Then how?"

"By how often I have time to stop at a kid's lemonade stand. By the friends I have and how often I get to do something nice for them. By the numbers of old people and kids who smile when I walk into a room. By the kind of woman who wants to be my partner."

Sandy felt her heart swell in her chest as he spoke. He was right, of course. So many of the things that had seemed important to her right out of college weren't important at all over the long haul.

"Think about it," Drew said, pulling her onto a bench. "Isn't that why you're back in Tyler, too? Because you decided that family was a better measure of a good life than money or power or prestige?"

Part of her didn't want to agree with him. Doing so seemed dangerous, threatened to pull them even closer together than they already were. And that was too large a risk. But she couldn't deny what he'd said. Tyler was where she wanted to be. Even though she missed the big city and had always dreamed of getting to the top of the marketing ladder, she realized more every day how special Tyler was.

Rather than admit that to Drew, she kissed him instead, right there on a bench in the middle of the city, where a dozen people waited for a bus.

"Aren't you tired?" she whispered.

"Tired? As in back to bed for a while?"

"You've worked so hard. You need your rest."

"You're right. How about it, Sandy Murphy? Let's spend the rest of our lives in bed together."

And she laughed, because he said it the way he said so many other things, offhanded and teasing, with that mischievous glint in his eye. At least, that was what she thought at the time. Later, she wondered if she had only heard it the way she wanted to hear it.

THEY RAN INTO the Tyler school superintendent in the lobby of the hotel as they were leaving the next morning. He was arriving for a convention and listened enthusiastically as they explained their successes on behalf of Yes! Yogurt. An explanation Sandy was more than eager to deliver, in order to dispel any suspicions.

The familiar face, gazing at them with such unabashed curiosity, seemed to prick the bubble of happiness Sandy had held on to so tenaciously their last day in Chicago.

They were heading home. It was over.

Drew, as he threw their bags into his car, acted almost as if he didn't realize that.

"You know, Britt's always telling me I don't have enough fun," he said as they headed through the morning traffic in Chicago. "I never realized how right she was until we took the day off. I mean, I love my work. But yesterday was totally for fun. And I feel like a different person. Thanks for suggesting it."

Sandy smiled, feeling the strain as he took her hand in his and squeezed. One last touch, she thought, before they arrived back on home turf.

Then, when they finally cleared the city and its endless suburbs, he insisted on talking about their successes at the food show. But the conversation didn't focus on what a good team they had been, past tense, but rather on what the future held.

"You know, these international clients are going to be a lot of fun for us," he said. "Don't you think? Between the two of us, we can take Europe by storm. What do you think, should we go over there sometime? Check out Venice or Vienna?"

She thought his conversation sounded suspiciously as if he expected them to be much more than colleagues.

"Maybe you and Jake should go," she said.

"Funny girl," he replied.

But now that they were coming closer to Tyler with each mile, his conversation grew increasingly disturbing. "You haven't seen the house I'm building, have you? Maybe we'll run over there tonight, after we get unpacked."

What was he talking about? How could he not understand what had to happen between them now? She didn't want to see his house. Couldn't bear the thought of seeing his house, actually. Because what had happened between them had to stop here. Could go no further. Surely he knew that.

She thought desperately over everything that had been said between them these past four days. Surely she had been clear with him. But she couldn't recall precisely what she had said. All she could remember clearly was how effortlessly she had gone into his arms, as if it were the only natural thing that had happened between them since the night they first met.

Gin. Gran. Sandy repeated the names silently, a mantra to remind herself that this fling might have been a small mistake, but that anything else was a prescription for disaster.

"Drew," she said, spotting the Tyler town-limit sign. What if people were already suspicious? What had she been thinking, staying an extra day? "We need to talk."

"We will," he said. "We will. Can you imagine what a ruckus we'll stir up if we tell everybody we're going to get married?"

Her throat closed in fear. She could barely squeak out a response. "If we *what?*"

"Okay. *If* was the wrong word. When. *When* we tell everybody we're going to get married."

CHAPTER FIFTEEN

DREW HAD NEVER realized he was one of those men who speak a different language from the one women speak.

Judging from all that had gone on these past few days since he returned from Chicago, he had no choice but to believe that must be his problem. How else to explain the fact that he had left Chicago one half of a couple in love and arrived in Tyler two hours later with the woman he loved not speaking to him?

"I don't get it," he said to Jake for at least the fourth time since his return to the office.

"Obviously." That was his cousin's idea of helpful input.

Drew had finally, in desperation, taken Jake into his confidence, although it didn't seem quite right to talk about such a delicate subject with Sandy's boss. But, hey, how much more screwed up could he possibly make things?

"You're no help, cousin," Drew snapped, aware that they were supposed to be going over the finances involved in stepping up production yet again, to meet the new contracts signed in Chicago. "You're a happily married man. I expected better from you."

Jake shoved his pencil behind his ear, leaned back in his chair and put his feet on Drew's desk. "Okay. Tell me again, what exactly was it you said that ticked her off?"

"All I said was..." Drew tried to remember, but discovered that his precise words had somehow been lost in the fury that followed. "Something about how surprised everybody would be when we got married."

"I see. And I assume this wasn't the first time you had used the M word."

Frustration flooded him. "Since when is marriage 'the M word'? I thought women liked to talk about getting married. I thought they were generally in favor of getting married."

Jake nodded his head and pursed his lips. "So this offhand mention was the first time you had brought up the topic?"

"Yeah. In those exact words. So?"

Jake shut his eyes and shook his head. "Such a bright guy, too. College educated. Capable of carrying his weight at work. Tell me exactly what happened next, Drew."

That request gave Drew no trouble whatsoever. The moments that followed his innocent comment would live in his memory forever. Like a victim of traumatic stress syndrome, he sometimes feared he would never again be able to drive across the Tyler town limit without reliving those moments.

Her exact words had been "What did you say?"

But it wasn't so much what she had said as how she'd said it. Her tone implied that he had suggested she sell her soul to the devil in return for some mindless personal pleasure that would benefit no one but him.

Instead of backing off and rephrasing the comment, Drew had disregarded the warning in her voice and repeated himself verbatim.

To which Sandy had replied, "Where on earth did you get the idea this was leading toward...toward anything like *that?*"

He could see now that Jake was absolutely right. She hadn't even been able to utter the evil M word herself, for heaven's sake.

Drew had tried to explain himself, redeem himself, even throw himself at her mercy during the rest of the drive. Nothing worked. By the time he pulled up in front of her garage apartment and she yanked her garment bag out of his trunk, he knew of only one more thing to say. The one thing, he'd thought, that always saved the day in the man-woman arena.

"But, Sandy, I love you," he'd declared earnestly. "Isn't that all that matters?"

Apparently not.

Sandy had stood and stared at him, wearing the baffled expression that had been his first clue they weren't speaking the same language. Then she'd set her luggage on the snow-covered ground, placed her hands on her hips and begun to explain things he still didn't fully understand.

"We work together, Drew."

So far, he was with her.

"I'm a professional woman, and whether you know it or not, protecting my personal and professional reputation has to be one of my first concerns."

That was where she'd begun to lose him. When had getting married become a reputation-ruining action? Was this some kind of morals clause he'd missed? Family-values legislation gone haywire?

"What happened in Chicago was special," Sandy had continued, while Drew stood by, himself now the baffled one. "And I'm not sorry it happened. But if you think I'd come back to Tyler after a weekend business trip with one of my co-workers and let everybody in town know what went on ... well, I don't even know what to say to you! How could you even think such a thing?"

By now, Drew was completely lost. "Sandy, I didn't mean we have to start sending out invitations in the afternoon mail, but—"

"Besides which, do you remember who we *are*, Drew Stirling?"

Drew had groaned. "You're not going to use that thing about Grandpa and your grandmother again, are you? Sandy, that's nuts. It has nothing to do with us. Can't you see that?"

Her expression said he amazed her more with each word he uttered. Then she picked up her luggage and said, "You are too obtuse for words. I'm going in. And I don't expect you ever to bring up this subject again."

Of course, he had. At least, he had tried. Without success.

He had sat in his car outside Yes! Yogurt the next morning, waiting for her to arrive. When she pulled up, he'd called out to her. She kept walking toward the building.

"Sandy, wait! Don't you think we need to talk about this?"

"I can't hear you, Drew."

Then she had closed her office door and left him standing in the hall in his dripping galoshes.

He brought her a hot dog for lunch, smothered in chili and cheese, just like the one she had been darn near orgasmic over at the street vendor's in Chicago.

"Does this cover the price of admission?" he'd asked, sticking his head through her office door.

"I can't eat that," she had said stiffly. "Have you ever heard of cholesterol?"

"You loved it in Chicago," he protested.

"Sometimes the things we indulge in out of town simply don't fly as part of our daily routine back home."

Remembering that one always hurt. Drew rubbed his forehead and said, "So what does that make me, Jake? On the same level as a hot dog? Something that gives her heartburn? Is that it?"

Jake stared at him a long time, then said, "You're going to have to leave her alone."

"I can't leave her alone. I love her."

"But she doesn't love you, Drew."

He sprang up out of his chair. "Hell, yes, she does!"

"She's not acting like it."

"Not now, maybe. Not now." But Drew remembered what it had been like in Chicago. The way she had looked at him when they made love. The way her touch had felt, so tender and filled with awe. The same way he'd felt when he touched her. He remembered the things they'd talked about, the discoveries of all the ways they thought alike, beliefs they shared. No, no matter what Sandy might be trying to convince herself of, Drew knew she loved him. He was as certain of that as he was certain that he loved her.

"She's the one, Jake. You've gotta tell me what to do."

"There's only one thing you can do when a woman gets cold feet."

"Okay. I'm ready. Give me the game plan."

"Leave her alone. The more you pursue her, the faster she's going to run."

SANDY'S SECOND greatest obsession was that someone would figure out what had happened in Chicago between her and Drew.

Her greatest obsession was Drew, plain and simple.

She thought with fear of that split second when he'd mentioned marriage and her heart had leaped joyfully.

Then she had remembered all the reasons why it simply couldn't be. Drew might think marriage sounded great now. But it was all too complicated, too jumbled up in ancient history and office politics. What would happen when their grandparents found out? What would happen when things started growing tense at work? What would happen when he realized it wasn't going to work out?

Then Sandy would be in disgrace, unable to hold her head up at work and responsible for breaking an old woman's heart.

So, no matter what her own heart told her, Sandy knew what she had to do.

All in all, she thought she was doing a pretty good job of pretending nothing had happened in Chicago, until Britt dropped by her apartment one evening. Sandy knew right away that something was up. Britt the homebody didn't go off and leave the family on a school night for an insignificant reason.

Britt had barely sat down on the futon couch before saying, "You want to tell me what's going to happen about you and Drew?"

Guilt and paranoia struck at Sandy's heart. Her old friend—her boss!—knew. And the only way she could know was if Drew had talked to Jake, and Jake to Britt. Sandy would throttle Drew.

Resigned, she told herself the best she could do now was come clean and hope to salvage her career. Sighing, she said, "Who told you?"

Britt smiled. "You did."

Sandy curled up in a corner of the couch, knees pulled tightly to her chest, arms locked around her legs. "Are you going to fire me?"

Britt chuckled softly. "Fire you? Whatever makes you think I'd fire you?"

"Not now, maybe. But later. When things get sticky."

"What makes you think things have to get sticky?"

Sandy let out a long, shuddering breath. The truth. It had been eating at her for days. "Because I don't think I can stay away from him." She forced herself to look at Britt, to gauge her reaction.

Britt smiled like a woman who had been there herself, and Sandy felt her defenses evaporate. She had worked so hard to avoid being with Drew, talking to him. But what was in her mind and heart was always with her, unavoidable and resolute. She was filled to the brim with Drew: his irrepressible humor, his certainty about what really mattered in life, his gentle spirit.

And his love for her.

That was the hard part. Remembering that he'd said he loved her.

All of it spilled out now, in the face of Britt's acceptance and understanding. She listened while Sandy told her everything that had happened, from that first meeting at Worthington House to her panic when he'd brought up the subject of marriage on the way back into Tyler.

"And I'm just so embarrassed," Sandy moaned. "Professional women don't do this kind of thing."

"Sandy, all women fall in love."

Sandy flinched. There it was again: love. She couldn't hear the word without feeling adrift, vulnerable, out of control. How could he have fallen in love?

Worse, how could she?

"That can't be what it is, Britt. It just can't be."

And there it was again, her friend's encouraging, understanding smile. A best friend's smile and a mother's smile all rolled into one. "Can't it?" Britt asked.

"Of course not. How could we work together?"

"The way Jake and I do."

Sandy sagged against the couch, ready to stop fighting but still unwilling to surrender. Britt could be right, of course. Maybe things like this didn't always have to end the way they'd ended for Gin. Look what a terrific team Drew and she had been in Chicago, even after they'd become lovers. No tension between them during work, and never a false move, as if they read each other like the nutrition label on a container of Yes! Yogurt. It did work for Britt and Jake, after all. Still...

"Sandy, most of the time this kind of thing is a problem because one of the people involved doesn't take it seriously. When it's only a fling."

Sandy thought about Gin, and how deeply she had loved Ted. Then she thought about Ted, and what a faithless so-and-so he had turned out to be.

"Now, we know Drew isn't taking this lightly. How about you?"

"Oh, Britt," Sandy said miserably. Could it be true, that what she'd seen happen to Gin didn't have to happen to everyone? Even if she could safely believe that, what about the rest of it? She groaned. "Oh, Britt, this is the worst thing that could have happened."

"What is it you're really worried about, Sandy?"

"Don't you see? What about our families?" Her insides began to churn just contemplating the consequences of her actions. "This just doesn't feel right. It's going to throw everybody into a tailspin. And then when it's over, our work will suffer and—"

Britt leaned forward and grasped her hand. "Sandy, one of the things I almost let get in the way of my marriage to Jake was my kids."

For a moment, Sandy lost her absorption with her own worries. "Really?"

"Especially Matt. He resented the heck out of the fact that his real dad was dead and I wanted to bring another man into the family." Britt looked down at the ring on her finger. "I almost let his anger wreck my chance at happiness. But I didn't, because burying myself with my kids wasn't the right thing for me. And you know how it's all worked out. None of the kids are closer to Jake than Matt."

Despite the certainty in Britt's voice and eyes, fear still roared loud and strong in Sandy's ears. "But it would break Gran's heart all over again."

"I don't know what happened between Mag and Drew's grandfather," Britt said. "I'm not sure anybody's positive about that, maybe not even the two of them. But a lot of the stuff I've heard revolves around their families' interference. You know, love isn't something you do for the other people in your family, Sandy. It's something you accept wholeheartedly because it's right for you."

THE NEXT AFTERNOON, Sandy drove by Worthington House three times, trying to work up the courage to go in and talk to her grandmother.

Three times she kept driving.

What could she say to Gran if she did go in? What did she expect her grandmother to say to her? Did she hope that by some miracle the facts of the story surrounding Mag and Clarence would have changed? For it was this that haunted her so, that hung so heavily around her heart.

Was history doomed to repeat itself? Gin's history? Gran's history?

The thought made Sandy shudder.

She kept driving, quickly finding herself roaming the countryside surrounding Tyler. The winter-bleak scenery suited her mood. She parked near the lodge and looked out over icy Timber Lake. Bare black branches silhouetted against a gray sky offered little hope of the spring that was endless months away. At this moment, it seemed as if the world would be frozen and bitter forever.

High above the lake, on the opposite shore, she could see the fresh-cut beams of a house going up. Drew's house. Her heart began to race, and to ache. He had wanted her to see the house, because he wanted to share it with her. And she wanted to see it. If only...

She stared, wondering if he was there. Wondering how much she had hurt him these past few days.

Suddenly, Drew's feelings seemed as important to her as her own. And that, according to Britt, was the way it should be when you're in love. Sandy remembered all the times she had respected Britt's opinions, how often she had gone to her for guidance during her college years. If she had trusted Britt to help her choose a major, to help her decide on a job, why not now?

It was then she heard indistinguishable voices farther down the shore. She craned her neck and saw Liza and Cliff Forrester tromping along the lake's edge, little Margaret Alyssa bundled up between them. The little girl squealed with delight when Cliff picked her up and swung her over his head, their laughter visible as their breath hit the frosty air.

The gray clouds that formed a backdrop to the happy family scene suddenly didn't look bleak or threatening, Sandy noticed.

She remembered when Liza had come back to town and fallen in love with Cliff, a troubled man with a troubling past. She remembered how everyone had talked and disapproved, predicting a gloomy outcome for the couple. The trio on the shore proved all the gossips wrong.

If Britt was right, true love was that way, able to defy all the odds. Lifting the people who believed in it to another, higher place where even the tough times weren't as hard to get through.

What else was it Britt had said? First you have to believe in it wholeheartedly?

With her heartbeat quickening, Sandy hurried back to her car. Blocking out the fears that had paralyzed her, she found the turnoff to Drew's new house within minutes and paused on the side of the road, hands trembling on the steering wheel as she tried to make up her mind. She didn't know, of course, that he was even around. But she had been drawn here. If Drew was at the house, wouldn't that be a sign that this was the right thing to do?

Holding her breath, she turned into the rutted, frozen drive. A solitary car sat near the house, which rose clean and simple out of the woods and toward the sky, feathered now with silvery clouds.

She found Drew on the second floor, sitting cross-legged on a thick cotton blanket, a patch of blue spread over bare plywood. The view from the floor-to-ceiling window took in the lake Sandy had just come from. He, too, was watching the Forrester family. Sandy stood in the doorway, admiring the way his hair fluttered in the crisp breeze wafting through the unfinished window. She remembered the way that hair felt against her fingers.

"They look happy," she said.

He nodded. "You didn't."

And neither did he. Sandy's heart thumped. What if it was too late? "I'm not."

"What are you going to do about it?"

"I'm here, aren't I?"

"And?"

"Any chance you still love me?"

He turned to look at her, and she saw the teasing light she had missed recently flicker once again in his eyes. "Sorry. I've been sworn to silence on that matter."

In all fairness, there was no reason he should make this easy on her, she supposed. She walked over and sat on the edge of the blanket. His closeness affected her instantly and powerfully. She wanted him. But that was less important now than what she'd come to say. For she realized, seeing him like this, that it had to be said.

"I was wrong," she said. "I was afraid and I was wrong. I—I love you, Drew."

The mischief drained out of his eyes and all that was left was raw emotion. "You're sure about this, Sandy?"

"I'm sure. I—I won't say it's not scary. But I can't hide from it any longer."

He let out a long breath and took her in his arms. "Thank goodness. I was afraid I was going to have to resort to something desperate."

His arms felt so right around her. "Like what?" she asked.

"I don't know. A magic charm? A pact with Cupid? Anything."

He kissed her, pulling her back to the blanket with him and cradling her in his arms, shielding her from the cold. He slipped his hands beneath her clothes, caressing her without exposing her to the weather, reminding her of all the ways he had shared his love those four days in Chicago.

They made love slowly and sweetly, then wrapped themselves in the blanket and lay back to watch the stars come out. They talked quietly, telling themselves long after their fingers and toes began to feel numb that it wasn't cold enough to get up and go home.

When the moon came out, a brilliant silver sliver, they rose reluctantly and headed for their cars.

"You won't change your mind when we get back to Tyler, will you?" he asked, brushing kisses across her forehead.

"I won't. But we'll have to tell them, won't we? Soon."

"Grandpa and Mag? Tell them what? That we're in love?"

"No. That we're . . . you know."

"Oh, no. I'm not making that mistake again."

"What mistake?"

"Saying the M word. This kid only screws up once before he learns his lesson."

"Okay, then." She drew a long breath. "That we're getting . . . married. Aren't we?"

"Is that a proposal? You know, I was hoping for more. Something tender. Romantic. Whatever happened to the woman getting down on one knee and—"

She gave him a jab in the ribs. "You're pressing your luck, Drew."

He laughed. "Okay. Yes, I'll let you make an honest man out of me."

"Drew? Can we . . . let's not wait around. I don't think I'm up for all the gossip and speculation. I just want to do it. Soon. Okay?"

"The sooner the better," he said. "So when do we break the news to the good folks at Worthington House?"

THE QUILTING CIRCLE was in session when Sandy and Drew arrived at Worthington House the next afternoon. Drew noted Sandy's worried frown, saw the hesitation forming in her eyes.

"You sit," he said, nudging her into a seat near her grandmother. "I'll go find Grandpa."

"But all these people—"

"Will make it easier," he whispered. "They'll both behave better with an audience."

He went off in search of Clarence, hoping Sandy would still be there when he returned.

She was, but she still looked worried. And Clarence grew even more agitated when he realized Drew was leading him into the midst of Mag's quilting circle.

"Whatever you have to say to me can surely be said in the privacy of my room," Clarence said, grinding to a halt right outside the activity door.

Before Drew could respond, Sandy jumped up and said, "Drew, you're certain—"

Before he could reassure her, Mag looked up and said, "What are you up to, young man?"

"If everybody will calm down, I'll be glad to clear this up for both of you." Drew walked over and put his arm around Sandy's shoulders. "Rather, *we'll* be glad to clear this up."

"Oh, dear." That was Sandy, under her breath.

A buzzing began from the women seated around the blue-and-red quilt. Clarence rapped his walking stick against the doorframe and said, "Quiet, everyone. Let's hear what my grandson has on his mind."

Mag's was the only voice that didn't grow silent. "You needn't come in here acting like you run the place, Clarence. And the same goes for you, young man."

"Gran—"

"Now, Alexandra, I think you—"

"Can we have a moment of silence, Mag, so that—"

Drew decided there was only one thing that stood a real chance of silencing this crowd. Raising his voice so it could be heard over everyone else's, he said, "Sandy and I are getting married."

The bickering went on another few seconds, then his announcement sank in. Clarence stared at them, almost losing his grip on his walking stick. Mag grew pale, her soft pink rouge standing out brightly against her white cheeks. The other women in the quilting circle couldn't decide who to stare at, so their gazes whipped rapidly from one to the other of the foursome. Not a needle moved.

"Now that I have your attention," Drew said, smiling down at Sandy, who finally looked relieved and calm, "I'd like to assure you both that we love you, but we also love each other. And we're hoping you'll give us your blessing and be with us for our wedding on February fourteenth."

Mag gasped, as did Emma Finklebaum. Clarence sank into the nearest chair.

"What did you say, young man?" Mag demanded, clutching the arm of her chair.

Sandy slipped from Drew's grip and took her grandmother's hand. "We're having a Valentine's Day wedding, Gran. Please be happy for us."

"Oh, Lord," Mag whispered, "not again."

Then she fainted dead away.

CHAPTER SIXTEEN

RELIEF WASHED through Sandy when Mag roused from her faint and instantly went on the offensive.

"You scoundrel," she snapped, her voice only slightly weaker than usual. She pushed herself up from the activity-room couch and pointed a mauve-tipped nail at Clarence. "You just couldn't stay out of this town and leave my family alone, could you?"

Sandy and Drew exchanged glances. Somehow, their certainty that they were doing the right thing had convinced them that their grandparents would rejoice with them. That the reality of this moment would overshadow events that had happened so long ago.

"I assure you," Clarence said, "I had nothing to do with this unfortunate set of circumstances. On the contrary, you are no doubt the one who sent for your granddaughter the moment my grandson arrived in your quaint little village, as innocent as a lamb to the slaughter."

Face-to-face with their grandparents' penchant for melodrama, Drew was trying hard not to laugh. And Sandy had to admit this feud between these two old people was beginning to seem a little extreme. After all these years, why couldn't they both forgive and forget, especially since it appeared that both of them might bear some responsibility for the bitter break-up?

Of one thing, however, Sandy was now absolutely, one-hundred percent certain: their problems had nothing to do with her relationship with Drew.

"...Be trusted not to go chasing after every young female who passes?" Mag was saying, dragging herself off the couch to confront Clarence nose-to-nose.

"Only if you can vouch for the fact that this young offspring of yours is after my grandson for some reason other than his professional status. Financial gain, isn't that what your family looks for in a match, Mag?"

"My granddaughter doesn't need—"

"Gran, please." Sandy put her hand on her arm. "Please, let's stop the fighting. All we want is for you to be happy for us. Can't you do that?"

She saw the uncertainty in Mag's eyes as she looked from her to Drew, then back to Clarence. Finally, she gazed at Sandy again and said, "Don't you see, Alexandra? It's happening all over again."

Sandy felt a momentary twinge of uneasiness when her grandmother said that. But she knew the rightness of what was in her heart. She had no intention of letting ancient history spoil it. She had thought long and hard about the unlikely set of circumstances that had brought her and Drew back to Tyler and she knew now that she'd been right all along—this wasn't entirely an accident. It *was* meant to be. But not for the reasons Gran wanted to believe.

"It's not like that, Gran. Look at it this way. Maybe this marriage is meant to be, to finally heal the bitterness from all those years ago."

Mag shook her head. "You don't know what you're saying, girl."

"Yes, I do. *We* do."

"Do you have any idea why you settled on a Valentine's Day wedding?"

Sandy linked her arm through Drew's. "I certainly do. Because it's soon and we don't want to live with months of gossip and speculation."

Drew smiled and added, "And because it's romantic."

"Ha!" Mag glared at Clarence. "You want to tell them why they picked that date?"

"The honor is yours, Mag."

Mag shook her head and reached behind her, groping for the arm of the couch. She sat again, still shaking her yellow curls, and said, "Because that's the date *we* were supposed to be married."

Sandy felt her blood run cold at her grandmother's words. "You—you don't mean that."

"Tell her, Emma."

Emma Finklebaum, who looked as if she wished she were getting all this down in a reporter's pad for future publication, smiled and said, "Oh, yes. She's absolutely right. Everyone in Tyler was in a tizzy about the prospect of a Valentine's Day wedding. And you know, I've heard the sale of Valentine cards has been below the national average in this town ever since." She chuckled. "Yes, I'd say Cupid has not exactly been popular in Tyler."

IN THE NEXT FEW DAYS, Sandy told everyone who would listen that the coincidence didn't bother her one little bit.

"Why, I might even wear the wedding dress Gran never got married in," she said to Sheila Lawson when she went out to Timberlake Lodge to make arrangements for a small reception following the ceremony.

Sheila gave her a funny look.

"It's a joke," Sandy said. "A little humor."

Sheila laughed weakly. Sandy told herself it didn't matter if no one else saw the humor in the situation, as long as she and Drew did.

Reaction around town varied from disbelief to horror to wide-eyed fascination. Annabelle Scanlon, when Sandy dropped by the post office to mail out the few invitations, said, "You know, everybody in Tyler who was there that day still holds the belief that Valentine's Day is bad luck for weddings. You sure you don't want me to hold these for a day, give you time to reconsider?"

"That's superstition, Mrs. Scanlon. I want those invitations in the mail."

As she left the post office, Annabelle called out, "You buy a dress you can get some other use out of, you hear me?"

Sandy knew, of course, that Tyler would talk of nothing else until the wedding was over. Some people—like Annabelle, and Marge at the diner—didn't mind telling her straight to her face that she was playing around with destiny. Others kept their talk to themselves, and ultimately Sandy found that more distressing. It was disconcerting to walk down Main Street and see a conversation between two people break off abruptly as she approached. Finally, after that happened three times in forty-five minutes, Sandy marched right up to Rosemary Dusold and Pam Kelsey and said, "No, we aren't worried that history is doomed to repeat itself. No, we don't feel there's any bad karma surrounding my relationship with Drew. Any other questions?"

The two women stared at her, speechless, for sixty seconds before breaking into slightly embarrassed but warmhearted laughter.

Gran was the only person Sandy truly worried about. She went by Worthington House every afternoon after work. Mag was mostly silent for the first two days after the announcement. But as Sandy was leaving on the third day, her grandmother said, "I let Clarence Stirling ruin a big part of my life. The one thing I'm not going to do is let him ruin my relationship with my granddaughter."

Sandy threw her arms around her. "Oh, Gran, you don't know how happy that makes me."

Mag patted her on the cheek. "I love you more than you can imagine until you have grandbabies of your own, Alexandra. I never expected any of my great-grandkids to have Stirling blood. But never mind. I'll be there on Valentine's Day, with bells on."

She probably meant it literally, Sandy speculated as she left Worthington House a few minutes later, her heart resting easier than it had in days. While she stood at the door, buttoning her coat and pulling on her gloves, Emma Finklebaum walked up and in a low voice said, "I wonder if I could have a moment of your time."

Sandy pocketed her glove. "Sure."

"I am, as you may recall, a journalist." Emma looked at her expectantly and Sandy nodded. "I was also very much involved in chronicling the previous . . . situation."

Her good mood dissipating, Sandy nodded again.

"What I am suggesting is . . . that is, I would very much like to negotiate for rights to your story."

Sandy wasn't certain whether it was anger or anxiety that shot through her so sharply. "What?"

Emma's smile was soothing. "In my professional opinion, this story is quite marketable. And I would like your permission to write it. Now, there are a number of ways we could handle this. An as-told-to story, perhaps, if you prefer. Although—''

Sandy shoved her fingers into her glove and grabbed the door handle. ''Emma, I'm not interested in telling my story. There is no story to tell. I'm getting married. Period. It happens every day. This is not something the supermarket tabloids are going to be interested in.''

''Oh, absolutely not!'' Emma's mouth grew round in horror. ''Alexandra, I am a legitimate journalist and I wouldn't dream of doing business with that kind of publication. I was thinking of a book, perhaps, with a serialization in one of the better women's magazines.'' She raised her right hand and fanned it in the air above their heads. ''I have the title in mind already—History Repeats: the Saga of The Modern-Day Capulets and Montagues.'' Emma paused and pursed her lips. ''You don't think people will have trouble recognizing the family names of Romeo and Juliet, do you?''

Beginning to quiver with the strong emotions she didn't want to inflict on this elderly woman, who no doubt meant no harm, Sandy opened the door and began backing out of Worthington House.

''Emma, history is not repeating itself.''

''But in case it should,'' the woman called after her as Sandy hurried down the steps, ''I just thought it would be easier if we negotiated now.''

Sandy didn't exactly run home, but she took the quickest route to her apartment and crossed the street midblock anytime she risked running into someone who might want to talk. When she finally locked herself in, she found herself face-to-face with the ivory-colored silk suit she had bought to be married in. She swallowed hard and ran the tips of her fingers over its soft, nubby surface. Tears began to gather in her eyes.

Not that she was worried, she told herself, but she was glad she had taken Annabelle's advice and bought something she could wear for some other occasion.

DREW TOLD HIMSELF he would feel better after he talked to Jake.

"I swear, Sandy's knuckles are getting whiter every day that passes," he said to his cousin. "She's getting such a case of cold feet, we're going to have to stash her standing up in the refrigerator case at the outlet store."

"It's normal," Jake said. "Happens to everybody."

"Not me."

"No?"

"No. If I'm having second thoughts it's only because I can see she's having second thoughts."

"Ah. So you are having second thoughts?"

"Well, no. Not actual second thoughts. More like thoughts about the nature of second thoughts." Was it just him, he wondered, or was he beginning to sound like a fool?

"Maybe you should wait, maybe make sure you're both one hundred percent ready."

"Wait? And give all this gossip a chance to work up a *real* head of steam? No way!" The thought of waiting terrified Drew much more than the thought of showing up in that church and... "You don't think she'll back out, do you? At the last minute or anything?"

Ah, damn! He'd gone and let the wrong thing slip out. After swearing he wouldn't allow the words to cross his lips.

But Jake looked and sounded calm. "You think history's going to repeat itself."

"No, no. Of course not." Drew tried to swallow, but his mouth was so dry. "On the other hand, I'd just as soon know now."

"As opposed to at the altar?"

So much for feeling better after talking to his cousin. "I think I'd better go pick up the rings."

"Besides," Jake said as Drew walked out of his office, "I thought it was Uncle Clarence who didn't show up at the altar. *You're* not going to pull a disappearing act, are you?"

Drew turned around and pointed a finger at Jake. "You repeat that anywhere else in this town and I'll arrange a leveraged buyout of Yes! Yogurt."

Jake grinned. "You're not a stockholder. There are no stockholders."

"I'm warning you, Jake."

"No, I'm warning you. If you do anything you shouldn't, Britt's going to disown you."

"I'm not backing out. I swear." He turned to his cousin one more time. "Unless you've heard something I don't know. You're not trying to tell me something, are you?"

"Go get the rings, Drew. You're making yourself crazy."

Actually, it was Sandy who was making him crazy. Or was it all the other people in town who insisted on behaving exactly as Sandy had predicted? They were talking about this wedding as if it were the second coming of the jilting of the century. Or maybe it was just his grandfather who was making him crazy.

"Have a plan B, son," Clarence said one afternoon as they took their first walk around the block since Clarence started physical therapy.

"I don't need a plan B, Grandpa. Plan A is going very smoothly."

"For the wedding day, I mean. To be sure, Mag appeared the picture of the glowing bride-to-be, right up until the rehearsal party the night before. Not a hint of trouble. Jitters, of course. They all have jitters. Or so I thought. Don't be taken by surprise, son."

Drew resisted the impulse to ask precisely how he might do that—not be taken by surprise if his bride decided not to show up at the altar. But he refused to consider the possibility, especially in the old man's presence.

"Drew, I want you to know that, no matter what happens, you remain my favorite grandson."

Drew grinned, his worries forgotten for the moment. "There's not much reassurance in that, Grandpa."

Clarence looked offended. "No?"

"I'm your *only* grandson."

Clarence chuckled. "Why, so you are."

When they got back to Clarence's room, his grandfather grasped his arm and said, "You can count on me, son. I'll be there. You want me to work on finding out whether she's planning to go through with it *before* you walk into that church?"

"It's not necessary, Grandpa."

Clarence shook his head. "I thought not, either. I walked into it blindly. Don't let that happen to you."

THE QUESTION was on the lips of everyone in Tyler as the day drew near. Would history repeat itself?

Liza Forrester thought it would. "I'm an incurable romantic," she said to her sister-in-law Nora, "and what could be more romantic than continuing this curse into future generations? Why, we could have Murphys and Stirlings jilting one another right into the next millennium."

Pam Kelsey, when she stopped by the boardinghouse, announced to her mother-in-law, "What a lot of nonsense! The chances of that happening again are nil. It's going to be a beautiful wedding."

Anna Kelsey taste-tested the pot of chili simmering on the stove, added a pinch of cumin and said, "That's assuming we know what happened the first time. Have you talked to two people who can even agree on that?"

Pam had to admit she hadn't.

Every penny of Renee Hansen's allowance went for good-luck charms. The rabbit's foot never left her pocket the week before the wedding. "Please, please, please," she whispered every night before she went to sleep.

Amanda Baron Trask, when pressed by brother Jeff to take a side in the debate, said, "The power of suggestion wins—that's my prediction. With so many people in Tyler *expecting* one of them to back out, one or the other is bound to cave in."

And at the high school, Matt Hansen overheard one of the teachers entering the faculty lounge talking about a pool that was being run. "If she doesn't back out, somebody's going to win a jackpot come Valentine's Day," the man said.

For a moment, Matt was so incensed that he made up his mind to tell his stepdad at the very first opportunity. But by the time Matt got home from school, his own problems had crept back into his head and filled up all the space there. He forgot all about Drew and Sandy.

He was probably the only one in town who did.

And as February 14 dawned cold and crisp and sunny, people in Tyler woke up and began pressing white shirts and polishing dress shoes. Everyone planned to get to the church on time, regardless of whether or not the bride and groom did the same.

Phil Wocheck expressed common sentiments when he told Sheila Lawson, "Wouldn't miss the fireworks for the world."

DREW WOKE UP with a knot in his gut and an ominous buzzing in his head. He lay in bed and stared at the tuxedo hanging from his closet door. What if it didn't fit, after all? What if there'd been a mix-up and he'd picked up the wrong tuxedo and this one wouldn't button? Or what if his clock was wrong and he'd awakened too late and...

He reached for the phone on his bedside table and dialed Sandy's number. He would tell her he loved her and she would say the same and he would feel better. Then he would get up, dress and meet Jake at the church. This would soon be over and they would wake up tomorrow in San Diego, Mr. and Mrs. Andrew Stirling.

Wouldn't they?

Or would Cupid's curse continue? That was what someone had called it two days ago, when he went in to make sure the rings were ready. The two words had spun around in his head ever since. At least he'd had the good sense not to repeat them to Sandy.

Her telephone rang and rang. Drew's heart began to pound a little too fast. Finally, the answering machine kicked in.

"Hi, this is Sandy. I'm not taking calls today, but—"

He hung up. He tried to remember if that was what the message on her machine normally said. Not taking calls today? What did that mean?

One version of the Mag-Clarence debacle surfaced in his memory—the version that said Mag had locked herself in her room the day of the wedding and refused to talk to anyone.

The knot in his gut began to tighten. He pulled the covers over his head. The phone rang and he almost didn't answer it. Then it dawned on him it must be Sandy. He yanked at the covers, had to fight them off, almost lost out to a particularly determined sheet, then snatched the ringing phone off the hook.

It was Jake. "You up yet?"

"She's not answering her phone."

"She's probably dressing. The way you're supposed to be." Jake sounded exasperated.

Drew let out a loud sigh. "You think?"

"Yes. Now get your butt ready. I'll pick you up in an hour."

"Jake, what if I can't? What if I can't do it?"

MAG AND CLARENCE RAN into each other at the front door of Worthington House. In honor of the day, Mag wore peach-colored silk instead of her usual bright tones. Her nails were the same color, as were her shoes and the silk flowers wound artfully into her blond curls. Ravishing, she thought, but not so ravishing she would show up the bride.

Mag had done that kind of thing deliberately in her youth, but she had mellowed with the years.

"You're looking dashing today," she said to Clarence with all the dignity she could muster.

"As are you." He moved his walking stick to his other hand and proffered his arm. "I would be honored to accompany you to the church, my dear."

Startled, Mag didn't know what to say. If asked, she would have said that never in a million years would she set foot in a church anywhere near Clarence Stirling. But he was a charming old goat—more so now than ever, it sometimes seemed to her—and perhaps this was the day to let bygones be bygones.

Mag looked at the limo waiting for them at the curb. "Well, I suppose it wouldn't hurt to ride together." She slipped her gloved hand into the crook of his arm.

He smiled down at her mischievously. "What say we give them the slip? It's such a glorious day, Mag, why not walk?"

"Why not, indeed? As I always say, give 'em something to talk about."

He laughed, and Mag discovered she felt far more gay this morning than she had expected to.

"At the risk of spoiling the day," Clarence said, "I fear there is something we must discuss."

Mag was silent. She had promised to support her granddaughter and she intended to keep her word.

"I spoke with Judson Ingalls yesterday," Clarence continued.

"Yes?"

"He tells me there may be some basis for your claim that you were the wronged party."

The words stopped Mag dead in her tracks. "He did?"

"Indeed he did, much to my regret."

He told her then what she'd been too immature and too wounded to listen to fifty years ago. Thanks to a flat tire on the isolated country road that in those days was the only way into town from Timberlake Lodge, Clarence and his best man, Judson, home on leave just in time for the wedding, had been late arriving at the church. So late that she had already left, in tears, to lock herself in her room. So late that the bride had gone away certain that the unsavory rumors about her groom and the best man's wife were true. "At the time, Judson and I both assumed you had decided not to show up yourself," Clarence said. "And I was in no state to talk to anybody at the church. By the time Judson found out what really happened, it was too late to inform me that you had been there that morning."

Mag sighed. "You'd already left Tyler by then. Without even talking to me."

"I tried to see you, Mag. I called every day for weeks."

"You did?" Mag remembered his calls that first day, which she had refused to take. "Mother never told me that."

"I fear our parents were the biggest hindrance to settling the difficulty."

"But they wanted us to marry. I know they did."

"Indeed they did. But the last weeks before the wedding, my father and yours were not on the most amicable of terms. There was heated debate, it seems, over when I would take over the businesses. Your father feared he was being pushed aside." Clarence looked down at her apologetically. "Knowing my father as I do, I fear your parent's concerns were probably well-founded."

She stared at him, stunned. "We should have eloped, after all."

He nodded and patted her hand. "Families are a troublesome business."

They continued walking toward the church, a mere half block away.

"So, Magdalena," he said as they reached the church steps, "your granddaughter *does* intend to show this morning?"

"Not if she takes my advice." And Mag smiled, a smile tinged with bittersweet.

The sunshine sparkled like diamonds in his laughing gray eyes. Oh, he was a handsome devil.

"An interesting day is in store for us all, my dear. A most interesting day."

SANDY STOOD in the bedroom where she'd spent all her nights as a little girl. She stared at the rock posters left over from her high school years, the team pennants, the mementos tucked into corners of the dresser mirror and tacked onto the corkboard over her desk. Notes from her best friends. A Polaroid snapshot of the pep squad. Her drooping, faded pom-pom.

She was frightened and there was nothing here to reassure her.

Britt popped her head into the room. "Time to get dressed."

Renee appeared next, her big eyes pleading. "You're going to be late."

Stalling, that was what she was doing. Sandy knew it. And from the look in Britt's eyes, her friend knew it, too.

"Renee," Britt said, "you run downstairs and tell the Murphys we'll be down shortly."

"But Mo-om..."

"No whining."

Renee backed out of the room, never taking her big blue eyes off Sandy. "Hurry, okay?"

When the two women were alone, Sandy sank onto her narrow childhood bed and said, "Britt, what am I supposed to do now? You won't believe what I heard at the bank yesterday. Somebody told one of the tellers it's payback time for the Stirlings."

"Payback time? What kind of nonsense is that?"

"It's not nonsense. They said the Stirlings are going to get their revenge today for losing everything they owned. Oh, Britt, I'm never going to make it. I can't go through with it."

CHAPTER SEVENTEEN

RENEE PRESSED HER EAR to the bedroom door and listened in horror.

The wedding wasn't going to take place and it was all her fault. She had forgotten to bring her rabbit's foot this morning and look what was happening.

Squeezing her eyes shut to hold back the tears, Renee stood frozen in the upstairs hallway and tried to figure out what to do. It was up to her to save the day. But how? What could a ten-year-old girl do?

Still not sure, she dashed down the stairs and out the door, jumping over puddles of melting ice all the way to the church. When she arrived, she had another shock. Drew hadn't arrived at the church, either.

Everyone in town, it appeared to her as she looked around, was there but the bride and groom.

Renee stood in the back of the church, thinking frantically, aware that her hair bow had come untied and the curls her mom had brushed so carefully this morning straggled every which way. Her white socks were splattered with dirty melting snow. She was going to be in big trouble for making such a mess of herself. But none of that seemed to matter now.

All that mattered was making sure the wedding went on as planned. And she couldn't think what to do.

The church door opened behind her and she whirled, hoping it would be Drew. Or maybe even, by some miracle, Sandy. But it wasn't. It was only their grandparents, Mr. Stirling and Mrs. Murphy. The tears she had fought back earlier filled Renee's eyes and started spilling over onto her cheeks.

"Why, sweetheart, whatever is the matter?" Mrs. Murphy lifted Renee's chin and looked her directly in the eye. "You tell Mag what the problem is."

"They're not coming," Renee said between sniffles, grateful that another grown-up now knew the awful truth. "Sandy already said she couldn't go through with it and now Drew's not here either and . . . I just know they're not coming."

Mr. Stirling and Mrs. Murphy looked at each other and frowned. Mrs. Murphy began straightening Renee's mussed hair. "This calls for action, Clarence."

"Now, Mag—"

"I know how my granddaughter feels about that grandson of yours. Can you say the same?"

"Well, yes, but—"

"And this whole ugly mess is our fault to begin with."

Mr. Stirling studied Mrs. Murphy and finally began to nod. "I can't deny that."

"Then what are we going to do about it?"

Mr. Stirling looked down at Renee. "Young lady, I want you to run to the boardinghouse right now and tell my grandson . . . well, let him know that . . ."

"Oh, for heaven's sake, Clarence," Mrs. Murphy said impatiently. "Tell him his grandfather and I are getting into it. Tell him the old fool's about to have a heart attack. Can you do that, child?"

Renee's tears began to dry. "Yes, ma'am. But what about Sandy?"

"You tell her that her Gran is creating the ruckus of all ruckuses at the church and if she doesn't get here soon she'll never be able to hold her head up in this town again. Did you get that?"

Renee grinned broadly. "Yes, ma'am!"

DREW WAS STARING at himself in the mirror, trying to figure out how much like his grandfather he was going to look in fifty years and whether he was willing to have the same regrets his grandfather did. He had reached for the tie that went with his rented monkey suit when he heard the front door of the boardinghouse slam shut.

"I hope this means you're coming to your senses," Jake said, glancing at his watch. "You realize the wedding is supposed to start in less than—"

The door to Drew's room burst open and a red-faced, panting Renee dashed in. "Drew! It's your grandpa. He's at the church and he's having a heart attack and he said for you to come, right now!"

"Oh, God!"

Drew stuffed the tie in his pants' pocket, snatched his jacket off the hanger on the back of his closet door and dashed out.

"Does this mean you're going to make it to the church, after all?" Jake called, heading after him.

SANDY SAT on her old bed, heedless of the fact that she was wrinkling the dress she had intended to be married in. Someone had called to let them know that Drew hadn't arrived at the church.

Britt had promptly called the boardinghouse, but there was no answer. "See?" she said. "He's on his way right now."

"Yeah," Sandy muttered. "On his way out of town."

Britt looked at her watch. "Put your shoes on, Sandy. If we leave now, we'll only be—"

The bedroom door was flung open, banging against the wall. Renee stood there, gasping for air, her hair flying.

"Young lady, what on earth—"

"It's your grandma. She's making a big..." Renee paused, screwed up her face. "A ruckus! That's it. A big ruckus down at the church. And if you don't come...they might have to...arrest her!"

Her mother looked skeptical. "Young lady, who told you that?"

"I was there. Cross my heart." And the little girl made the solemn sign.

Sandy started slipping her feet into her running shoes. "She's probably right, Britt. With Mr. Stirling there, there's no telling what Mag might do."

Britt grabbed one of the running shoes and handed Sandy an ivory-colored pump. "Why don't you wear these? Just in case."

Sandy looked skeptical. "But—"

"Wear the high heels, Sandy."

She wore the high heels. And when she got downstairs, she went to the refrigerator where her bouquet was stored. "Just in case," she said to Britt as they dashed out the door.

"A woman has to be prepared," Britt said, smoothing out the wrinkles in the back of Sandy's dress as they went.

The first person Sandy saw when she reached the church was Drew, standing in the vestibule and looking as flustered as she felt. He called her name the instant she called his.

"You're here," she said, noticing that he looked a little disheveled. His tie dribbled out of a pocket and his cuffs weren't buttoned.

"Of course I'm here," he said.

"But you weren't. You changed your mind, didn't you?"

"I didn't change my mind. I—I tried to call you this morning and you weren't there and . . . I got scared."

"Me, too," Sandy said in a whisper, suddenly realizing that almost everyone in the church had turned to watch. She smiled. "They got to us."

He took her hand. "I guess they did."

"Young man!" They both turned at Mag's command. "Young man, I think it's time you corrected the mistake your grandfather made."

"Now, Mag, if you'll recall, the truth of the matter is we were both left standing at the altar."

Sandy exchanged a worried look with Drew.

"But I was left standing first," Mag said.

"As a gentleman, I must concede."

Mag slipped her hand through his arm. "A wise decision. Now, you two, do what we should have done fifty years ago. Quit worrying about what's coming out of all those flapping jaws in this town and tie the knot."

Drew looked troubled. "But Grandpa, your heart?"

Clarence squared his shoulders. "My heart has never been better, son. At least, not in fifty years. True love, Andrew. It's the best medicine." He glanced down at Mag, whom Sandy would have sworn began to blush. "I hope you young people can see now what happens when you listen to unfounded rumor?"

Sandy saw him wink then, and she turned in the direction of his glance. Renee, struggling to smooth her hair, stood in the doorway grinning. Before Sandy could react, the dapper-looking elderly couple wheeled, walked down the aisle together and took seats near the front.

Sandy looked at Drew, saw the smile play over his lips as he watched their grandparents. She put a hand on his arm. "We've been tricked."

"Or maybe we've just been taught a lesson," he said, taking her hand in his.

"We don't have to be manipulated into this, you know," Sandy said, still wanting to be sure.

"I don't feel manipulated. Do you?"

"No, it's just . . . it's not too late to back down."

He kissed the tips of her fingers, and she felt the tenderness clear down to her toes. "How could I do that?" he murmured. "I've decided you're right, after all. It is destiny."

Sandy smiled now. "You always do come around just in time."

"I may not be a genius, but I'm pretty darned smart."

He kissed her lips then, a soft, slow kiss that nevertheless would have ruined her lipstick if she'd ever finished putting on her makeup. Then he said, "I love you, Sandy. I haven't doubted that for a long time. But unless you feel the same—"

"And I love you, Drew. I can't deny it's a little scary. But Gran always told me to follow my heart—that the only thing that would get me in trouble was not doing so."

"So what now?"

From the front of the church, the solemn tones of the wedding march began. Sandy grinned. "Gran always said give 'em something to talk about."

They looked down at their disheveled attire and grinned. "I'm game," Drew announced.

"Let's march."

As THE TOWNSFOLK poured out of the church a half hour later and watched the newly wedded couple climb into the limo and head toward Timberlake Lodge, the stories were already starting.

"I told you he was all set to back out," Johnny Kelsey told his wife, Anna. "I knew that when Jake went flying up those steps after him this morning."

"Nonsense," said Tillie Phelps. "Sandy was the last to show, didn't you notice? Mag told her to run and I'd say she was all set to do just that."

"Ha!" said Annabelle Scanlon. "Run *after* him, that's what, if you want my opinion."

The only two who weren't discussing what must have happened behind the scenes at the wedding were Mag and Clarence, who walked out of the church arm in arm, as they had entered it. They had a more pressing argument to settle.

"Remember, I told you when I left town that this silly feud would be settled someday," Clarence said. "The curse is broken, precisely as I predicted."

"Why, you did no such thing!" Mag exclaimed. "You said you'd see my whole family in . . . well, you know . . . before we ever spoke again."

"Magdalena, you have it all wrong, as usual."

"I remember it very distinctly, Clarence. You were wearing that gray sharkskin suit that was so becoming and . . ."

They debated all the way out to Timberlake Lodge. They never did agree. But they had a delightful time arguing.

Hometown Reunion

continues with

Hero in Disguise

by Vickie Lewis Thompson

Here's a preview!

HERO IN DISGUISE

"SHEILA!" Abby Triblett grabbed Sheila's arm. "Look!"

Sheila Lawson glanced up from the Timberlake Lodge registration desk, where she'd been helping Abby untangle a booking error.

"The guy heading for the bar," Abby said in the same urgent undertone.

Sheila looked toward the bar entrance and caught her breath. A dark-haired hunk in tight buckskin breeches and a formfitting buckskin shirt strode into the dim interior, his moccasined feet making no sound on the polished wood floor. "Be still, my heart," Sheila whispered.

"Who do you suppose he is?"

Sheila edged down the length of the registration desk and leaned over the far end to track the man's progress into the bar. "One of the reenactors from the encampment, I guess," she said in a low voice.

"You didn't say any of those history nuts would look like *that*." Sheila grinned at Abby. "Ready to make a foray down to their encampment by the lake?"

"First let's find out if he's the exception or the rule."

"How do you propose to do that?" Sheila watched him skirt the tables and saunter over to the bar. He propped one foot on the brass railing running in front of it as he gave his order to the bartender, then shifted his weight, stretching the buckskin tight across his backside.

"One of us will engage him in conversation." Abby nudged Sheila with her hip. "Don't hog the view." As she craned her neck for a better look, she sighed. "He has nicer buns than Joe Montana."

Sheila agreed. She also took note of wavy hair a little too long to be fashionable but just right for a woman to comb her fingers through. "He could have an ugly face."

"God wouldn't do that to me."

Sheila poked Abby with her elbow. "You realize this conversation is sexist and superficial."

"I won't tell anybody about it if you won't. I'll just bet he's single. Sheila, we have to think up a reason for one of us to go in there and talk to him."

"That's easy." A thrill of anticipation shot through her. "We'll ask about his costume. Trust me, history buffs love explaining things like the origin of fringe."

"Okay. Let's flip for it to decide which one of us goes in there."

Sheila won the coin toss and began to frame her first question as she entered the bar. *I couldn't help noticing your costume.* Now there was an understatement. *Who do you represent?* Or was it *whom?* Oh, well. If he cared that much about grammar, she wasn't interested, anyway. She reached up to tap him on the shoulder just as he put down his empty glass and turned, nearly colliding with her. She gasped. "Mr. *Wagner?*"

Startled, he stepped back. "Why, it's Sheila. Sheila Lawson. Sixth-period government."

"Class of '83," Sheila said automatically as she stared in dismay at her high-school history teacher. Her married high-school history teacher...

HARLEQUIN ⬦ PRESENTS®

HARLEQUIN PRESENTS
men you won't be able to resist falling in love with...

HARLEQUIN PRESENTS
women who have feelings just like your own...

HARLEQUIN PRESENTS
powerful passion in exotic international settings...

HARLEQUIN PRESENTS
intense, dramatic stories that will keep you turning
to the very last page...

HARLEQUIN PRESENTS
The world's bestselling romance series!

Harlequin® Historical

If you're a serious fan of historical romance,
then you're in luck!

Harlequin Historicals brings you
stories by bestselling authors, rising new stars
and talented first-timers.

Ruth Langan & Theresa Michaels
Mary McBride & Cheryl St. John
Margaret Moore & Merline Lovelace
Julie Tetel & Nina Beaumont
Susan Amarillas & Ana Seymour
Deborah Simmons & Linda Castle
Cassandra Austin & Emily French
Miranda Jarrett & Suzanne Barclay
DeLoras Scott & Laurie Grant...

You'll never run out of favorites.

Harlequin Historicals...they're too good to miss!

HH-GEN

HARLEQUIN®
I N T R I G U E®

THAT'S INTRIGUE—DYNAMIC ROMANCE AT ITS BEST!

Harlequin Intrigue is now bringing you more—more men and mystery, more desire and danger. If you've been looking for thrilling tales of contemporary passion and sensuous love stories with taut, edge-of-the-seat suspense—then you'll *love* Harlequin Intrigue!

Every month, you'll meet four new heroes who are guaranteed to make your spine tingle and your pulse pound. With them you'll enter into the exciting world of Harlequin Intrigue—where your life is on the line and so is your heart!

Harlequin Intrigue—we'll leave you breathless!

INT-GEN

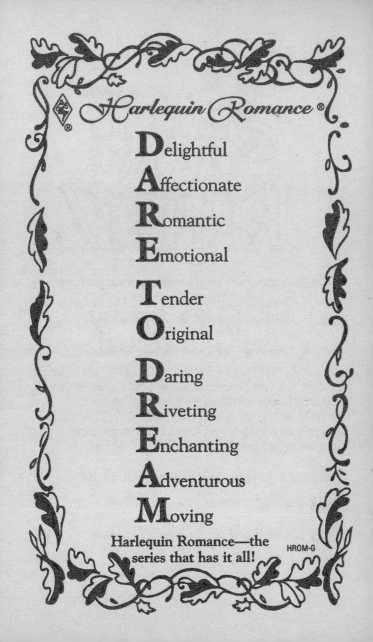

Harlequin Romance ®

Delightful

Affectionate

Romantic

Emotional

Tender

Original

Daring

Riveting

Enchanting

Adventurous

Moving

**Harlequin Romance—the
series that has it all!**

HROM-G

Readers just can't seem to get enough of
New York Times bestselling author

Sandra Brown

This May, a mother searches for

A Secret Splendor

(previously published under the pseudonym Erin St. Claire)

Arden Gentry is searching for the son she was forced to give up. But finding him could resurrect all the half-truths, secrets and unspeakable lies that surrounded his birth. Because it means finding the man who fathered her baby....

Find out how it all turns out, this May at your favorite retail outlet.

 MIRA The brightest star in women's fiction

What do women really want to know?

Trust the world's largest publisher of
women's fiction to tell you.

HARLEQUIN ULTIMATE GUIDES™

I CAN FIX THAT

A Guide For Women
Who Want To Do It Themselves

This is the only guide a self-reliant
woman will ever need to deal
with those pesky items that
break, wear out or just don't work
anymore. Chock-full of friendly
advice and straightforward,
step-by-step solutions to the
trials of everyday life in our
gadget-oriented world! So, don't
just sit there wondering how to
fix the VCR—run to your
nearest bookstore for your copy now!

Available this May, at your favorite retail outlet.

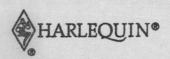

HARLEQUIN®